Grace

Grace

a fictional memoir

Robert Ward

Golden Books

NEW YORK

Golden Books®
888 Seventh Avenue
New York, NY 10106

This is a work of fiction. All individuals (with the exception of members of the
Ward family) and circumstances recounted in this book are completely fictitious.
Any resemblance to individuals, living or dead, is completely coincidental and
unintentional.

Designed by Gwen Petruska Gürkan
Photographs courtesy of Robert Ward

Manufactured in the United States of America

10 9 8 7 6 5 4 3 2 1

Library of Congress Cataloging-in-Publication Data
Ward, Robert (Robert Mason)
    Grace : a fictional memoir / Robert Ward.
        p.   cm.
    ISBN 0-307-44007-9
    I. Title.
PS3573.A737G73   1998   97-24088
813'.54—dc21   CIP

This book is dedicated with love to my son, Robert Wesson Ward, in order that he might understand where he came from and that courage, character, and compassion will never go out of fashion.

Acknowledgments

*F*irst and foremost, I want to acknowledge the contributions of my old and dear friend, my editor, Bob Asahina. Over the past twenty years, Bob has consistently been my best friend and a strong critical presence for my other books, even when I was working with other publishers. *Grace* came about largely because he remembered a story I'd told him eighteen years ago about my grandmother's quietly heroic life. Thanks, good friend, and God willing, we'll have twenty more years of laughs and good conversations together.

I also want to thank my wife, Celeste Wesson, for her courage and honesty, and for insisting I not give up on this book, even when people were telling me it was "too small, too personal." (Frankly, I've always wondered how something can be too personal. Seems to me most writing nowadays is too corporate, but that's another story. . . .)

Thanks, too, to my mother, Shirley Mason Kauffman, for her tales of her own young married years and her relationship with Gracie.

Thanks to my agent, Richard Pine, whose wisdom, editorial sense, humor, and kindness helped steer this project true north.

And thanks as well to my motion picture agent, the literate and unflappable Ron Bernstein.

The writing of Grace would not have been possible without the following books:

First is the wonderful *The Baltimore Book: New Views of Local History,* edited by Elizabeth Fee, Linda Shopes, and Linda Zeidman (Temple University Press, 1991). I'm especially indebted to Chapter 8, "Radicalism on the Waterfront," by Linda Zeidman and Eric Hallengren, which refreshed my memory concerning stories of union organizing on the Baltimore docks, stories I first heard from my grandfather, Robert "Cap" Ward.

I'm also grateful to *The Bay,* by Gilbert Klingel (The Johns Hopkins University Press, 1951), and William W. Warner's *Beautiful Swimmers: Water-*

Acknowledgments

men, Crabs, and the Chesapeake Bay (Atlantic–Little, Brown, 1976). Both of these books are classics and are essential reading about the Chesapeake Bay.

My reading on Gandhi included *Gandhi, an Autobiography*, by Mohandas K. Gandhi (Reprint: Beacon Press, 1993); *Gandhi, a Memoir*, by William L. Shirer (Simon & Schuster, 1979); and *Gandhi on Non-Violence*, edited by Thomas Merton (Reprint: Shambhala Press, 1996). And, of course, I'm grateful for Taylor Branch's unsurpassed biography of Dr. Martin Luther King, *Parting the Waters* (Simon & Schuster, 1988).

I'm also grateful for the invaluable and fascinating reference work *The Penguin Dictionary of Symbols*, edited by Jean Chevalier and Alain Gheerbrant (Penguin Press, 1969), and *The Dictionary of Symbolic and Mythological Animals* by J. C. Cooper (Thorsons Press, 1995).

Thanks, too, to my late grandparents, who seem more alive and fully human in spirit than many people I meet still walking around:

To Robert "Cap" Ward, my grandfather, for his courage and surprising tenderness.

And, especially, to my grandmother, Grace Allan Ward, for her generosity of spirit, kindness, and great courage. Even with her flaws, she was the embodiment of all that is best in humanity, and it was an honor and an inspiration to be her grandson.

Grace and me, 1950

Among those who knew her well, my grandmother Grace was famous for three things: her intelligence, her kindness, and her "weird spells." As a child, however, I had experienced only the first two. All I knew about the spells was that occasionally Gracie would cancel on a dinner or a family movie outing saying she had gotten a cold or was exhausted. My father would look at my mother and say, "Ma's had another one of her weird spells." My mother would give my father a knowing look, shake her head sorrowfully and say in her heavy Baltimore accent, "It's such a shame, hon. Such a turrible shame." Then, just when things were getting tense and interesting, they'd both become very quiet. And that would be the end of that, until the next time it happened.

Though I was too well bred to say anything, my father's comments irritated me. I worshiped my grandmother, thought her incapable of anything less than the finest, most virtuous behavior, and couldn't tolerate picturing her as subject to weird fits, like some kind of helpless mental patient. I suppose a psychiatrist could make serious hay out of "grandmother worship," but the plain and simple truth is everyone who knew my grandmother well was either crazy about her or was temporarily furious with her for her gentle but firm insistence that they be better people than they felt they could be (or, in some cases, wanted to be). In the end, though, most people tolerated Grace's high-mindedness because she seemed to embody the best in life: civic virtue without pretense, and a real humility, not goody-two-shoes Christianity, like the big-haired jokers who these days troll for your bucks on "Christian television." In spite of the fact that Grace was good and kind, she was also effortlessly witty and occasionally even acid-tongued. Even though she had character by the bushels, she was fully human in a way that now seems almost quaint, or even perhaps extinct.

I seek to remember Grace's story, though, not to preach the lost art of living virtuously, but to celebrate a life lived deeply and truly, and in the end bravely.

It's the story of the year I learned not only of my grandmother's struggle to escape poverty, to find a life for herself, but the tale of her secret history, a story that forever changed my view of her and of myself.

I only hope that in my own life I have exhibited half of Grace's courage.

First, I remember her front porch, the place where we sat and dreamed and talked as a family. There was a white picket rail around that porch, and on the front of the fence was a cameo picture of a clipper ship. That cameo was painted by my father and nailed to the porch by Grace herself as her way of providing her family identity. Her family was the Wards, and they made their living on the high seas, for my grandfather, Robert Roland Ward, was a ship's captain. His nickname and the only name I ever called him was Cap, though Grace called him Rob, and the sailors who served with him called him Captain Rob. Grace and Cap had two children: my father, Robert Allan Ward, a navy man, an intelligence officer in World War II, an early computer expert, and a painter; and Ida Louise Ward, a nurse and later the highest-ranking woman in the Department of Health, Education and Welfare in Washington, D.C.

This was her home, their home, a redbrick row house at 544 Singer Avenue, just a block or so off one of the main roads that run from Maryland to Pennsylvania: Greenmount Avenue or, as it becomes called farther up the old Number 8 streetcar line, the York Road.

G r a c e

My father, Robert, and my mother, Shirley, and I also lived in a row house, a redbrick row house in another Baltimore neighborhood called Northwood, only ten minutes away by car. Even though the neighborhoods were similar—redbrick row houses built side by side with twenty others in the block, small but comfortable front porches, a little patch of lawn, and a grassy hill that sloped down to the sidewalk—I always felt that my grandmother's home was roomier and yet, paradoxically, snug and cozier as well. Which, of course, had everything to do with Grace and very little to do with architecture.

Not long ago, I drove my rented car by her old home, catching my breath as the memories came flooding back, and I was shocked to see just how small the house was, what a hardscrabble little lawn lay in front of the place. Only one thing remained the same: the little dandelion-covered hill in front of Grace's porch. It was as steep as I remembered it, and holding my breath I could see a younger, thinner, and more desperate version of myself pushing Grace's old hand lawn mower up that hill, then pulling it gingerly back down, careful that the sharp blades didn't roll over my foot. Indeed, I could hear her voice from the old porch swing, saying, "Now, keep control, honey. We don't want my grandson running around toeless. That wouldn't do at all."

Strange how all else had changed. The front porch, which seemed almost luxuriously wide as a child, now looked no bigger than a postage stamp. It seemed impossible that on summer nights my whole family— mother, father, grandmother, grandfather, aunt, and myself—would sit on that porch, telling stories and waiting for a roar to go up from Memorial Stadium, signaling that one of our beloved Orioles had made a great play. I could see the lights of that old stadium, shining over the flat tar rooftops— lights that turned the sky an alien blue-orange. I could taste Grace's hand-squeezed lemonade, her apple dumplings with fresh-shaved nutmeg and real cream. As we sat there on the old wooden steps with my grandmother, who sometimes sweetly stroked my head, I would think, This is perfect. If things could only stay this way, all of us together, on Grace's front porch.

Grace

That old sweet world was so slow, and so filled with loving family moments that it seemed life would indeed go on and on in its predictable and sustaining rhythms. Go on, day after good day, and never change.

And yet, even as I savored the sweet happiness of that moment, there lurked inside me the knowledge that it wouldn't, couldn't remain the same.

But in the good days of the late '50s and early '60s there was always Grace's Sunday dinner, the piano, and the hymns. I remember my happiness on Sunday morning as my father and mother and I dressed for church. Red-brick Northwood-Appold Methodist Church was at Cold Spring and Loch Raven Boulevard, only five blocks away from our home, and I genuinely looked forward to attending Sunday school while my parents went into the chapel to listen to black-haired, square-jawed Dr. Robert Parker preach. I remember some of the other kids walking toward church, then veering off to hang at the Medic (short for Medical Center), a drugstore in the little shopping center across from our church. There the hookey players smoked cigarettes and laughed at the "squares" who still attended church. Many of these boys were friends of mine from school, but back in that long-gone world, I wasn't usually among them. The truth was, I wanted to go to church with my mother and father. Why? Because I believed in the Methodist Church. I believed that God was knowable and that our little church was the very embodiment of His Word. I didn't question why this was so; it was a given. Now, thinking back on it, I think that I believed it so fervently because my parents seemed to believe it, and I know that their faith was largely based on the rock of my grandmother's.

Of course, it was also true that my family and I believed in the church because it was the '50s, a time of blind faith in not only religion but government, law and order, America First . . . but that's only a sociological truth. Even then there were families and individuals who were less religious. I knew several self-proclaimed agnostics in our little row-house community, and people were tolerant of them, even if we thought their lack of faith a sad thing.

G r a c e

Still, the real reason my family believed in God and our church was because of my grandmother. She didn't go to Northwood-Appold, but a church in her own neighborhood, First Methodist, and she was involved in many church affairs. She helped the "needy" by going to the poorest neighborhoods and taking part in charitable efforts; she was involved in the Methodist Women's Council, which oversaw students from "foreign lands" coming to study in America. She collected money and clothes and "supplies" (which, in my youthful mind, somehow equated to medicine, canned tuna fish, and Ivory soap) for missionary work. What's more, she believed in educating the poor, which meant taking needy kids to the symphony, and to art exhibits at the Walters Art Gallery. In casual conversation or in written speeches that she gave occasionally at church or in other liberal havens throughout the city, she always stated that since Christ was the maker of all things, great books and classical music were His true higher manifestations; therefore, a true Christian should read and listen to the very best.

There was another, even more personal reason that I liked going to church. I liked the social convention. I liked seeing my parents dress up, my father in his light blue Botany 500 sport coat, his red-striped rep tie, my mother in her two-piece, gray wool suit with a sprig of violets on the lapel. I thought them both handsome, and I remember sitting snugly in the back of our old green Studebaker, feeling warm from the car heater, safe and at peace.

It was a feeling, I now realize with something of a shock, that I took for granted. We were a family, and we were going to our church as all families did, and after church we would talk to the Reverend Parker and our friends in the neighborhood for a while, then take our car back home, where we'd put on our casual clothes (for Dad and me, khakis and button-down sports shirt), hop back in the Stude, and drive to Gracie's for Sunday dinner.

I remember the trip to her house as well, down row-house Winston Road, past the houses of my friends—Kevin Higgins, whose father owned and operated one of the most fashionable clothing stores in town, the Oxford Men's Shop; John Littman, the neighborhood's only Jewish boy and a great basketball player; Ronnie Stumpfel, whose parents had followed us when we moved from our old neighborhood, Govans, just across the Loch Raven Boulevard, only a mile or so away. At the end of Winston Road we would take a left turn out onto the Loch Raven Boulevard, with its wide expansive grass plot, drive back up past Northwood-Appold, and cruise down a rolling hill, then up again, until we turned right just across from the brand-new Eastgate Shopping Center.

I can still recall the excitement I felt as we approached the shining rows of stores, all of them under one gleaming corrugated metal canopy, and the expansive parking lot. There was the Music Mart, where I first bought an Elvis record, "Don't Be Cruel"; the Hecht Company, where I bought my first baseball glove and had it autographed by Oriole catcher Gus Triandos; Kresge's 5-and-10, where my pals and I could eat twenty-five-cent banana splits. And there was also the local grocery store chain, Food Fair, where my parents shopped, the largest and cleanest store I'd ever seen, completely stocked with every kind of food imaginable. Food Fair featured a new "frozen foods" section with my two favorite dishes: TV dinners, which my parents and I ate on special copper-colored brittle-legged TV trays, so we wouldn't miss Ed Sullivan, Sid Caesar, or the great Gleason; and the most amazing new invention in frozen-food land, "Fresh Frozen Fish Sticks." To be precise, Mrs. Paul's Fresh Frozen Fish Sticks. Now I'm amazed that we ever ate them at all, considering that even then I thought they tasted like pure sawdust, which I had to smother with tons of ketchup to make barely edible. What you must realize is that my family and I were living in early '60s Maryland, the home of the then-nonpolluted Chesapeake Bay, which had the greatest crabs and oysters in the United States. Yet instead of buying fresh fish, we eagerly ripped open boxes of frozen, tasteless fish sticks. What could we have been thinking?

Then again, taste was not what fish sticks were about. Fish sticks were modern, one of the first television foods, the first wave of many products that made us feel part of the great new glamorous electronic reality that was slowly and insidiously supplanting the human warmth of neighborhood and family. Fish sticks even came in a cardboard box with a frame of a wood-paneled television set surrounding the "food" on the cover. It stuns me when I think of it now; we were actually optimistic and innocent enough to believe that frozen foods would not only save us time but somehow taste better and maybe even be better for us than fresh food. And beyond that patent absurdity, we believed that if a smiling man came on television and said, "Hey, Mom, they're tasty, they're modern, and they're time-savers. Everyone in your family will LOVE fish sticks," he was probably telling the truth. We liked the TV guy and we wanted to believe him. After all, he was one of us, wasn't he? He was white, he was neatly dressed, and maybe he was even a Methodist. In the parlance of the time he was probably a "good guy," so how could we not believe him?

However, not everyone in our family felt this way. Sometimes, Grace would come shopping with us. I remember her face when we filled our cart with frozen foods. Her eyes narrowed and there was a bemused smile at the corner of her mouth.

"Why are you buying that stuff, honey?" she asked my mother.

"Oh, everyone gets them now," my mother said, in a slightly superior tone.

"Really?" my grandmother asked. "Why?"

"Well," my mother said, suddenly not at all sure. "They save time."

"Oh? To do what?" my grandmother said.

"Watch TV," I said, eagerly hanging on the shopping cart.

"I see," my grandmother said. But it was obvious that she did not see, that she would never see.

And even then, I think part of me knew she was right. But I didn't want to believe her. I loved my family, I loved my church, I loved the Orioles, I loved the shopping center, I loved Baltimore and America, and, by God, I wanted to love fish sticks, too.

It may have been an uncritical time, but if we were blindly optimistic, we were also tentative. We were afraid of criticism, any criticism, because, I think, not so very deep down we knew we were blind, and if someone made a rent in the fabric, then the whole cheap cloth might tear to shreds.

G r a c e

It was an age when it was important not to be too critical of fish sticks. Or anything else.

For the most part, the family trip to my grandmother's was a happy occasion. We chatted about the neighborhood, about my schoolwork, about my father's new job at the Aberdeen Proving Ground learning the first great computer, Univac, a wall-sized monster that was like something out of a '50s sci-fi epic.

We were a happy family taking a trip toward the happiest of destinations, Grace's.

One exception was the Dannons. Tad Dannon, a burly happy-go-lucky boy in my fourth-grade class, had awakened one morning with pains in his arms and chest. He was diagnosed with polio. Six weeks later he was dead.

As we drove past his wealthy parents' modern stone home, my mother would look at my father and say, "Poor Mrs. Dannon, I don't know how she can go on living."

I would look up at the Dannons' old elm trees hanging over the street and think, The polio trees . . . God save me from the polio trees. A few seconds of panic would ensue, in which I would feel my muscles turning to mush, and the casket lid being lowered over my head.

But within a few more seconds we were clear of the Dannons' tragic home and we would begin chatting happily again.

I mention this because, looking back, it now seems to me that during my early adolescence polio was my only cataclysmic worry. I suppose the atomic bomb did scar our psyches in some undefinable way, but even though I recall bomb drills ("Duck and cover, and don't forget to put your books over your head to protect your hair from fallout"), I don't remember taking death by atomic bomb seriously.

Why not? Because our dads had beaten the Germans and the Japanese, that's why. Without once saying it or perhaps even consciously thinking about it, we knew that America was king of the world. We had TVs and dads who learned Univac and the Baltimore Orioles and the Methodist Church and fish sticks and nobody could really hurt us—ever.

The Russians? Come on, we would clobber the lame Russians. How could we lose? They had big flabby bodies, wore ratty-looking car coats, had super bad haircuts and giant spaces between their front teeth where all the horrible boiled potatoes they ate got stuck. We had President Kennedy and sexy, glamorous Jackie, too. Enough said.

After surviving the polio trees, we would cross Alameda Boulevard and start the descent down 39th Street toward Waverly. As we came closer to Grace's, I would feel happiness spreading through me like some kind of elixir. Perhaps that sounds a little excessive, but there was a headiness and sweet excitement about going to Gracie's house that made all of us a little giddy. Our car chatter would become more lively as my mother would wonder just who Gracie might have over for dinner this Sunday.

Often my aunt, Ida Louise, would show up, the only college graduate in our family. Sexy in her tight college-girl sweaters, and darkly beautiful like the actress Laraine Day, she was a nurse, a graduate of the University of Minnesota. She worked at Union Memorial Hospital, had her own "efficiency apartment" on Calvert Street, and dated a marine named Clay who had won the Congressional Medal of Honor for wiping out a North Korean machine-gun nest. Sometimes Clay joined her at the table and I liked his big broad face, the friendly way he joked with me. He was a true hero, a man's man, the real-life version of John Wayne. And just like the guys the Duke portrayed in the movies, he never bragged about his war exploits but was content to let someone else bring them up. Then he would act like the modest and humble fellow he really was—which only increased my boundless admiration for him.

As for my aunt Ida, I was simply in love with her.

By my early teens, I could barely speak when she looked at me. Her eyebrows were dark and dramatic, she had sensual red lips, and when she spoke I could often see a little tip of her tongue. Once when she was leaving my grandmother's, I suddenly kissed her on the lips, and she said in the sexiest voice imaginable, "Well, well, look who's getting bigger." I visibly blushed and ran to the backyard, feeling like a fool, the heat of her lips still burning my own.

But by the early '60s, I saw less and less of her, for she had moved out of Baltimore and its limited horizons, to Washington, D.C., where she could become a policymaker rather than a nurse. I was deeply proud of her, but I also missed her terribly, and beyond that I felt a certain fear when she left. Until she moved away, it had never occurred to me at all that things could change for our family. Ida's moving to D.C. proved that they could and would. Yet she was still close enough and I saw her often enough to maintain the fantasy of family permanence.

Sometimes my grandmother had exotics to dinner, like Mr. Oh, a very thin and devout Buddhist from Japan, or Mr. Pran, an eager and very talkative Indian mystic from Delhi. I was a bit too young to benefit from the wisdom of Mr. Oh, but I recall Mr. Pran very well. He was a Methodist Church–sponsored exchange student, replete with purple-and-red turban, a big black beard, and a full set of gleaming yellow teeth. He often brought a gift for my aunt and my grandmother—one time a carved ivory elephant, another time saris. My sexy aunt Ida tried on hers after dinner and did a fake Indian dance, barefoot, while the family laughed and I felt hot, overwhelmed with sweaty desire. Mr. Pran told us stories of his country, especially of his own youth, and of Gandhi's nonviolent movement, ahimsa, which his own relatives had taken part in. The stories were inspirational, the triumph of the good and spiritual Indians over the mercantile and snobbish, empire-building Brits. We loved the Indian people, we worshiped Gandhi, and we loved the purity and subtle humor of dear Mr. Pran.

After one dinner, Mr. Pran told us in a high-pitched voice that the secret of Gandhi's power was meditation. Everyone wanted to know more about it, so he took us all into the living room, made us sit in the lotus position, and taught us all how to breathe for "deep spiritual satisfaction." Thus, long before hippies and Deepak Chopra, my family sat and breathed deeply as a real live Indian mystic told us how to "get our chakras up." I remember my own spiritual breathing, sucking in great cubic centimeters of Baltimore air in order to "receive enlightenment" and "to be as pure as Gandhi."

I meditated like a true believer for twenty minutes, and got a headache for my troubles.

Usually my grandfather didn't make these family gatherings. He was nearly always away at sea, on a freighter in Galveston, or a tanker in New Orleans. Five foot nine, and built like a fireplug, Cap was a seafaring man, a freighter captain since his youth. I had known him first, of course, as my granddad, a nice old guy whose main physical attributes were his "sea legs." He walked on land as he did on a ship's deck—that is, he wobbled back and forth like Popeye, looking comical and slightly ludicrous.

But no one ever said so to his face, for there were other stories, tales of his toughness, of battles he'd had with my father as a boy, many of which revolved around Cap's wild, destructive drinking. Even at this time, when he was in his '60s, the family held their collective breath when he came back from the sea. Would he or would he not go on a bender? Would he end up in a brawl, or disappear for two days, only to be found sleeping on the tar roofs of the garages behind his own house? So, while I loved him and was proud of him, I felt tense and uncertain when he appeared.

But in September 1961, my grandfather was getting a lot of work, so he was usually away at sea. During most of our Sunday afternoon dinners, he would call us on a ship-to-shore phone. The family and our guests would gather around the telephone, and Cap would call from some place on the high seas. As I listened in awe, he'd tell us of a "big wind" they'd just gone through, or a "little hurricane" he'd managed to steer through off Mobile. Then, invariably, his voice would break up from the static, and he'd say "Love you all" and be gone. I remember the feeling I'd have after the phone calls. It was exciting, exotic, and most of all it was manly. Indeed, as I turned fifteen years old he had become a secret hero to me. He was a seaman, by God, out there on the Atlantic, roughing it, while we sat in his cozy living room, eating our apple dumplings, drinking iced tea and coffee, and listening to Mr. Pran tell us about Gandhi. And even then I would think, What Cap does makes all the rest of this possible. And I loved him for it.

Another familiar guest was Grace's friend and constant companion, Sue Retalliata. My grandmother had taught her in Sunday school, so she must have been at least twenty years younger, but she was already an "old maid" and seemed to be Grace's contemporary. Sweet, round-faced, with heavy-lidded brown eyes, friendly and quietly intelligent, she adored my grandmother, and the two of them spent endless hours working on church projects, going to Bible study groups, and attending liberal political meetings.

Like my father, Sue was also a painter, but unlike him she hadn't given it up. She had worked for years as a legal secretary, and now that she was retired she'd taken up the Baltimore folk art of screen painting again.

Screen paintings were and still are a Baltimore tradition that had started in Highlandtown, a section of the city quite far from Waverly, my grandmother's neighborhood. Sue had grown up there, and learned from her mother this complex and tricky folk art created by actually painting on window screens. Typical screen paintings showed rustic barns, waterwheels, or cows and horses in sylvan pastures. Once the screen painting was finished and sold, the owner would put it in his window, where it could be seen from the street. Highlandtown's row houses were even smaller and narrower than those in Waverly, and the paintings broke up the monotony of the gray formstone-covered row houses and the mostly treeless streets.

Sue had only recently resumed practicing the family art form, and to her great surprise she was now gaining a local reputation as a folk artist, which delighted both her and my grandmother. She had even been interviewed for the *Baltimore Sun* Sunday magazine, where she'd been called "an authentic Baltimore primitive" by some overeducated art reviewer. Both Sue and Grace loved that, and Sue had written the words "Cave Woman" over her little workshop in an abandoned warehouse in Waverly.

G r a c e

Sue's other distinguishing feature was a problem with her left leg. She limped badly and needed a cane to walk. Though I never knew exactly what had happened, there were subtle family suggestions that Sue had hurt her leg in some dramatic way, though like my grandmother's "spells" no one would openly discuss it. As a young kid I was only vaguely interested, but as I entered my teens, I was now beginning to question family propriety. What were my grandmother's spells all about anyway, and why did no one ever talk about how Sue had hurt her leg?

Wesley Brooks was the pastor of my grandmother's church, First Methodist, located eight blocks away. The round-faced minister with sagging jowls (he was only in his mid-thirties, but looked like a much older man) often joined our happy Sunday family get-togethers, a fact that made my grandmother proud, and me slightly sick. Officious and pretentious, with an overly pink complexion, a balding head, and tiny eyes that sat in his head like two frozen Birds Eye peas, Brooks seemed to me a bloodless, sexless man. Indeed, though I could scarcely admit to myself (in those distant days bad thoughts about a minister were tantamount to cursing God Himself), I disliked him at first sight. He rarely smiled and seemed slightly patronizing to everyone he met. No matter what anyone did for him— whether offering him fresh cinnamon rolls or knitting a sweater for his doughy-armed daughter, Alice, he always drummed his munchkin fingers and said, "Fine, fine. God's work. Just fine." No one could inspire me to do God's work less than Reverend Brooks.

My grandmother, on the other hand, was devoted to him. He was her minister, her spiritual leader, which was, for her, proof enough of his ultimate goodness, whatever his shortcomings. Whenever I was overly critical of him, Grace quickly recited a litany of the many charitable works he'd done for the poor. When I grumbled that "he probably only did it to show everyone how perfect he was," my grandmother said I "lacked charity" and gently reminded me that "we all have our strengths" and "everybody can't be as uproariously amusing" as I was. She said this with a gentle smile, and though it was clearly a reproach, she gave the last part a special emphasis, just to let me know that she really meant it. To *her*, I was uproariously funny, with my mimicry and parodies of authority. But that in no way conflicted with her love and respect for Dr. Brooks, and she didn't appreciate it when I mocked him.

Far from being a wise-guy rebel, I stood chastised where Dr. Brooks was concerned and tried my best to think well of him. Usually at my grandmother's Sunday dinner that wasn't too hard, for Grace's spirit of generosity, sweetness, good cooking, and flat-out fun made it easy to think the best of everyone in the room.

I remember the great mounds of mashed potatoes, the huge porcelain bowl of delicious gravy, the plate full of fried oysters, the great Smithfield ham, lima beans smothered in butter, and mounds of red, ripe, stewed tomatoes, a Maryland delicacy, which Gracie always made in the same half-cleaned pan. "You need to keep a little of the old grease to keep in the flavor, honey."

Yes, the food had everything to do with our good times. But I have since been to many more sophisticated dinners where the food and wine were all first class yet the party arrived dead. What was it that made my grandmother's table so inspiring? I can only say that it was she herself, though she never talked of herself at all. Instead, she led the discussions, from art (she loved van Gogh, Renoir, Gauguin, hated Picasso because she thought he defiled women, thought Jackson Pollock a "talented infant") to social philosophy—she quoted John Locke and Rousseau—and politics (she was strictly a Roosevelt Democrat and, of course, revered Eleanor; indeed, Sue Retaliatta had once called her "the neighborhood Eleanor" and Grace thought it the finest compliment she'd ever received) and, of course, literature. Grace's passion for books was that of a broad-minded, curious adult who had found great literature late in life, when she finally had some time to read. She now read Thomas Mann—she adored *The Magic Mountain* —Shakespeare, Tolstoy, and especially Charles Dickens.

When I started reading *Great Expectations* in the ninth grade, she called me every night to ask me how far I'd gotten, and we would end up having a two-hour discussion about Pip and his friends. We would laugh happily at all the fantastic and wonderful twists of the plot. I remember those phone calls even now: her voice would become almost girlish, and her infectious laughter would infuse me with such happiness that it never occurred to me that talking to one's grandmother for two hours on the phone about books was an uncool thing to do. Just the opposite, actually: she was the coolest person I knew.

One rainy Sunday we ended up in a family discussion of Shakespeare, and my grandmother suddenly began to recite from memory lines from *King Lear.* This happened spontaneously and put the family in mild shock. No one at the table, including my father, had any inkling that she knew the Bard well enough to quote him from memory. Later, when I asked her about it, she said that she didn't talk about Shakespeare often because she "wasn't sure she understood him. Will's a little brighter than I am, honey." It was a typical witty and self-deprecating Grace remark, but I didn't really believe her. As far as I was concerned, no one was smarter than she was.

And I wasn't the only person who felt that way about Grace.

Around her neighborhood, Grace had almost unwittingly become a counselor. Sixty-five-year-old, overweight Hazel Richardson would come to her door to discuss why her roses didn't grow like Grace's (not enough nitrogen in her topsoil, Grace would explain). And retired miner Harry Martin would call to tell her how his son was doing in the army in Germany. And old Pop Crakowski, owner of the corner store, would come by occasionally to discuss, of all things, baseball, and times he'd spent watching the greats like Ty Cobb and Babe Ruth. Grace surprised Pop and me by knowing a tremendous amount about Ruth's boyhood at the St. Mary's Home for Boys and Girls, which was, of course, right in Baltimore. His subsequent years with Boston and the Yankees—the years that made him Babe Ruth—didn't really interest her. Her only real concern was the drama of his rise from poverty and a drunken bartending father to becoming someone. The fact that the someone happened to be a great athlete made him slightly less interesting. But she listened carefully as she pruned her roses, and Pop Crakowski trundled off to his home, five doors down, with a smile on his face.

I won't say that my grandmother loved all her neighbors. She wasn't a saint—though for a long time I often mistook her for one—and she admitted to me that occasionally she found her neighbors' repetitive woes boring. But she never turned any of them away. And I believe she tried not only to hear them all out but to love them as well.

After Sunday dinner, the women would clear the plates and help Grace in the kitchen, while the men retired to the living room or the front porch to talk sports or politics. And I would wander out onto the front porch, with its cozy green metal glider, and sit with my feet up, gently swaying back and forth. The streets were generally quiet in those days, but I could see the surreal glow of television sets in the houses across the way—in Johnny Brandau's house, a boy who'd become a friend almost on the order of my own neighborhood pals; into the living room of big Sherry Butler, a huge Polish woman whose husband, Stan, had left her for his secretary. Sherry now lived as few women in our world did then, alone. There had been rumors about her—that she had men visitors at night, that she had been drunk for weeks, that she'd been fired from her job at the phone company, that one of her new boyfriends was fond of beating her up—and, absurdly, I tried squinting my eyes, as if by doing so I might gain X-ray vision, be able to see through her cheap flower-print curtains, into the unusual anarchy that was her home.

Sherry Butler had another fascination for me as well. She was one of the few people who I knew disliked my grandmother. They had had words several times over, Sherry being loud and screaming foul language in the streets. Grace was no busybody, no Mary Worth. She didn't seek out people or problems. On the other hand, she never shied away from them, and when Sherry got unruly and drunk and acted out in public, Grace wasn't afraid to talk to her face-to-face.

But Sherry wasn't the only person who had problems with Grace. In one falling-down row house just across the street from my grandparents lived the sprawling, drunken, and criminal Watkins family. Inside that dilapidated building dwelled drunken and mean grandfather Jerry Watkins; his daughter, the middle-aged Cherry Watkins, a once sexy woman who had now gone completely to seed; and her two sons: Nelson, who was in his mid-twenties and had already done a two-year stretch in the Maryland State Penitentiary, and his younger brother, Buddy, my age.

Though I liked to think at the time that we were a typical American family in every way, the Watkins-Ward feud seemed like something out of another century, a citified and not quite as vitriolic version of the Hatfields and the McCoys. I didn't know why it had started, and everyone in our family was too ashamed of it to even dignify its existence by talking about it, but to the best of my knowledge the whole thing had begun with the two grandfathers. What it was between them I had only the dimmest idea. All I knew was that my grandfather's drunken bar fights had reached their most legendary and violent apogee when he battled Jerry Watkins in a famous, knock-down-drag-out street battle two years before I was born—a battle that had started at the Oriole tavern around the corner on the old York Road, spilled out into the street, and ended up at the corner lamppost where Cap had smacked Jerry Watkins's big bloated head on the curb until blood ran out of his nose.

The Baltimore city cops had come to put in their two cents, but Jerry Watkins, like everyone else in the neighborhood, didn't "talk to no gendarmes." Police weren't exactly hated, but no one ever took them for friends. The neighborhood fought its own battles, and took care of its own, without outside help.

Needless to say, I didn't hear about these battles from anyone in my own family. Gradually, as I spent more and more time at my grandmother's house, the story leaked out from the local boys I had befriended, Johnny Brandau and Big Ray Lane. When I asked my father about it, he said it was "all a myth. The two men had a slight disagreement, and maybe a couple of drunken punches were exchanged." My father was a bad liar, though. He always rubbed his nose when he was fibbing. He nearly rubbed the skin off the end of it that day.

Whatever had happened, bad blood had come down through the generations. The daughter, Cherry, hated my father, and her sons, Nelson and Buddy, hated me. I, who was not allowed to hate my enemies, tried simply to ignore them, but that wasn't easy to do. For they lived outside of their ramshackle home, hanging out either on their fallen-down front porch, where they constantly threw a ball around, or more usually on the street corner, by the light pole, right on the very spot where my grandfather was said to have pounded their grandfather into the curb.

Though it was a time when it was fashionable to explain every single evil known to man as a "product of an unfortunate environment," I never believed such bunk when it came to the Watkins brothers. They had high simian foreheads, deep-sunken brows, and heavy-lidded eyes. Nelson, especially, looked like the legendary Missing Link, and he had the prison record to go with it. At eight he'd started a fire in another kid's house, nearly burning the place to the ground. When they asked him why, he said, "The kid had better comics than me, so he deserved it." That little act had earned Nels a trip to reform school, where he had spent two years and learned his true calling, breaking and entering. Around the neighborhood it was well known that he was a cat burglar, that he spent a lot of time across the York Road in Guilford, the wealthy old section of town with mansions and the Baltimore aristocrats. There was even some pride in Nelson's work among the locals. "Did you hear about old Nelson? The boy robbed the swells over in richtown. Got his mother a silver tea set. No stopping him." The problem was that Nels wasn't very good at it; he'd been busted twice, and the last time he'd spent two years downtown in the state penitentiary, where he'd added "dope dealer" to his repertoire. Now not only was he a thief, but he also sold drugs to high school kids. In short, he was mean, dumb, and bad, and he was busy teaching the tricks of his various trades to his little brother, Buddy, who was short, wide, and had a conspicuous gap between his eyes. Buddy hated everyone in the neighborhood except his running mates, the two horrible Harper brothers, Butch and Mouse.

The Watkinses and Harpers, who lived a few blocks away, spent nearly every night hanging down on the street corner, making cracks at anyone who happened to want to get by them to shop at the corner grocery store, Pop's Place. I feared them, especially Buddy, whom I knew I was destined to have a run-in with. It was really just a matter of time, because making peace with him was definitely not an option.

With the exception of that old and mysterious feud, though, peace, kindness, and generosity flourished at Grace's. As I sat on the porch listening to the men talking of the Orioles' chances to escape the cellar, I experienced a deep warmth, what I now believe was the glow of inclusion. We were part of a family, our family was a good one, kind, decent, smart, but not overly intellectual, caring of others and minorities but not self-righteous or smug about it. In short, in those happy days, I felt that we had a place in the world, maybe not the highest or most exulted, but a respectable and very real place in our neighborhood, in our city. And though I didn't think in such grandiose terms, if you had put the question to me, I would have said, "Yes, of course, we have a place in America, too."

For I believed that the world was based on families like ours. There were problems, of course, with the U.S.A., just as there were problems in our own family, but by and large, just as our family was decent, so was our neighborhood, our city, and our country.

A feeling, incredibly, I think now, that I took for granted in those bright, warm, and innocent years. But by late 1961, the year I turned fifteen, the feeling that the world made sense, that people meant well and were basically good, that we all belonged, was gone from my life, my grandmother's life, indeed our whole family's life, forever.

Mother and me, 1953

I suppose the serious trouble with my parents had been there for a long time, years maybe. But I had never seen it. That fact alone astonishes me. I like to think that I was a sensitive, observant kid, that little or nothing passed me by. And yet, for a long time, I had no inkling that there was a problem with my family. Did I miss it, or did my parents just keep it from me, to protect me? I've asked both of my parents since, and the not-so-surprising answer is that they don't know either. Neither of them could tell me when things turned bad, but I can certainly remember when I first became aware of the situation.

The year I turned fifteen the cracks began to show. My father started working late every night at his new job in the civilian computer unit at the army base at the Aberdeen Proving Ground. He'd worked late shifts before, so at first I thought nothing of it, but during the second week of June my mother stopped sewing, watching her favorite shows on television, or even reading one of her A. J. Cronin novels. Instead, she sat in the dark kitchen, alone, her hands folded on the Formica-topped table as if in prayer. After I watched her spend two nights in utter silence, I ventured in from the couch where I had been watching Lloyd Bridges as Mike Nelson in the old under-water adventure series *Sea Hunt*.

"Mom," I asked, "is something wrong?"

G r a c e

She looked up and smiled faintly in the darkness.

"No, sweetie, I'm just tired, that's all."

"You're not sick or anything?" I asked.

"No, of course not," she said.

I shuffled in behind her, put my arms around her shoulders, and hugged her tightly.

"I love you, Mom," I said.

"I love you too, sweetie. More than anything in the world."

I sat down with her at the table. The kitchen door was open, and through the screen we could see the fireflies glowing in the darkness, hear the crickets chirping in the backyard grass.

"It's nice sitting here," I said, trying to sound optimistic.

But my mother didn't answer, and I felt a dread that I'd never known before.

"I like the crickets. Don't you, Mom?"

My mother said nothing to that at all. She just looked up at me and smiled weakly.

"Yes," she said. "That's a good sound, their song."

We sat that way for a while. I felt the dread opening like a poison flower inside me, and it was such a new feeling that it struck me as curious. It was as though I was a third person watching it bloom, and though it was intensely painful, it seemed interesting, nearly beautiful. After all, I was young and in love with any new sensation. Especially since I had the naive confidence that any negative ones would soon pass away, and all would be right with the world again.

But my mother's pain was something else again. I could see it in her eyes, in her sagging shoulders, and I suddenly felt afraid and then furious. But at whom I wasn't certain.

Suddenly, outside, from across the little woods in front of our home, there came the sound of Elvis Presley singing "I Want You, I Need You, I Love You," and both my mother and I were startled.

"It's the rec center," I said. "The dance over at Northwood school must be starting."

"And you should be there, hon," she said, putting her hand over my wrist. "Not stuck in here with your old mother."

"Ahhh, who needs it?" I said. "I'd rather be here with you."

Suddenly, feeling desperate to make her happy, I jumped up.

"You want to dance, Ma?" I said.

"No . . . come on."

"Last chance," I said, holding out my arms.

Then she smiled and got up, and I held her close to me, stealing the self-conscious hug of a fifteen-year-old boy who is supposedly "too cool" to need them anymore. My mother was a big woman, overweight by twenty-five pounds or so, but she was terrifically light on her feet, and we two-stepped around the kitchen twice, then took a turn around the dining room table, and moved neatly and quickly into the living room.

As the song ended, I pulled away from her and did my best imitation of a formal bow, and my mother held the edge of her dress, curtseying and smiling sweetly.

"I am charmed, dear sir," my mother said, managing a smile.

"No, madam," I said, "the pleasure is all mine."

Now the music floating across the moonlit woods was another ballad, Jerry Vale's "You Don't Know Me," then secretly one of my favorite songs, though I would never have admitted it to any of my friends.

I sang to my mother as we danced, and then she stopped halfway through the song.

"What's wrong, Ma?" I asked.

"Nothing at all," she said. "Just that song. There's a lot of truth in that."

"I guess so," I said. But I didn't like the sound of that.

"I'm very tired tonight," she said. "That's all."

"Well, why don't you go up to bed then, Ma," I said. "I'll lock up down here."

"No, honey. It's all right. I've got to do a little work on my patterns. I'm going down to the cellar and sew for a while. You really ought to go over to the dance."

"Ahhh," I said. Actually she was right. I wanted to go, but I wasn't sure about my dancing, especially my jitterbugging, so I stayed at home on Thursday night, rec night, and listened to the music, only fantasizing about the girls I would meet from school, the beautiful Diane Hooper, or Pam Hoschild, or the perfect, black-haired Ruth Anne Muir.

"I'm kinda tired," I said. "I gotta cut Gracie's lawn tomorrow. I think I'll go on up to bed."

"Sure, honey," she said.

I hugged my mother again and kissed her on the cheek, and I was starting up the stairs when she called to me.

"I love you, Bobby," she said.

"Me, too, Mom," I said.

I smiled and tried to pretend both to her and myself that I hadn't heard the desperation in her voice.

It wasn't long before it was impossible to pretend things were the same. My father came home later and later, and on the few nights he managed to make it for dinner, he was surly and furtive. My mother was never a good cook. At her best she was able to do a passable meatloaf or a decent stew, but when things were going right for our family, it hadn't seemed to matter. Now, though, her shortcomings as a cook seemed to be forever on my father's mind.

"Meatloaf again, Shirley? Typical."

"Leftovers? Yeah, this is real cuisine we have here, Bobby."

From the quintessential happy '50s family, we suddenly fell into a parody of ourselves. My father would come in and go directly into the bathroom, where he would wash himself for over an hour. Much later in his life, we understood that he'd been a victim of obsessive-compulsive disorder, a disease that I myself suffered from only a few years later. He'd had a brief bout with it as a boy, thinking that he'd drunk poisoned well water and becoming so obsessed with the thought (this days after the "poison" had failed to kill him or even make him sick) that he had missed school for a week. Indeed, I would have given anything to know such a disease existed in those days, for then I'd have been able to forgive him for his hours spent alone in the bathroom. As it was, I came to the all-too-obvious conclusion that something had gone wrong with all of us—perhaps, foremost, myself. I was growing up, I had pimples on my face for the first time, and I was starting to notice girls, and in a year I would be going to high school. I badly needed emotional support and desperately needed to talk to him about what I was going through.

But suddenly he was gone, either working late hours or locked behind the bathroom door.

I remember making a fairly sensational catch in a neighborhood football game once—I thought of myself as the Northwood version of Raymond Berry—and I rushed home to share my triumph with my father. When I arrived, breathless and exuberant, I ran to the bathroom door, opened it quickly, and said, "Dad, I have to tell you about the football game. I made this really great catch, and—" I never finished the sentence. My father was naked down to his boxer shorts, his head covered with salves and cotton balls. He must have seen the shock on my face, because he said, "Don't ever come into this bathroom without knocking again. You see my face? I'm cursed, Bobby. Cursed. I've got to use all my time to fight the curse, you hear me? So get the hell out and leave me alone."

I turned and walked toward my bedroom, convinced that he was a mad man and that he hated me.

Now, of course, obsessive-compulsive disorder can be treated with a psychotropic drug like Paxil and group therapy sessions, and most of these destructive mental states can be greatly reduced or nearly eliminated. I've used the drugs and attended the sessions myself, and as a result I have little or no trouble with it, after half a lifetime of my own such problems. (In my own case blasphemous words repeated themselves in my ear for an entire year, until I finally thought about committing suicide, but that's another tale.)

Unfortunately for my father and our family, no such help existed then. Instead my dad really believed that God had laid a terrible curse on him and that, like Job, he had no choice but to go through his life in this terrible agony.

Grace

*   *   *

Eventually the bathroom became his whole life. In the morning, he would spend an hour and a half washing himself again and again with special soaps, cleansers, and alcohol-soaked swabs before driving to his job. Curiously, he told me much later in life, the obsessions didn't bother him much at work. As long as his mind was occupied on solving computer problems, he was fine, functional, even a unit leader—the same bright, witty, and sweet guy we'd always known. Insidiously, the disease took hold as he was driving home. He would begin to think about all the dirt in the air, all the germs he'd been exposed to while working in a crowded office, and by the time he arrived at home, around six, he was quietly panicked, convinced that his very existence depended upon repeated but useless washings. Useless, for as soon as he was clean, he would become convinced that he'd missed an area, near his ear, that the curse was upon him again, and he would begin rubbing the "filthy area" until the germs were "dead"—only to soon find another area, this time near his right nostril, that he'd "missed." And so the whole crazy ritual would begin again.

My mother, who worked as a secretary for a typewriter company, a lousy job with low pay and a bullying jerk of a boss, would come home, herself dispirited and half-dead, and cook dinner. She'd say the magic words "Dinner is ready," and my father would be forced to come out of the bathroom. The meal itself had become a tension-filled agony. Gripped by his compulsion, my father felt that while he was eating, he was wasting precious time, that the insidious germs he'd missed wiping out were doubling their efforts, making their way back across his face.

Filled with huge and incomprehensible anxiety, he unloaded on my mother and on me, knocking the food ("This damned burger is so overcooked it could be used to play step-ball. Why don't you take it outside and bounce it for a while, Bobby?"), rebuffing all efforts to talk with him ("I work all day. I don't have time to discuss inanities like the Baltimore Colts, son"). Within a few torturous minutes he'd be back in the bathroom, with the door locked, and my mother would be sobbing at the kitchen table. And

G r a c e

I would be in the front room with a huge lump in my stomach, a lump that radiated pain all through my body.

Their arguments raged all night. From my dark bedroom I could hear them tearing at each other, my mother mocking him for staying in the bathroom, my father lashing out at her that she "didn't understand," that she "never understood anything" except her "own pathetic reality."

I would lie in bed, feeling numb, frightened, telling myself over and over that this couldn't be happening to us. We were good people, happy people—a family. I'd shut my eyes and think of good times, of my father and mother and me swimming together out at Beaver Dam, of picnics we'd gone on down at the Magothy River, and of those perfect Sundays at my grandmother's. Meanwhile, my parents continued their endless battle just outside my bedroom door.

"You don't love me anymore, Robert. Why don't you come right out and say it?"

"You'd like that, wouldn't you? Then your martyrdom could be complete."

Inside my bedroom, I jammed my pillow over my head, sweat breaking out on my neck and face. I could barely breathe, but it was better than listening to them tear each other to shreds.

Luckily, I have always had a talent for escape. I knew, for example, by the time I was five that I was going to be a writer, or I was going to be nothing. I remember my uncle Clay saying to me one day, "What do you want to be when you grow up, Bobby? A cowboy? A fireman?" and my answer was dead-certain: "When I grow up I'll write books. I'm going to be an author." My uncle smiled in a condescending way and said, "Well, buddy, how *can* you know a thing like that at your age?"—a question that produced in me a desire to smack him in the face. Lacking the words to explain what I nonetheless knew to be unequivocally true, I sputtered and blurted out, "Well, I *am* going to write books, and that's all there is to it." Though I was acting childishly, I knew that somewhere inside of me there was a talent for storytelling, an appetite for language, and that nothing and no one must get in the way of it. Indeed, the very words "I'm going to write books" seemed to come from some older, wiser place inside of me, some place already adult. In no other aspect of my life did I reveal any sign of precocious maturity. Quite the opposite. I was a silly kid and often played the class clown. But in a secret place in my heart that I discussed with no one, I knew that reading and writing were my destiny.

I'm sure that this is what gave me the idea to go to Grace's. A simpler explanation would be that my parents were making my life hell, and so I escaped to my kind and sweet grandmother's. But that wouldn't be the whole truth.

Aside from the terrible pain of seeing my family suddenly disintegrating, the thing that bothered me most of all was that when my parents battled, I couldn't hear my inner voice anymore. I couldn't concentrate, I couldn't read my sports novels (my favorites being Duane Decker's Chicago Blue Sox novels, which featured a new book for each position, and the wonderful Tomkinsville books of John R. Tunis, *The Kid from Nowhere* and *The Kid Came Back*), and I couldn't sit peacefully at the old rolltop desk in my bedroom and make up my own stories. Indeed, though I felt devastated for them and for us as a family, I also felt a terrible fear, maybe even a greater fear, that as they destroyed themselves they would destroy not only "me," the boy, but the inner me as well, the writer, the artist who was just beginning to try out his wings. Since I knew I had to be a writer, that nothing or no one must stop me, I also knew I had to get away from people who were trying to drive me mad. As the battles roared on, night after night, I began to talk to myself under the covers in an ironic and distancing voice. I would say to my imaginary friend, Warren, "This is bad, Warren. This is very, very bad. They are going to drive me mad." And Warren (whom I always pictured as having curly red hair, a red-and-blue-striped T-shirt, jeans, and black high-topped Keds) would answer back in an equally ironic voice, "They're trying to drive you crazy. They don't care if you become a writer or a plumber. Are you going to allow that to happen, my good man?" And there the argument would stop, for I could only imagine escape as running away from home, something I knew would be pure folly. What was a fifteen-year-old going to do out in the world? The problem seemed insoluble, and I began to dread going home from school, knowing that the dinner tension would soon burst into the full-fledged nightly scream-out that would often rage on until well after midnight.

The answer to my problems came in the nick of time. As my home life became an unbearable thicket of parental accusations and reproaches, I began to feel a tension growing inside of me that made my head feel as though I was filled with a strange gas. I remember a day in school when I knew the answer to a riddle our beautiful redheaded health teacher, Miss Mercer, was proposing, but I couldn't get her to call on me. I sat on the edge of the chair, waving my arm furiously. I'd figured the damned thing out when no one else had. I had to tell her. I desperately wanted her to ac-knowledge me, but she turned to others, none of whom knew the answer. Finally, she sighed and told the class the answer herself, which threw me into despair. Indeed, I began to sob and mumble to myself in a tragic voice, "But I knew it. I knew it . . ."

Seconds later, tears came flooding down my face, and my mood went from sad to furious. Why hadn't she called on me? What the hell was wrong with her? I knew the goddamned answer, didn't I? I was overwhelmed with an intense and surprising loathing for Miss Mercer (whom I'd always adored). I wanted to run up to her and scream at her, "You never listen to me. Never!!"

Instead, I sat at my desk with my arms wrapped around myself, as if I was wearing an invisible straitjacket. If I could just squeeze myself tightly enough I might not kill anyone.

I barely made it through the rest of that school day. My classes and classmates floated by me as though they were phantoms.

And as I walked through the little woods off Herring Run, it oc-curred to me that I couldn't go back home, not tonight anyway. So, without knowing where I was heading, I began to walk south instead of east, through a muddy field of tract homes at the Alameda and Winston roads.

I remember the scene even now:

G r a c e

The great sea of mud, the half-built houses, the rolls of tar paper,
loose nails, old scraps of fast-food wrappers left by the workmen. Suddenly
I thought this was where I belonged, this was who I was. I walked into one
of the half-constructed houses and found a fully done kitchen, a room with
gleaming metal faucets and bright-patterned linoleum on the floor. I sat
down, shaking with an unnamable fear.

Someone else would live here, I thought. Someone else who had
a family, and who would be a family, a real family like ours used to
be . . .

I felt sick then, and I threw up on the floor. Afterwards, I felt some
measure of relief, and for the first time the solid world outside my head
seemed to come back into focus. Things lost their translucent weirdness,
and I suddenly knew where I was going.

Why hadn't I thought of it before?

I would go to my grandmother's, to Grace's, and I would stay there.
For how long, I didn't know. Maybe a few days, maybe a whole week.

Maybe for as long as it took my parents to miss me. If they did miss
me at all . . .

I got up and looked around at the gleaming metal faucets, the
spanking-new stove covered in plastic, and I felt a kind of hyper-happiness.
I would live with my grandmother where things were quiet, where I could
think again, read and write, become who I wanted to be.

I'd miss my parents, of course, but they could always come and see
me. And I'd have the peace I needed to remain sane.

Perfect.

By the time I had walked all the way from school to Grace's front
porch my mood had swung again, and I was no longer confident. It seemed
terribly strange to be going to her house with the intention of staying. I already missed the walk up my own street, the fact that my mother would
soon be home, the sweet familiarity of the living room furniture, and especially my own room.

I walked into her house (this was when people felt no need to lock
their doors) and called out her name:

"Gracie, it's me."

"Bobby? That you? I'm upstairs," she said.

I trudged up the steps and went into her airy front bedroom. She was sewing a blouse, moving her foot up and down on the old Singer treadle. Her black alley cat, Scrounge, sat on an embroidered pillow next to her. The two of them were inseparable. Gracie treated the cat like a baby, talking to him, petting him, giving him special treats.

"Honey," she said. "This is a nice surprise."

"Yeah," I said. "Hi."

I walked over and kissed her, felt the softness and smelled the sweet odor of her skin. Just hugging her made me feel solid, as if by touching her I could get the character and confidence I lacked.

"I was wondering if I could stay here tonight?"

"Of course," she said. "Have you told your father and mother yet?"

I looked down at the floor.

"No. I guess I should call them."

"Yes, you really should. Is anything wrong, honey?"

"No," I said, feeling at once guilty for lying and at the same time unable to tell her what a nightmare our home life had become. "Everything's fine. I just thought you might need some company."

"Well, I always welcome company from my grandson," she said. "And I bet you could use a snack. I have some fresh apple butter downstairs. And some cold milk."

"Great," I said.

"And let me think," she said, smiling. "Tonight I bet I could find a couple of crab cakes. And some coleslaw for us. Of course, I don't know if you eat real crab cakes anymore. But if not, I could always go out and get us both some of those frozen fish sticks you're so crazy about."

I began to laugh, and she broke into her lovely, infectious smile.

"No, I guess homemade crab cakes will have to do," I said.

"Now go call your mother and father. And then you can go play outside for a while."

"Great," I said.

I went over and kissed her again, and she patted me on the head.

"You're getting so big," she said. "Yes, sir, I should have done it when you were little."

"Done what?" I said.

"Put those books on your head, that's what."

I smiled and felt bathed in her affection. That had been the family joke since I was small. "We don't want you to get any bigger," my grandmother would say. "So we're going to pile books on your head so you can't grow." Everyone would smile at this sweet, sentimental little joke, including me. But now as I stood next to my grandmother, it didn't seem so funny anymore. After all, I was practically grown up, and no one *did* seem that happy about it. It occurred to me that when I was little my parents hadn't acted as if they despised one another, so maybe my getting older was partially the cause of their troubles. That thought depressed me all over again, and I got the call home over with as quickly as possible, so I could hustle out to the street, find Johnny Brandau, and play some ball.

Gap-toothed, brown-cowlicked, freckle-faced Johnny Brandau and I passed his Johnny Unitas model football to each other up and down Singer Avenue. We made sensational catches as we both provided a running commentary on our brilliance:

"Brandau goes out, runs left . . . cuts between the Nash Rambler and the green Studebaker. Ward goes back, dodges a lineman, and rifles a bullet which is . . . CAUGHT by Brandau at the Redskin 10. First down!"

"Ward goes out, cuts left, fakes out the Lions' defender, and grabs the ball just as it's about to smash the Hargroves' back window. He refuses to be denied. Touchdown!"

As the sun went down and the streetlights came on in Waverly, I felt peace and kindness descend on me like a benediction. Tonight there would be no screaming, no threats, no "I wasted my whole life on you, you bastard," no "I'm cursed, I'm cursed, you don't get it, you've never gotten it, you bitch," and the thought of that (or was it from sheer hysterical relief?) suddenly made me start to laugh.

Grace

The laugh began as a giggle, but quickly developed into a full belly laugh, and then went beyond that to a kind of hysterical babble, which was more like a scream.

Johnny looked at me, scratched his burr haircut (or his "wiffle," as we used to call flattops back then), and shook his head:

"You are totally crazy," he said. "Crazy, man, crazy."

"I know," I said. "I just feel . . . happy."

Which didn't begin to get what I was really feeling—a combination of exuberance and flat-out, hysterical desperation. Finally, the fit of laughter subsided, and I was able to get my breath.

"Hey," I said, trying to return to normal, "I'm going to hang around for a while so maybe we could get a tackle football game up tomorrow."

"Yeah, well, we usually get Ray Lane and some of the other guys and go over behind City and play."

"Great," I said. "I get home around three. I'll come over, and we can go over to the field together."

"Okay," Johnny said.

"Hey, throw me one more pass. A long one."

He sped down Singer toward the York Road and cut left. I cocked my arm and let loose with a bullet pass. Though Johnny was athletic, the ball skimmed off his hands and smacked into the rear window of a car. I grimaced as it hit, and waited for Johnny to take a look at the window.

"It's okay," he said. "Man, am I glad that you didn't break *that* window."

"Yeah" came a voice from the front porch behind Brandau. "You're real lucky it didn't break, Ward."

I looked through the twilight and felt myself shiver.

It was Buddy Watkins and his big brother, Nelson. They slouched on their crumbling, unpainted front porch. Their D.A. haircuts, short on top and long in the back, hung like gleaming black worms. Buddy wore a pink-and-black silk jacket hanging open to reveal his black T-shirt, garrison belt, Levi's, and motorcycle boots. Nelson was dressed in a dirty white T-shirt, brown pants, and black Cuban-heeled, pointy-toed shoes.

I swallowed hard and felt that there wasn't enough air left on the planet.

"Hey, Buddy, that your car?"

"My mother's car, Ward. You think you can come down here from your big-time neighborhood and pound your goddamned football on people's cars? That it?"

Nelson said nothing but grinned and revealed a couple of blackened teeth. Johnny Brandau stared down at his feet.

"No, that isn't it," I said fiercely. Though I was scared, I was determined not to let them bully me.

Buddy walked down off his porch and scuffed his way toward me. I stood glued to my spot, too frightened to move. He stopped a few feet away and glowered at me.

"What are you doing over here anyway?" he said. "This ain't your neighborhood."

"I'm visiting my grandmother," I said. My voice cracked on "grandmother."

"Your grandmother," he said. He twisted the word "grandmother" in such a way that it sounded obscene. "How do you like that, Nels?"

"That's very sweet," Nelson said. "That's maybe the sweetest thing I've ever heard."

"Yes," I said, "my grandmother. And don't say anything about her, you hear?"

"Whoaaaaa," Buddy Watkins said. "Listen to that, Nels. Tough guy. 'Don't say nothing nasty 'bout grannnnnny.'"

He walked toward me and with both hands pushed me hard in the chest, knocking me back into the streetlight.

I felt frightened, strangely disconnected from my body.

"What are you going to do about it, Ward?" he said. "Tell me what you're gonna do."

"Yeah, do tell us, tough guy," Nelson said, laughing at me.

I looked down at the ground. It was hopeless. He was bigger, twice as strong, and he'd kill me.

G r a c e

"Screw you both," I said.

Buddy turned toward his brother.

"Whoaaaa," he said. "Ward's breaking bad."

I felt a wave of fear sweep over me. My first night at my grandmother's and I was going to get my ass kicked.

Just then I heard a voice, Grace's voice, from her front porch:

"Bobby, it's time for dinner. Come on in."

I turned and looked up on the porch. Grace stood there looking down the street at us. I knew with her poor eyesight she would have no idea what was happening.

"Saved by granny," Buddy said. "But there'll be another time, Ward. Meanwhile, go play in your own neighborhood, asshole."

"Hello, Mrs. Ward," Nelson yelled from the porch. "How nice to see you today."

My grandmother said nothing, but looked in my direction, squinting.

Buddy sneered and turned away from me, and I felt such an intense shame that I wanted to die. Because it was true: I had been saved by my grandmother. And there *would* be another time, another time when there was no one around to save me. And I knew, to my shame, that I couldn't save myself.

The next few days, however, were better, and I managed to put both Buddy and my parents' troubles out of my mind. I was too involved in schoolwork to worry about anything else for long. I had an essay to write for English, and I had to work with a friend, Paul Cross, on our science project, which was the study of apes. (All of whom, I noticed, really did look like Buddy and Nelson.) I had little time when I got home from school but still managed to work in a good tackle football game with the Waverly gang, all friends of Brandau and Lane.

My plan seemed to be working. I was able to sleep. My grandmother made me wonderful dinners and was generally delighted to have me around. And, in turn, I was thrilled and relieved to be with her. Each night, after I'd eaten and finished my homework, Grace would play the piano, and together we would sing hymns or old songs. The regular piano player at her church had come down with "the grippe," and Grace had agreed to spell her for a few weeks, a promise that now worried her.

"Lord, I've forgotten everything," she said to me. "I doubt if I can play a note."

"Of course you can," I said.

I smiled at her, and we sat down together at the old piano stool. The song was "The Old Rugged Cross," and my grandmother had trouble sight-reading the first few chords. After that she rattled the song off as though she'd been playing it every day for the past fifteen years. In a few minutes she began to sing. She had a surprisingly powerful alto voice, and when she sang the song, there was something in it that sent chills up my spine. I don't mean because her voice was great; it was only average. But there was sincerity and a nearly frightening intensity in the way she sang the song that bespoke the mysteries of Christianity, mysteries that told of the sea of troubles, the nails in Christ's hands, both the fear of death and the everlasting hope of the Resurrection. When Grace sang there was something ominous in the song, something beautiful but barren, forlorn.

When she was done, I told her as much.

She looked at me and nodded seriously.

"You're right. There's a lot of desperation and fear in that song," she said as we sat together on the piano stool. "Think about the words, 'There on the hill stood the old rugged cross, a symbol of suffering and pain.' That's the truth. Jesus died on that cross, to save us from sin . . . sins we commit anyway. Hurting ourselves, the ones we love. . . . It's a dark world sometimes, Bobby, and we all commit trespasses. Which we need to be forgiven for."

"Not all of us," I said, smiling with goofy affection toward her.

"If you're referring to me, you've got it wrong. I've got feet of clay like every other person."

"Sure," I said. "I didn't mean you were perfect or anything like that."

"Far from it," she said. "And you better believe it."

"Oh, I know," I said. "You're one of the great sinners of the world."

She laughed and kissed me, but then added seriously, "You'd be surprised."

On other nights Grace and I would sit down and talk. These conversations always ended up being rambling philosophical discussions, but they never started out that way. There was no self-consciousness to them, no "Now it's time to let me teach you a thing or two, young fellow," the kind of lame approach most adults lay on kids, which often turns them off from learning altogether. Instead, we would usually start talking about a book she was reading. It might be Dickens, or it might be the nonviolent writings of Gandhi, whom she admired nearly as much as Jesus. She explained to me his philosophy of ahimsa, a nonviolent protest based on love of humanity. Her face lit up when she quoted him: "'We must love the British even as we fight them.'"

"The Negroes use Gandhi's ideas, don't they?" I said.

"Yes, they do. Martin Luther King is a student of Gandhi's."

"Do you ever think about going out there to demonstrate with them?" I said.

She smiled, and suddenly looked away from me.

"Only every day," she said.

Her answer surprised me.

"Really?"

"Yes, but I'm a little old to be riding in freedom buses. So I try and collect money, and I've written a few letters to the *Sun* when I see one of their conservative columnists unfairly attacking the civil rights movement, but that's the extent of it, I'm afraid."

"Dad told me you were involved in other movements, though," I said. "I forget which ones."

She smiled, and patted my head.

"That was long ago," she said. "In another time."

"I'd like to hear about it," I said.

G r a c e

"Some other night," Grace said. "You have a school day tomorrow."

I nodded and hugged her. I knew that the real reason she wasn't telling me about her past was that it was so heroic, and she considered bragging a venial sin. But I resolved as I went off to bed that someday I would get her to tell me all about her glorious youth.

Sue Retalliata, me, and Grace,
1955

It was the seventh day at Grace's, Sunday morning, and we were going to church together. I was looking forward to it; going to church with Grace was a special treat. After the Reverend Brooks, she was one of the most eminent people at First Methodist. She sang in the choir, played the organ in a pinch, and taught Sunday school. She was also the co-head of the Methodist Women's Council, something I knew very little about, but which was obviously an important organization. She received calls at all hours from the other women in the group, calls about charity drives, church suppers, raffles, study groups. I knew about all of this in only the most sketchy manner, but it was exciting to go to church with her because it seemed serious. When Grace was in church she was in her true element, the place where, more than any other, she felt deeply at home. And especially during this unmoored and frightening time for me, I needed that security, that feeling of kindness, the old glow of inclusion, which suddenly had been turned off in my life.

I remember that Sunday more clearly than I remember where I was yesterday. My grandmother wore a green wool suit and a black comb in her hair. I had gone home for a few minutes early on Friday (when my parents were both at work) and grabbed some of my clothes, my football, and some books. So this day I was ready, dressed in my navy blue blazer, grey slacks, and penny loafers. My tie was a blue-and-red rep, which I had bought at Kevin Higgins's father's store, the Oxford Shop. I brushed my crew cut to attention and my grandmother and I walked from her house down Greenmount Avenue the few short blocks to the church. I remember walking out to the porch, seeing the Brandaus heading off to the Catholic church. I waved to Johnny and he waved back, then Grace joined me on the porch and we set off, walking together, her arm in mine.

We were halfway down the block when we heard the screams.

"You bastard, give me that damned bottle."

Startled, both Grace and I looked up and saw Sherry Butler through her upstairs window. She was wearing a slip, her dirty blond hair was a mass of springs, and she fought violently with some man over what looked like a whiskey bottle.

"Gimme it, bastard."

"I won't. You'll only drink it all, you damned drunk."

"Look who's calling who a drunk."

I stood in amazement. Though my parents had their troubles, there had never been a physically violent confrontation between them. Now I watched as the man raised his arm and brought it down on Sherry's head.

Grace stopped, looked up at the window, and shouted:

"Don't you hit her again!"

I felt my throat constrict.

"Gracie," I said. "This isn't our—"

"You hit her again and I'm calling the police," my grandmother called.

The two struggling people in the window stopped and looked out, their bloated, drunken faces incredulous.

"Who's 'at?" Sherry said, peering down into the street as she pulled her straps up.

"Grace Ward," my grandmother said.

The man, a big lug with a red slab of a face, now peered out as well.

"You oughta mind your own business, lady," he said.

"You heard what I said," my grandmother responded. "The two of you stop that behavior right now. Before someone is hurt."

I felt an overwhelming sense of embarrassment, mixed inextricably with a flush of pride.

No one could have pulled this off but Grace.

"Go mind your business, lady," the man said. "Nosy old bag."

He laughed at my grandmother, but she stood stock still staring up at him.

"Are you all right, Sherry?" Grace said.

"Yeah, I'm okay, Mrs. Ward," she said, and suddenly there was timidity and a sweet vulnerability in her voice. "We just got to drinking too much, 'at's all."

"That's no excuse for hurting each other," my grandmother said.

"You hear that?" Sherry said to the man in the window.

"I didn't hurt nobody," the man said. "I just wanted a drink is all."

"Try coffee," Grace said, and turned smartly away, once again taking my arm as we headed up the street.

After that rather astonishing and upsetting beginning, I was relieved to get to the safety of the church. I liked seeing the families walking toward the church doors. They came from all directions, everyone dressed in their Sunday best, modest suits and sport coats. There was a security and kindness in knowing that we were all there together, that we thought as one. The only possible blemish on our common purpose was my feelings toward the Reverend Brooks himself. As we headed for the lovely old stone church on the corner, I tried to push all uncharitable thoughts from my mind. I told myself that I had misunderstood him, that I had judged him superficially, and I prayed that I might have the strength to be honest and see people for their better selves, like Grace did. As we waited for the light on the corner across the street, I suddenly realized that there was something different about today's service. Just outside the open church doors, a small group of Negroes (as they called themselves then) stood, talking quietly. This was not news in and of itself. As the neighborhoods "changed" south of 33rd Street, Negroes had started coming to First Methodist. They usually congregated together just before the service on the little grassy knoll outside

the church, talking and laughing with an apparent ease and good humor
that I, in my ignorance, envied.

But this Sunday they weren't laughing, and they weren't talking to the
whites. Indeed, they looked grim-faced, quietly determined . . . angry, and
anxious. I should add that all of this registered in an almost subliminal way
as we walked up the steps and my grandmother greeted her many old
friends. As we got near the door, Grace's great friend, Sue Retalliata, limped
over to us, leaning on an old wooden cane.

"Oh, Grace," she said, "You brought Bobby. Hi, sweetie."

Sue reached over and hugged me hard, almost choking me with her
cheap rose perfume and lilac-scented face powder. But I didn't mind. I had
always liked Sue.

"How are you, honey?" my grandmother said.

"Wonderful, Grace," Sue said. "I've sold three more screen paintings
this week. That's nine houses in my neighborhood."

"Nine? That's wonderful," my grandmother said. "You're turning into
a regular Grandma Moses."

Sue blushed and shook her head. Like all good Methodists I knew she
was anxious to keep her light under a bushel and that she felt embarrassed
(and even guilty) by even a modicum of worldly success.

I was happy for her, and as we headed inside and found our pew, I was
glad she was with me, because my grandmother was going to play the organ
for the hymns. Sue patted me on the arm as we sat down together and
picked up our Bibles from the back of the pew in front of us.

"I heard you've been staying with Gracie, Bobby. Is everything okay at
home?"

"Sure," I said. "Everything's just fine."

"I'm glad to hear that," she said.

I could tell at once that she knew otherwise, which meant that Gracie
and she had been talking about my parents' difficulties. The revelation was
not very shocking; of course, Gracie knew . . . and yet I found that I was
shocked anyway. I didn't like to think that people were discussing my family
as "troubled" or "a problem family." Such labels scared me; they were for

other people, "the unfortunates who had broken homes" and whom people patronized in magazine articles. I wanted to believe, needed desperately to believe, that my family was capable of righting ourselves, working out our problems, that everything would be fine again.

Now, as I watched people file in for the church service, it occurred to me that maybe it wasn't true. Maybe we wouldn't be fine at all. I wondered if my own parents were going to church together today, and I felt a twinge of guilt that I wasn't there to help keep them together.

It was a quarter to ten, fifteen minutes before the service was to begin, when the seven Negroes came in. Traditionally, they sat in the last two pews of the church; it never occurred to anyone to question this. That was simply the way things were done. What was odd, I thought, was that they were coming in so early. Usually, they waited until the rest of the congregation was seated, then they quietly filed into their seats in the back pews. But today, to everyone's astonishment, they didn't sit down in the back pews at all. Instead, they came directly into the church and headed for the front, which was not yet filled. The seven of them, four men and three women, slid into the third row of the church and took their seats.

The moment was electric. The quiet, humble little church was quickly rife with whispers. But Sue Retalliata, sweet, slightly daffy soul that she was, had somehow missed the whole startling turn of events.

"What's happening, honey?" she asked me. "Why's everybody so loud all of a sudden?"

"Look," I said, nodding my head toward the third row.

"At what . . . oh, my! My goodness!" she said.

I couldn't help but laugh at her sweet-natured surprise.

"What are they doing?" she said.

"I think it's called 'nonviolent protest,'" I heard myself say. "Or maybe you could just call it going to church."

Sue said nothing to that. Her mouth had dropped open wide.

Just then, I saw two beefy-faced men, men I recognized as neighborhood guys who served as ushers, rush up the aisles toward the third row.

One of them was Edward Moon, a fat, ham-hocked man in his early forties with a blond marine haircut and wearing a shapeless brown suit. He was a churchman through and through, always the first to sign up for every committee.

He reached the third row and stood staring at the Negroes with his hands on his wide hips. In his shock, indignation, and arrogance he looked like a giant slab of beef. A steer in a suit. He stared, then shook his head in disbelief. For what seemed like an eternity, the seven Negroes kept their eyes front and center, totally ignoring him.

Finally, he was forced to speak, and as he did, the whole church was deathly still.

" 'Scuse me," he said, his voice sounding like a gong. "What are youse people doing?"

Though there was a man sitting on the very end of the row, it was the young, attractive black woman sitting next to him who answered Mr. Moon.

"We have come to praise Jesus Christ our Lord, same as yourself," she said.

I was aware of the civil rights movement in those days but I never thought I'd see it firsthand. I saw it on television like everyone else, and lately my grandmother and I had started discussing it. However, up to that very moment I hadn't known quite what I felt about it all. But when I heard those words with their quiet, dignified, but nonetheless rock-hard commitment and sincerity, I found myself breaking out into a wide and involuntary smile. I felt like cheering. I instantly knew, as only the young can know, that I was with these people, that I wanted them to sit there until Mr. Edward Moon's eyes popped out of his moronic Waverly head. My family had always instinctively pulled for the underdog, against the bully, and here, it was abundantly clear to me, Mr. Moon was the force of stupidity and unbridled arrogance.

But my joy was short-lived. The church was again buzzing, and I heard a woman behind me say, "What is the world coming to? Niggers don't even know their place no more, hon." And the rejoinder from the sixtyish man sitting beside her was, "Commies put 'em up to it. I totally blame Russia. The whole thing is Russia's fault."

I looked up near the pulpit, and I saw my grandmother standing next to the preacher, Dr. Brooks. I was intensely curious as to what he might do in this situation. But before he could act, Edward Moon decided to take matters into his own hands.

"You . . . you people do not sit here," he said "You have seats provided for you in the back. Now I'm going to ask you nice one more time. Will you get out of those seats and go to the back where seats are provided?"

This time the black man on the end of the pew answered. He had a soft, mellow voice.

"These are the seats we have chosen. And we are staying in them for the rest of this service, sir."

The "sir" was brilliant, I thought. An ever-so-polite punch in the gut. Edward Moon's face seemed to puff up like a blowfish. A blue vein throbbed furiously in his temple.

"Then I will be forced to remove you bodily from these here seats and from this church."

"You do that, Mr. Moon," the Negro said coolly, "and you will be sued in court. If you want to remove us, you will have to call the police and have them arrest us."

"Good idea!" a man called from the back.

"Hell, yes, call the cops," someone else yelled.

"This is awful," Sue Retalliata said. "Just awful."

I looked up at my grandmother and saw that she was talking to the Reverend Brooks. He listened intently, then nodded and walked up to the podium.

"Friends," he said. "This is the house of God. There will be no violence here. And no police."

But the noise didn't cease. He spoke again, louder, with a tinge of desperation in his voice.

"Listen to me, friends. Please. Everyone sit down. That includes you, Mr. Moon. This can all be worked out among ourselves. No one call the police. Please be seated, and let this Sunday's services begin."

But Edward Moon did not sit down. He stared with unabashed hatred at the seven Negroes and especially the man on the end who had dared challenge him.

"This ain't right," he said. "It ain't right, and it ain't gonna happen. Not in my church, it ain't."

He stared at the Negroes for a while longer, as though he were trying to will them out of their seats. Then he turned toward Dr. Brooks and shouted, "I cannot believe that you would side with them over your own people!"

"We are all brothers and sisters here, sir," Brooks said, his voice trembling.

It was a courageous and daring thing to say in the face of all the raw animosity staring up at him.

"Wrong," Edward Moon said. "These people are no brothers or sisters of mine. I told you that we shoulda never let them in the door inna first place. Give 'em an inch, they take a mile."

Suddenly, my grandmother walked up to the podium.

"Sit down, Mr. Moon," she said. "You're not giving the sermon, Dr. Brooks is."

That brought a loud and much needed tension-breaking laugh from the congregation. But Edward Moon was not going to give up so easily.

"I will not sit down in this church as long as these . . . these people are sitting where they should not be sitting. I'm leaving and I urge every other member of this church who finds this kind of thing . . . un-American . . . I urge you to walk out with me."

Then, scowling at the Negroes one last time, Moon turned and walked out. And in short order so did at least twenty other people. I watched them come out of their pews, some quickly, as though stung by bees, and others slowly, their heads bowed down, as though they were ashamed of themselves but had to leave nonetheless as a matter of principle. I looked up at Gracie and caught her eye.

I had never seen her look so deeply upset. Her face was a mask of pure pain. I thought for a moment that she might cry, something that was unheard of.

But she held on. And quickly sat down at the piano and began to play.

"Hymn 348, 'The Old Rugged Cross,'" Dr. Brooks said. "Let us stand and sing."

Which we did. That is, all fifty or so of us who were left, including the Negroes in the third pew. And it seemed to me, as we sang those old words, that the song had a whole new meaning now, that carrying that cross was no longer going to be just a "symbol of suffering and pain" but that every single person in the congregation was about to learn what it truly meant to climb that long, torturous hill in the rain.

After his service, the Reverend Brooks usually opened the church rectory for a coffee-and-pastry session, a little meeting where people caught up on their neighbors' businesses, found out what each other's children were up to, and picked up the schedule of church events. Usually, about ten or fifteen people attended the coffee hour, and it was almost always a casual and relaxing affair.

But not today. Now half the church crowded into Dr. Brooks's study. I found my grandmother with an excited group of women, one of whom was the well-dressed Annette Swain. I was always surprised to see Annette Swain at my grandmother's church. She lived only a few blocks away, but they were blocks on the other side of Greenmount Avenue, beyond the low brick wall and green hedges that led into the wealthiest and most exclusive enclaves in the city—Guilford and Roland Park. Here were the homes— or rather mansions—of the rich, the CEOs of Baltimore's leading industries, and their illustrious families. Their children went to wealthy private schools like Gilman or St. Paul's, Friends, or Boy's Latin, and then Hopkins, Harvard, or Yale. They sailed together, schooled together, made money together, and usually went to the Episcopal church on

G r a c e

Roland Avenue together as well. Annette Swain was something of an anomaly. She had grown up dirt-poor in Fayetteville, West Virginia, and came to Baltimore looking for work as a waitress. Instead she found a man named Bill Brisbane, a local hotshot and ex-lacrosse star at Johns Hopkins University. Now Brisbane was the president of the huge ad agency of Dillard and Brown. No one really knew what he saw in her, but before long she had shocked Brisbane's blue-blood, white-collar family by running off with Bill to the marriage capital of the East Coast, Elkton, Maryland. Everyone in the church knew this story, mainly because Annette loved telling it so much.

When someone had asked her why she chose to come across the York Road to First Methodist rather than go to the good old rock-solid, mon-eyed All Saints Episcopal Church in Roland Park, she said, "'Cause I grew up a Methodist, and I don't like their damned hymns. They don't even sing 'Silent Night' at Christmas." It was a charming but only partially true answer. Grace always suspected that Annette came to First Methodist because in our church her voice would be heard, while over at All Saints she would be considered an interloper, someone who got into the club through the back door. Yes, she was in, she had the money, the car, the club member-ships, but she would never be taken seriously . . . a bitter pill for a climber like Annette to swallow.

Now she buzzed around the little room, shaking her head and talking in her loud, high-pitched voice:

"Well, I know they've been put upon, poor dears, but this is not the way . . . definitely not the way. Coming in the house of God and disrupting a church service? I mean I wonder what they hope to accomplish. It's very, very sad that they chose this tactic. I know a thing or two about coming from poverty, from people whom the better educated classes wouldn't spit on, and I must tell you, a person's got to pull herself up by her own boot-straps, not by asking for some special attention."

To my surprise there was a general buzz of agreement to this claptrap. People nodded their heads as they drank their weak coffee and ate their lemon cookies.

G r a c e

I looked at Grace expectantly. If ever anyone had offered her a more perfect setup line, I couldn't imagine what it would be. I thought of the way she had handled Sherry Butler and her drunken boyfriend, and I was positive she'd rip into Annette.

But she said nothing, only sipped her coffee and looked away.

I found myself scratching my head. Maybe, in all the excitement, she simply missed what Annette had said. Encouraged, Annette went on, this time addressing Dr. Brooks:

"Believe you me, Reverend, I know what these people are feeling, 'cause I've been down to the well and found it dry more than once. But you don't get respect by demanding it. You get it by working for it, like any other person. Only way to get success in this world is to work at it. And that's the truth."

Yes, I thought, and almost blurted out myself, either that or marry into it. That would be just the thing for the seven Negroes at our church. If they could just all marry rich Wasps in Roland Park or Guilford, everyone would spend all night and day gloving their hands and shoeing their lily-white feet.

I looked over at Grace again. Annette was like a pitcher in batting practice offering up meatballs over the center of the plate. But Grace, so artful and so eloquent with her rejoinders, didn't swing at any of these fat, easy pitches.

And this time there was no doubt that she'd heard.

"Well," the Reverend Brooks said. "this has been a trying day, and I don't pretend to have all the answers, but I want to thank all of you for staying today and for coming in here to talk. Before we say anymore, though, I want you to know that I'm going to pray for guidance in this matter, and I hope each and every one of you will also."

"That's fine, Reverend," someone said. "But what are we gonna do about it?"

The Reverend Brooks smiled weakly.

"Well, I think we all are in agreement that the Negro has suffered greatly. And as Christians we must not turn a blind eye to any person's suffering. Absolutely not. On the other hand, there is a practical question. Black people have only just joined our church, and the policy set by the Methodist Council of Churches in Maryland is that they should be afforded seats in the rear of the church, until such time as . . . as . . ."

Suddenly, Grace smiled. "Until such time as they choose not to do it anymore. Like today."

I took her hand when she said that, and felt a swell of pride in my chest.

"I wish it were that simple, Grace," the Reverend Brooks said. "But I'm afraid that we can't run a church according to our emotions. No, the real answer is until such time as the governing body of the Methodist Church changes its position and allows them to sit where they please."

"And how would that happen?" I suddenly heard myself say.

Grace looked at me and at first I feared I'd blown it, but she nodded as if to say I'd asked the right question.

"It would happen, young man," the Reverend Brooks replied, "at policy meetings of the Methodist Church, which will be this summer at Asbury Park. I mean if someone wanted to bring it up, that would be the time to do it."

"Yes, Reverend, but these people don't want to wait. I mean what will you do if they come back next week . . ."

"I don't really know, young man," he said, and there was more than a little outrage in his voice. Who was this kid, not even a regular church member, asking him questions?

"Well, I'll tell you what ought to be done," Annette Swain said. "They should be met at the door by Baltimore City Police and they should be removed from these premises, for their own good."

Again there were more than a few mumbles of assent to this asinine suggestion.

I looked at my grandmother, but she had turned silent and seemed to be lost inside herself again. Fortunately, someone else, a young mother named Sally Callahan, spoke up.

"For their own good?" she said, her voice incredulous. "I must be getting old. Maybe you can explain that to me, Annette?"

Annette Swain felt that she was up to the task.

"Of course. Look. The Negroes want public opinion on their side, right? But if they disrupt church services, the place where ironically quite a few people are already praying for their side to get the justice they deserve . . . then they will set themselves back at least ten years. Because no one likes a pushy mob of . . . of . . . people telling them what to do in their own church, and I'm surprised at you, Sally, for not already knowing that."

I was in shock. There were holes in Mrs. Swain's argument big enough to let a Colt fullback run through.

"Wait," Sally Callahan said. "There are only seven Negroes. So who is the mob you're talking about? Seems to me it might be us."

"Ridiculous," Annette said. "Utterly ridiculous. We're the mob? No, I don't think so. This is our church, and *they* are the troublemakers."

"Next you'll be saying they should all go back to the churches they came from downtown . . . or maybe they should all go back to Africa? Is that it?" There was real passion in Sally's voice, and a tone very close to contempt.

"My goodness, my goodness!" Sue Retalliata said. "Goodness gracious! My-oh-my!"

"I have never said anything of the kind," Annette Swain said. "I don't know why you are getting in such a huff. Because all I'm really saying is that these Negroes don't live in this neighborhood, so they're our guests here, and as guests I think they should show some manners. Would they like it if I went down to, say, Pennsylvania Avenue and broke up one of their gospel services or whatever it is they do?"

"That's ridiculous," Sally Callahan said.

And this time she looked directly at Grace for support. But none was forthcoming.

I couldn't understand it. I knew my grandmother was sympathetic to the Negro cause, and here was her chance to add her voice, yet she said next to nothing.

Grace

There were a few more angry exchanges, then the crowd slowly drifted out as the Reverend Brooks extracted a promise from them "not to forget to pray."

Grace, Sue, and I were almost to the church's front door when the Reverend Brooks caught up with us.

"Grace," he said, looking breathless and exhausted. "There's something I really need to talk to you about. I almost forgot it in all the excitement. Could I see you for a minute in my study?"

"Certainly," she said. "You can go on home, honey. I'll be fine."

"No. I'll wait," I said. "See you out front."

I went outside with Sue, holding her arm as she made her way slowly down the concrete steps.

"What a day," she said "My-oh-my-oh-my."

"Yeah," I said, troubled. "Looks like the movement has caught up with the Methodist Church in good old Baltimore."

Sue shook her head.

"I don't know what to think," she said.

"Come on," I said, losing patience. "You and I both know the Negroes are right. They should be able to sit anywhere they damn well want."

"Bobby, you shouldn't curse," Sue said.

"I'm sorry," I said.

"Well, I suppose you're right, though. But people don't change easily. Believe you me, they don't."

"Which is why they have to do what they're doing," I said.

"I suppose . . . ," Sue said. "I just wouldn't want to see anyone get hurt."

"Hurt?" I said, again flying off the handle. "Who's going to hurt them—Reverend Brooks? What's he going to do, smack them with a lemon cookie? Or maybe Annette Swain? What a complete and total self-righteous idiot she is."

"No," Sue said shyly. "I was thinking more of Edward Moon. He looked like a madman to me."

G r a c e

She had me there. In the excitement I'd temporarily forgotten about Moon and the look in his eyes. The same mad and intolerant look that was in the eyes of some of the people who'd walked out with him.

"Well, honey, I have to get home," she said.

"Can you make it to the streetcar?" I said.

"Of course," she said. "You take care of your grandmother now. She's the best."

"I know," I said, giving her a hug and a kiss.

I watched her limp down the street and felt my heart go out to her. Alone, approaching middle age, with her two cats and her screen paintings. It wasn't an easy existence, yet she never complained and worked hard at her art.

Sue was, in her own quiet, shy way, very brave, I decided.

But what had happened to Gracie?

I waited in the rich fall light. I watched as the last of the congregation left First Methodist. I sat on the church steps and thought of all I'd seen. It was clear that a real revolution had begun. There was no doubt about it. The civil rights movement in the Deep South that I'd heard so much about had actually come to Baltimore. I tried to sort out my feelings. It seemed crazy, impossible to me. The Deep South—Mississippi, Louisiana, Alabama, places "like that"—were cracker states, filled, as everyone knew, with racists, ugly and mentally deficient morons like the guys in the Ku Klux Klan. But Baltimore had always prided itself as a mid-Atlantic state where tolerance was the watchword. After all, the state, as we had all been at great pains to learn in history class, was founded by Catholics. The Calverts were the first great family, and they founded the state so that they might practice their religion without fear of reprisal. Other states might have had a Negro problem, but we had been taught that we races could get along. Indeed, there were only a few of the meanest rednecks I knew who even used the term "nigger."

Then I remembered the Watkins brothers, Nelson and Buddy. I thought of Sherry Butler and her "boyfriend," drunk on Sunday morning. I thought of kids I knew from Woodbourne Junior High School, kids with skinny, undernourished faces, bad skin, and few clothes who were always bumming a quarter for lunch money.

And I knew that they could all go either way. They could end up on the right side, like Ray Lane or Johnny Brandau, or they could end up with the haters, the Edward Moons of the world.

Sitting there in the chilly air, I realized that this might be one of the most important days of my life . . . the day I found out things about myself and about those good Christian people around me.

And what of Grace? The question haunted me again.

I shook my head. Maybe she was biding her time. Maybe this very talk with Brooks was about the race problem, and she was going to perform her magic like a ward politician behind closed doors. Whatever the answer, I could barely wait to talk with her about it, how she felt, what she might do . . . and for that matter what actions I might take myself.

The church door opened, and my grandmother came outside. The Reverend Brooks shook her hand and smiled at her warmly.

"Keep it in mind, Grace, okay?"

My grandmother smiled, nodded and then turned toward me.

"Lord," she said, "you must be starved. We've got to get home and get you some lunch."

"Sounds good to me."

She put her arm through mine and we started the walk home. I was happy to hang on to her, feel the sureness of her grip.

"What was that all about?" I asked.

"Oh, not a whole lot," she said. "Dr. Brooks wanted to remind me about choir practice this week. He's determined to keep the regular schedule going in spite of all the turmoil."

"Oh," I said, disappointed. "I thought he was talking to you about what happened with the Negroes."

"Well, yes and no. He's basically supportive. But he doesn't want the radical contingent to set the agenda for the whole church."

Though I was confused, what Grace said made a kind of tortured sense to me. It was understandable to me that Dr. Brooks wouldn't want outsiders to tell him what to do with his own church.

Still, that was purely theoretical. The truth was that when I thought of the Negros walking up the aisle and imagined the courage that had taken, I felt inspired, stunned by their example. I remembered the people who'd walked out of church, and it occurred to me that I'd been shocked and that the shock was just starting to register now, hours later.

How could people be so ignorant? So stupid?

Maybe I didn't know anything at all about anybody . . . or how rotten the world really was.

When we got home, I was anxious to get Grace to tell me about her meeting with Dr. Brooks, but she didn't want to talk about it. So I settled for her big, bountiful lunch of crab cakes and potato salad, and then went by myself to the Waverly Theater, to see *Attack of the Crab Monsters* and *Earth Versus Flying Saucers*. Afterwards, I ate a bag of ten-cent cheeseburgers at the Little Tavern and then went back to Gracie's house. I fell asleep early that night, with visions of demons and strange soup plates attacking the earth. Then the dream faded and I began to sleep peacefully, deeply.

Until I heard a terrifying moan.

It was a low aching moan, more like the sound of a sick animal than a human being.

I thought for a moment that it was a dream fragment, an aural piece of the nightmare-in-progress, and I half-slipped under the bizarre sound into unconsciousness.

But the drone persisted, louder, more insistent, and seconds later I was fully awake. Shaking my covers off, then sitting still, I listened intently for the source of that painful cry.

I looked out the window at the moonlit trees, the garage roofs across the alley. Was it an injured cat or a dog? Maybe my grandmother's cat, Scrounge?

Then, finally fully awake, I realized that the sound came from my grandmother's room.

I felt panic overtake me as I jumped from the bed and ran into her room. Maybe all this had been too much for her, and she was having a heart attack.

I went to her door and looked in, frightened to go any farther, not sure of what I would see.

And what I finally did see scared me even more deeply. Grace was sitting up in her bed, her eyes wide open, her gray hair let down long behind her head.

Her eyes were staring in extreme fear, and she was pointing with her right hand at some invisible phantom in front of her.

The sound she was making was so guttural, so unlike her normal speaking voice that it seemed to come from some other person . . . or some other thing that possessed her.

For a second the sight of her—looking so much like a possessed witch that she might have stepped right out of "Hansel and Gretel"—scared me so badly that I couldn't move from her door.

I simply stood there, in terror myself, watching her as she pointed and groaned this terrible sound . . .

"*Ahhhhhhhhhh . . . Winnnnnnn . . . Gateeeeeee Noooooooooo!* God. Win . . . gate . . . no!"

She threw up her hands as if protecting herself from some invisible blows.

Finally, I forced myself to move forward, and seconds later I was at the bedside, holding her by the shoulder, gently shaking her.

"Gracie, Gracie!" I said. "Wake up. Wake up . . ."

The sound continued for another six or seven unbearable seconds. I was shaking myself, terrified. . . . She had to stop this . . . she had to . . .

"Grace, Gracie . . . please. Stop! Wake up!"

And then slowly she seemed to come back from that dark, terrible place. She blinked and turned to me.

"Bobby?"

"Yes," I said. "It's me."

"Oh, honey," she said. "Honey."

Then she put her head against my chest and began to cry, sadly, deeply.

"It's all right," I said. "It's all right. You must have had a nightmare, but you're okay now. It's okay, Grace."

"Yes," she said. "Yes, a nightmare. That's all . . ."

And she slowly stopped crying.

"Could you hand me a tissue, honey?"

I pulled a Kleenex from the box next to her bed. She wiped her eyes, blew her nose.

"You're not in any pain, are you?"

"No. I'm fine."

"It must have been one heck of a dream," I said.

"Yes," she said. "Ghosts . . ."

"Really?" I said. "Did you recognize them?"

She shook her head.

"No . . . no, my dreams are never that clear. Just fear . . . terror. Something coming for me. Stalking me."

She stopped and looked at me.

"I must have scared you to death, honey. And after all you've been through lately. I'm terribly sorry."

"Cut it out," I said. "You couldn't help it."

She sighed and managed a smile.

"No . . . of course not," she said.

I fluffed up her pillow for her, and she lay back down.

"I love you, honey," she said.

"I love you, Gracie," I said.

Then I kissed her forehead and patted her on her worn cheek.

"Good night, honey," she said.

"Good night, Grace."

I smiled and quickly left the room. But I didn't go to sleep for a long time. I had finally seen it and heard it with my own eyes and ears: one of Grace's famous "spells." What could it mean? Where did such paralyzing fear come from in one who had been so brave? It didn't jibe with the woman I knew.

But then, neither did her failure to talk on the Negroes' behalf at church. What had all that been about?

And what about the meeting with Dr. Brooks just after the protest? She'd seemed nervous when I asked her about it. And he'd seemed excited as he approached her. . . . I found myself wondering if there was something more to it, something she hadn't told me about.

But I dismissed the idea and felt a pang of guilt for my disloyalty.

Just before I fell asleep I thought of my parents again. I would have bet my life that they were happy, that they would always be together. Now, I knew it not only wasn't true anymore, but worse: maybe it had never been true.

Maybe they had been putting on an act for my sake. Or maybe it was always there, the anger and tension between them, but I was just too young and unconscious to see it.

Maybe they just lied. I knew a bright kid in school, Teddy James, who swore that adults were all skilled liars. One wise guy I knew in my own neighborhood, Denny Blake, told me once that you weren't really an "official adult" unless you lied about something important twice a day.

Then I had an almost unbearable thought. Maybe, maybe it was the same for Grace as well. Maybe she had a good act down, but when it came to putting herself on the line, she wouldn't tell the truth to anyone, especially not a mere kid.

Bobby Ward, 1955

*H*aving gone to bed doubting my parents and my beloved grandmother, I woke up convinced, as only a teenage boy can be convinced, that my latest intense feelings were dead-on (they had to be, because they were my latest feelings): all the adults had betrayed me, and the best and most intelligent thing I could do was forget what any of them said or promised. Forget the civil rights movement, which was after all not *my* movement, and simply go to school, learn what the teachers had to teach me, chase girls, play sports, and be a normal, fun-loving teenager.

As I climbed onto the Number 8 streetcar on the way to school, I told myself that I felt much, much better. I believed in nobody and nothing, and I was never going to take a chance on anyone or anything again.

I was going to be normal, by God, happy, and to hell with civic duty, morals, and all that other complicated junk. After all, most of my friends didn't seem to be struggling with this torturous stuff, so why should I?

That morning at school I felt a tremendous sense of freedom. All I had to do was pay attention in class and do well on tests. A snap for a basically smart guy like myself. I told myself that I'd get into my studies, that I'd blank everything else out. After all, hadn't everyone said that school had to be number one? And from now on it would be. To hell with anything else—Negroes, parents, and especially tricky grandmothers.

Grace

This new strategy worked brilliantly for three periods, right up to lunch. After eating a hot meal in the school cafeteria, I went out with the rest of the kids for recess, sat on the stone wall, and watched my classmates playing basketball. I was a pretty fair shooter myself and sometimes played in the daily game. In fact, I was debating whether or not I should join in when Howard Murray, a black boy my age, ran up to me.

"Hey, man," he said. "You gonna play?"

"I don't know," I said. "I ate so much lunch I feel like a beach ball."

He laughed and hit me on the arm in a friendly way. I told myself not to be overly friendly back to him because I wasn't going to get involved with any more Negroes. It was too confusing, and I was on my new be-a-regular-guy kick.

"Know what you mean," Howard said. "That corn bread and stewed tomatoes is good. Not as good as my mama makes it, but pretty good anyways."

I laughed, and so did he. It occurred to me that whenever I talked to Howard we were both usually laughing. Which made me sad, because I wasn't going to be involved with Negroes ever again.

"Where do you live, Howard?" I said.

"Why, you gonna come and rob my house?"

I laughed and felt a flush of warmth for him. I immediately told myself to negate it. Do not get involved in any of this . . . be happy.

"Over on the Harford Road," he said. "Up by Cold Spring."

I knew the neighborhood and was surprised. It was a white hillbilly neighborhood, filled with guys who made Elvis look like a fraternity boy. D.A.s, chopped and channeled rods, hoods who wore Luckies rolled up in their T-shirt sleeves and had girlfriends with big hair courtesy of tons of Spray-Net. Fast girls who chewed gum triple time while they were doing the backseat boogie at the Timonium Drive-In.

"Man, that's hairhopper kingdom over there," I said.

Howard smiled.

"Not on my block," he said. "We're the second black family to move in."

"Wow," I said. "Have there been any problems?"

He looked down at the ground, hesitated.

"Nothing much," he said finally. "Some big mouths blowing off steam is all."

I nodded then and looked back out at the guys running a fast break. Something was happening to my newly found resolve. My morning nihilism was breaking down. I felt real affection for Howard. Damn.

"You want to play ball over at Waverly Rec sometime?" I said. I couldn't believe I had said this. Hadn't I just told myself to avoid complications? Hadn't I just sworn to myself to be simple, a normal mindless American sports-loving girl-chasing teenager?

"They got any problems with integration over there?" he said.

God, I hadn't even thought about that. Here was my chance to get out of it. All I had to do was say, "Yes, Howard, they seriously hate niggers in Waverly," and he'd turn me down.

"Tell you the truth, I don't know," I said.

"You ever seen a Negro play there?"

"No, but Ray Lane plays there, and Johnny Brandau. You know those guys from school. They won't let any of the assholes hassle you."

"How 'bout you?"

"Me either," I said. "I'm with you."

He laughed.

"Damned hairhoppers can't shoot baskets anyways. Let's give 'em a lesson."

"Good, we'll do it soon. Hey, if you're the first Negro, we'll have integrated the place."

"Cool," Howard said. "Let me know. Meanwhile, I'm gonna get in the game."

He headed out to the basketball court, and I smiled and gave him a little wave of encouragement, and then thought, "What are you doing?" Indeed, in less than four hours I had broken every vow I'd made that morning. I had sworn off complexity, told myself I would never put myself out on any moral limbs again, but from some perverse, unknowable depth in myself, I had asked a Negro to come play ball at a redneck rec center, a place where he and I might both run into serious trouble.

Not only that, he knew it, I knew it, and we both still wanted to do it.

I was sick, that was all there was to it. I was sick and craved moral complexity, drama, confrontation, even though I knew I was essentially cowardly, gutless, and a teenage fool.

As the bell rang to signal the end of recess, I felt ugly, strange, weak, and heroic all at the same time.

I hadn't been home in nearly two weeks. My mother had called once but I'd been out, and when I called her back, the line was busy. I called three more times and still got the busy tone. Whoever she was talking to was getting an earful.

Finally, on Wednesday, two weeks after I'd moved to my grandmother's, I decided to pay a visit to my home.

The walk home from school with my old friends Don Hoffman and Kevin Higgins was weird. Only two and a half weeks before, it had seemed pleasantly routine. Me and my pals walking to our block together—what could be more normal? Now it was as though I was a visitor from some other neighborhood. There was an unnatural silence as we walked. The guys started talking about a great catch Hoffman had made playing tackle football over at Tom Mullen Little League Field, and I felt the sting of omission.

My house on Winston was the first one we reached, and we usually stopped for a moment to finish whatever conversation we were having before I went inside. But today my two friends looked at me in a strange, confused way.

"What's the deal, Bobby?" Kevin said. "Do you live here or down in Waverly now?"

"Hey, I'm just visiting my grandmother for a little while," I said. "It's nothing. I still live here."

"Is it going to be weird for you to go home?" Don said.

"No," I said. "Not weird at all. I mean it's still my home. Haven't you guys ever visited your relatives?"

"Sure, in the summertime," Kevin said. "But not during school."

He rubbed his burr haircut and sighed.

"You gonna stay here or down there with your grandma?" he said.

"Ah, well . . . my grandmother's not feeling very well right now," I said. "So I'm looking after her."

"Well, since you're here today, you want to play ball over at Morgan?" Kevin said.

"I don't know. I have to talk some stuff over with my mother," I said. "Maybe. I'll call you in a half hour or so."

They both nodded, and Kevin hit me on the arm as I went back up the steps to my parents' redbrick row house.

I watched my friends carrying their bookbags down the street and felt suddenly dizzy and sick to my stomach. It occurred to me that my disappearing had upset my friends as well as me, and that made me want to cry.

I used the key, which I wore around my neck on a string, and let myself into the house.

Of course, my mother wasn't home. She didn't get home for two hours. I didn't know why I had told them I had to talk things over with her before I could play ball. That sounded ridiculous. It was as if I wanted her to be in there, waiting for me. I was like a damned baby.

"Oh, Mommy, please be there at home to snuggle with me."

What was wrong with me? I was revolted by my childishness. I was fifteen, practically in high school, and I could take care of myself. Or at least I should be able to. Jesus . . .

I walked through my house, feeling my sense of panic rising. Everything was the same, the TV, the blue-striped sofa, the piano next to the stairs, the blond Danish Modern dining room table and the four blond chairs. The little serving table with my record player on it and my stacks of 45s neatly piled next to it. Just as I recalled it, but the light was wrong. There was a waxiness, a kind of alien sheen on everything. A sheen of strangeness.

Grace

It was as though our home had been sold, and all the tables and chairs and magazines and lamps had been placed in there by some phantom real estate lady to make it look like a "typical Baltimore family's dwelling place."

I could see and hear her as she walked through the house, dressed in a two-piece wool suit.

"This home used to belong to a typical Baltimore family, the Wards. A father, a mother, and a child. They were happy here for a time, until . . . well, let's be gentle and just say bad luck overtook them. Now they're gone . . . no one knows quite what happened to them. You can make a very nice deal on their house. Furniture and 45 collection included."

I sat down in the suddenly too-white kitchen, looked at the startling sunburst clock on the wall.

Then I put my head down on the cool Formica table and fell fast asleep.

My mother woke me when she came in from work. She ruffled my hair and smiled at me when I looked up.

"Well, hello there, stranger," she said, trying to affect a jaunty tone.

"Hi, Mom," I said. "Guess I fell asleep."

"Your grandmother isn't letting you stay up too late, is she?"

"No," I said. "Just a busy time."

She took off her old gray overcoat and folded it neatly over the back of the kitchen chair.

"You have a snack?"

"I'm not hungry," I said. "I tried calling you, but the line was busy."

My mother sat down and folded her hands.

"Guess I've been on the phone a lot lately," she said.

She looked old, tired; there were new wrinkles on her face, crows' feet that I swore hadn't been there just last month. And her hair had a few new iron-gray strands in it.

"I may as well tell you," she said. "You're old enough to know the truth."

I bit my lip and squeezed my hands together. My fingers were cold.

"Your father's having an affair. He's not home at night because he's out with another woman."

I felt as though someone had punched me in the chest.

"Who is she?" I said, amazed that I could say anything.

"Someone named Helen. Someone at his office. She's older than him. He always wanted a mother to take care of him like Gracie did. Now he's got one. She babies him, tells him he's a great man."

I said nothing but reached out and held her hand.

"What's going to happen?" I said.

My mother shook her head and began to cry.

"I loved him so much. . . . When he was away in the navy at Pearl Harbor, I could have gone out on him, you know. I had plenty of men ask me. . . . Once in a bar where I went with my friend Flo, two marines on leave picked us up. They took us to some friend's apartment, down on Charles Street. Flo was pretty drunk and she went right into the bedroom with the one called Bill. I was in the front room with the other one. His name was Ted. He was from Seattle. He kissed me on the lips. I wanted him to . . . go on. God help me, I did. But then I remembered I was married and I felt dirty and cheap. I pushed him away from me and walked right out of there. It was snowing outside. I wanted to get a cab and go home. But I didn't want to leave Flo with two men, so I went back in to get her. She didn't want to leave, but I told her I'd be waiting outside until she came. I just sat down outside on the curb. It was freezing, the wind was like a knife; it whipped up my dress, freezing my ankles and legs. Flo didn't come out for an hour. And when she did, she laughed at me. Said I was an idiot for sitting out in the cold, that I should have been inside partying with them. At the time I thought they were awful, but you know what, hon? She was right. Flo went down there every time Bill came into town. Marty and the kids didn't know anything about it, and I didn't blame her. I wished I'd done it now. I wished I'd gone down there with her every damned time."

"No, Mom," I said. "Don't say that."

I held her hand. But she pulled it away.

G r a c e

"You were right to go live at Gracie's. All we do around here is scream at each other. Go back there if you want to. I don't blame you."

I looked at her once beautiful face, and I felt things breaking inside of my chest.

"Are you and Dad gonna . . ." I couldn't finish.

"Get a divorce? I don't know. I don't know about anything. You . . . you should go back to Gracie's for a while. I mean while we sort things out."

"Okay," I said.

I got up from the chair.

"You don't have to go now," she said. "You could eat dinner here. It'll just be the two of us, you can count on that."

"Sure," I said.

I sat back down, and suddenly I started laughing. I felt like a puppet, popping up absurdly, then collapsing in a heap.

"We'll have dinner together," my mother said. "It'll be nice."

"Yeah," I said. "Good."

I looked up at the clock, figuring exactly how long I'd have to stay.

The shock of my family's overnight disintegration left me reeling, and yet I was strangely functional. Instead of freaking out I performed a kind of emotional lobotomy on myself. I guess the classic psychoanalytic term is "denial."

In short, rather than fall apart, I not so simply told myself a little story as I left that night. I remember saying to my imaginary friend Warren, "Well, Warren, old friend, it's you and me and Grace now. (And let's just hope she hasn't completely copped out, too.) Because Rob and Shirl have lost it. They're finished. The family is dead, and we've got to move on."

The cynical, wise-guy voice I used was an amalgam of old movie voices, tough guys on television. I was some kind of fifteen-year-old Boston Blackie or Bogart's Marlowe. I kept the feeling inside me (like some giant crater of black ash that threatened to engulf me) at bay by jiving with myself in heroic movie voices.

G r a c e

I know now, of course, that this desperate and purely intuitive strategy could only work for so long . . . that, in fact, by turning myself into a wise guy, by denying the pain, I was only buying myself time. In the end, when bad things happen to us, we pay; and when your family cracks up, you pay for the rest of your life.

You never really trust people again, never really believe they are going to hang around. From that day forward, my life has been a battle to regain trust. It's a battle I'm still fighting . . . and to be honest, I don't know if I'll win it or not.

But I'm jumping ahead. Way ahead. Which is, a wise friend once told me, another problem. . . .

That night, as I made my way back to Grace's, I didn't feel the pain directly. I was simply glad to be out of my home, happy I had some place to go.

I told myself that I wasn't going back home again. If they wanted to go mad, they could, but I wouldn't let them get to me. No way, no way . . .

I lay in bed that night and told myself I would keep at least one of my new resolves. Maybe I couldn't help myself by getting into moral complexities, but I'd still work hard in school, become brilliant and successful, and then all my relatives would be so sorry they'd messed with me. . . .

Bobby Ward, boy genius.

To that end I spent the next days doing my schoolwork, losing myself in history, math, English. It was Thursday afternoon, and I'd just seen the first fruits of my labor. I'd received an *A* on a short essay I'd written on *Silas Marner*. I carried it home as a badge of my new seriousness in school. I knew that Grace would love it and would tell me I was wonderful . . . the "perfect grandson". . . words, frankly, I was dying to hear.

I burst into her house, paper in hand, and was shocked to see a huge Negro man sitting in Grace's old green reading chair, a copy of Gandhi's works in his massive hands.

G r a c e

When he saw me, he stood up and smiled, and I must have looked like an idiot. I'm certain my jaw dropped flat-open.

"You must be Robert, Grace's grandson," he said.

"Right," I said.

"I'm the Reverend Josiah Gibson," he said, "from African Methodist. Just come to pay a visit to your grandmother, and she's been nice enough to invite me to stay for dinner. She's gone up to the market to get some crabmeat."

"Oh," I said, brilliantly. "That's nice."

Everything about the Reverend Gibson was larger than life. He looked to me like Gene "Big Daddy" Lipscomb, the Baltimore Colts' great defensive tackle, which turned out not to be such a wild guess after all, because the minister had played college ball at his alma mater, Morgan State, the Negro college that was only five blocks from my parents' home.

He frowned at the paper I was waving in my hand.

"What do you have there, son?"

"Oh, this? Just a little essay I wrote for English class. On *Silas Marner*."

"Is that an *A* I see emblazoned on the top?"

"Yes, sir," I said.

"Good for you. Did you like the book?"

"I liked getting it read."

He laughed in a generous way.

"Good answer. I read old *Silas* when I was in school, too. It's about the power of love, its regenerative and spiritual power, but the thing I remember best is it's about a hundred pages too long."

Now it was my turn to laugh. The minister laughed with me, and I felt his warm presence sending out sparks in the nearly dark room.

"Guess you're wondering why I'm here," he said.

"Yeah, sort of."

He began to pace the room then, and I swear the old floorboards shook.

"Well, I'm not sure if you're aware of this, but your grandmother's a pretty well-known lady in church circles."

I smiled and nodded.

"Fact is," he said, "when it comes to politics and church matters, there's no one who can make a difference quite like your grandmother—"

Just then, Grace appeared carrying a bag with celery stalks sticking out. I quickly went and took it from her.

"The reverend was just telling me how well known you are," I said.

"So I heard," she said. "Now Reverend Gibson, if you are going to brainwash my only grandson into thinking his grandmother is some kind of saint—"

"Listen to you," Dr. Gibson said. "A typical Methodist."

"What on earth does that mean?" my grandmother asked.

"Hide your light under a bushel," he said.

"Well, I never," my grandmother said.

"Mrs. Ward, you know I'm telling the truth," Reverend Gibson said. "Now you take the Catholic Church, for example. What do they do when they want to build a monument to God? They build the Sistine chapel in Rome, that's what. Full of magnificent art, fantastic architecture, a towering monument to their faith in the Lord."

"No. A towering monument to their huge Catholic egos," Grace said.

The minister laughed with delight and hopped on one foot. The floor shook.

"You're making my point for me, Grace," he said. "You see, as Methodists we disdain shows of ego. Our churches are simple country church houses by comparison. Even our oldest churches, like First or Lovely Lane, are modest affairs compared to the Catholics'."

"Which is the way it should be," Grace said. "We're not trying to impress the world . . . all that material wealth . . . it's got nothing to do with faith. Quite the opposite."

"True," Dr. Gibson said. "But sometimes our modesty gets the best of us.

"Anyone who stands up for others like you do should still be leading the troops into battle, not acting like a meek little lamb. Now I don't love the Catholic Church and I happen to agree with you that their love of worldly power and wealth has often led them astray, but still, if they had a warrior like Grace Ward working for them, they would know exactly how best to use her. Whereas we modest, unassuming Methodists . . . we're afraid to show off our talents for fear of being thought vain. How many times have you heard a Methodist say, 'Don't be a show-off,' or 'Let your light glow warm but low.'"

"Or 'The meek will inherit the earth,'" I said, laughing.

My grandmother shot me a look.

"And with good reason," she countered. "Vanity is a sin. And to my mind, not a small one. It leads to the love and worship of appearances rather than truth."

"Yes, well and good, but losing one's passion is a bigger one," the minister said, and smacked his huge fist into his hand. "And we Methodists are prone to that one. We try so hard to be modest and spiritually pure that we forget that Jesus Christ himself threw the moneylenders out of the temple. Yes, he did! For he was a passionate man!"

The Reverend Gibson smacked his big fist into his palm again, and I stood there in total silence. I had never thought about the issues he was bringing up, but I recognized them at once as essentially true. All my life I'd been told not to be too loud, not to make waves, to be modest, useful, a helper. Never once in my life had anyone said to me, "You're brilliant. You're smart. Take the bull by the horns and lead."

Modesty—quiet, decent, boring, unmemorable modesty—was the Methodists' watchword.

And where did it get you, I thought? My father goes out with some woman at the office named Helen who tells him he's a god. Maybe that was it . . . maybe my father had gotten tired of being so damned modest.

My grandmother looked at me.

"If you'll be so kind as to bring that food into the kitchen, I'll make us all some dinner. And we can hear Reverend Gibson here enlighten us some more on the wonders of the Catholic Church!"

I looked at Dr. Gibson to see if he had taken offense, but on the contrary he was smiling.

"Not my intent at all," he said. "Just wanted to discourse on the virtues of blowing one's own horn and keeping passion alive. Praise God!"

My grandmother made a *harrumph* kind of noise and led me into the kitchen. Dr. Gibson followed. I could hear him chuckling. He seemed the kind of man who enjoyed upsetting the applecart, and I didn't quite know what to make of him. Nor, I think, did Grace.

As Grace made dinner, the Reverend Gibson smiled and leaned his huge frame in the kitchen doorway, completely blocking out the view into the dining room. I sat at the kitchen table shucking peas.

"I bet young Robert here has inherited some of his writing talent from you," the minister said, winking at me. "I've read your essays in the church paper."

My grandmother blushed, then looked at me.

"What's he talking about, honey?" she said as she took a plate of her crab cakes from the icebox.

"I got an *A* on my *Silas Marner* essay in English," I said.

"That's great!" she said. "You certainly worked hard on it."

She came over and kissed me on the head, then turned toward Dr. Gibson.

"I'm very proud of this young man," she said. "He's got a lot of artistic ability."

"Yeah, I'm going to be the next Hemingway," I said, rolling my eyes. I felt my cheeks redden. But Dr. Gibson completely ignored my discomfort and looked at me with his big luminous green eyes.

"If you have any talent, you should push it to the limit," he said. "To be the best you can you have to make demands of yourself. I do some writing myself, for the church and for various movement papers, and I know how hard it can be."

"Really," I said, "Is it hard for you, too?"

"Writing is always hard," he said, "but I'll tell you a secret. I find its difficulty is in direct proportion to what I have to say."

"How do you mean?" my grandmother said.

Dr. Gibson sat down at the table and picked up some pea pods. They disappeared in his hands, then three popped out at once and plopped onto the plate.

"Well, take Bobby's English project, *Silas Marner*. When I read that back in school, I found it dreary reading, so writing about that would be drudge work. But when I'm writing something that I feel passionate about, like, say, integration, and what's going on with voter registration down South . . . well, then, it's not half as hard. Because I've got a passion for the subject, I can't wait to share it, and sometimes the words just roll right out."

"Makes sense," I said.

But my grandmother shook her head.

"Yes, I can see your point, but passion for your words can create some of its own problems."

"Really?" Dr. Gibson said. "I'm afraid I don't quite understand."

My grandmother stopped cooking for what seemed like a long time, and her face was thoughtful. When she finally spoke, I felt it was as if some great effort was being expended.

"The problem with passion is that anybody can claim it," she said.

She stopped then, and in that moment she looked every bit her age.

"Some of the most despicable people I have ever known overflowed with passion," she said. "And some of the worst crimes have been committed in its name."

She stared at the floor and seemed to be lost in thought. There was a long, uneasy silence.

I felt dizzy, confused. Not by what she had said but by the anger in her voice.

"Yeah," I said finally, to break the silence. "Look at the Nazis. They were really passionate about genocide."

"I would disagree with you there," said Dr. Gibson. "I think real passion is always guided by reason. Bigots are filled with anger and hatred, but that, to my mind, is not passion at all. Duke Ellington is a passionate man. Adolf Hitler was an insane man. That's the difference."

G r a c e

My grandmother stirred the vegetables on the stove and smiled at him, a kindly but nevertheless challenging smile.

"You're right, of course," she said. "But there's a thin line between passion and insanity. We've seen that in the arts for years. Take van Gogh. He was a passionate genius, but he was also insane. He cut off his ear and eventually committed suicide."

"Because no one bought his paintings, and he was alone," Dr. Gibson said. "No one appreciated him. That's too much to ask of anyone. Not even a great artist can live in the world alone. We need each other as brothers and sisters."

I thought I knew where he was going. It was obvious the minister was steering the conversation back to the civil rights movement . . . just as obvious as the fact that Grace was steering the conversation in the opposite direction.

Later on, I followed the two of them into the dining room and helped myself to my grandmother's cooking, but that night I scarcely tasted the food. The Reverend Gibson told my grandmother that he had been in touch with the great civil rights leaders Dr. Ralph Abernathy and Dr. Martin Luther King and that the movement was spreading almost faster than the leaders' ability to chart it.

He talked about how Rosa Parks had started the Montgomery bus boycott in 1955, how she had called her friend E. D. Nixon, president of the Pullman porters' union, and a white lawyer named Durr, and how everyone agreed she was the perfect person to test the laws of Montgomery. My grandmother and I were fascinated.

The Reverend Gibson went on to discuss the movement's different strategies for different states, how Alabama's laws varied from Mississippi's, and what might happen when demonstrations erupted in each state. I sat there dumbfounded, listening without opening my mouth. My grandmother mainly listened as well, but when she did speak, she held her own and seemed to understand complex legal strategies that left me in the dust.

Grace

To say that I was surprised by what I heard that night would be too tame a description. I realized that I knew nothing at all about the civil rights movement and next to nothing about Negroes. Indeed, as I listened to Dr. Gibson explaining court decisions and the kinds of planning and coalitions the black leaders had formed and how they had to anticipate what President Kennedy might do (and how little he had actually done), it occurred to me that "civil rights" was too bland a phrase for their struggle, that what Gibson was describing was nothing less than a strategy for war. It so happened that I was studying the American Civil War in school that semester, and what I was hearing here was not unlike that conflict. As I sat there eating crab cakes and helping myself to seconds of mashed potatoes, I began to understand for the first time that the Civil War and the current struggle were all part of a continuum, that Negroes were still in many ways "slaves." Negroes were fighting a battle that had begun when they were brought to this country in chains from Africa, a fight for their dignity, their families, their very lives. And they were fighting a war in which the other side had most of the money, all the guns, truncheons, fire hoses, and Jim Crow laws on their side. The Negro generals—Martin Luther King, Jr., Roy Wilkins, Ralph Abernathy, and many others I didn't know—had only their own courage, cunning, and passion.

To win this war, Negroes not only had to have mind-boggling courage; they also had to be smarter than whites.

That thought was like cold water in my face. Everyone knew that Negroes were brave, but few whites understood that they also had to be more intelligent than the white lawmakers, too—smarter than college-educated lawyers, smarter than sharpie businessmen, and smarter than savvy, racist politicians.

Smart like the Reverend Gibson was smart.

I sat there silent, learning more in one night than I had in a lifetime about my black brothers and sisters. And by the time dessert was served, I was in awe of their brains and courage. Now I understood, all at once, how amazing the nonviolent movement really was. How truly great King and Abernathy and all the others were. . . .

As the evening wore on, we moved into the living room, and Grace poured Dr. Gibson coffee.

"Grace, this has been a wonderful evening," he said, his eyes shining. "It's heartening to meet a person with a fine mind *and* a passionate spirit."

They both smiled at his reference to their short philosophical debate.

"You know," Dr. Gibson continued, "Jesus Christ was Himself a fighter for the underdog. I have even heard some people say He was a revolutionary."

Grace smiled.

"I've heard that, too," she said, "but it's the kind of line usually spouted by Communists."

They both laughed again, but I was sure now that Dr. Gibson was feeling her out. He wanted to ask something of her, some favor . . . but what would it be?

I didn't have to wait long.

"Grace, I'll be frank. I'd love you to meet with some of my friends in the movement. There's a good group of people in town who are really starting to get the ball rolling. You know Baltimore isn't as bad as Alabama or Mississippi, but there's a lot that needs to be done. There's even a small part of the movement happening at your church."

Aha, I thought. This is it . . . and why not? Who else would the Negroes turn to at First Methodist? Annette Swain or Pastor Milquetoast? Given all I had learned tonight, I felt an intense pride that they had come to my grandmother. They were asking her to be a small part of history, and I was sure Grace would rise to the occasion.

But instead, her voice dropped and she fidgeted in her chair. She looked distinctly uncomfortable.

"Yes, it has," she said, but with little enthusiasm in her voice or manner.

"That's right," the Reverend Gibson said, "and we wish to lend any support we can to the brothers and sisters at First Methodist. Without upsetting the Reverend Brooks too much. 'Cause we think that essentially he's a decent man. That's just one of the things we wanted to talk with you about."

Grace nodded, but there was no enthusiasm in it. She looked tired, even afraid.

"I'll be honest with you," she said. "I'm very busy right now. I'm about to take on new responsibilities at church, and I've got this young man here to see to, at least for the time being. I don't know how much I'll be able to do."

"Gracie," I said. "You don't have to worry about me. I'm fine, and if you want to—"

But Dr. Gibson interrupted me.

"Anything you could contribute would be appreciated," he said. "And I think you'd really like the people in the circle. There're university professors, and doctors, lawyers, and a few local reporters . . . a very eclectic and sophisticated crowd."

My grandmother hesitated again, then shook her head.

"I'll have to think about it," she said. "I have many commitments. But thank you for asking me. I'm honored."

For a second the Reverend Gibson looked confused, then managed a polite nod. It was obvious to me that he was a man who wasn't used to being turned down. And that this visit had not gone at all the way he had expected.

"We're going to have a meeting in ten days at Lovely Lane Methodist Church. Wednesday night at seven o'clock. I hope you can make it."

"I'll give it serious consideration," my grandmother said.

"That's fine," the minister said.

He turned to me.

"There's room for you, too, young man," he said. "If you'd like to come."

"Really?"

"Really. We have many young brave and idealistic people in the movement. You might find this an educational experience that will be a little more interesting than *Silas Marner*." He smiled, and we shook hands.

Then he turned and nodded in a rather formal way to my grandmother, and was gone.

Grace

After he left, the living room seemed diminished, as the air itself does at the end of a summer thunderstorm. I felt elated but also worn out . . . and disturbed. Why didn't Grace jump at the chance to get involved? It was obvious to me that she had so much to give. I thought of her "spell" the other night. Could that have something to do with it?

She walked into the kitchen, and I followed behind her.

"He was great, wasn't he?" I said. "That was fascinating."

"Yes," she said. "It was quite an evening."

"Well!" I said eagerly. "What are you going to do? Do you think you're going to go?"

She looked at me with tired eyes.

"I don't know," she said. "I'm not sure."

"But why?"

She sighed deeply.

"It's just as I said. I have a lot of commitments. At the church and with various organizations I'm already in. I'm not twenty-five years old, Bobby. I can't spread myself too thin."

"Oh," I said. "I guess not. . . . It's just that I thought this is such a great movement, that you'd want to be part . . ."

"It is a great movement," she said. "But it's not my movement. It's their movement. The Negroes are doing well. They need money, and they need laws changed. Which means they need powerful people on their side. I'm neither rich nor powerful."

"Yeah, but Dr. Gibson came here especially to see you. That must mean he thinks you have something special."

She smiled and patted me on the shoulder.

"No, he makes a lot of these visits. What it really means is I have a grandson who has a very oversized picture of his grandmother."

"No, I don't," I said. "I'm goofy and I've got a lot of things wrong . . . God, I found out a whole boatload of things I didn't understand just tonight . . . I'll admit that. But I know you're not like everyone else. You're better. I know it."

But even as I said it, I doubted it was so.

Grace

My grandmother hugged me.

"It's been a very instructive evening," she said. "Now get to bed. You've got school tomorrow."

"Yeah," I said. "Hooray."

I smiled at her, she kissed my forehead, and I went off to bed. But I lay there again for a long time, wondering what was going on in Grace's heart. There was something stopping her, but I didn't know what. I replayed in my mind what she'd told the Reverend Gibson. She'd said she had "expanded duties at church." Was that just a line? She hadn't mentioned anything of that kind to me.

What could stop her from helping the movement? It made no sense to me. Finally, exhausted from worry, I fell into a troubled sleep.

Robert "Cap" Ward

*D*uring the next week I had three tests in school,
so I vowed to study and somehow put all my other
worries on the back burner.

During the day I worked hard at school, and in the afternoon I concentrated on history dates, Nathaniel Hawthorne (yes, *The Scarlet Letter*, a
book I hated then as much as *Silas Marner*, but which I completely failed to
understand and now love), alluvial plains, and hogbacks. At night my
grandmother worked on her sewing and read from the Bible or *Anna Karen-
ina*. I remember her comforting shape sitting under the old reading lamp as
I came out from the dining room where my studies were spread out before
me. Sometimes we would talk for a few minutes before getting back to our
own reading, but often we would merely smile at each other, and I would
feel something close to the old glow of happiness again. Then I would go
back to my schoolwork, redoubling my efforts after being inspired by my
grandmother, who often said to me, "One of the greatest, persistent joys in
life is being a perennial student."

Life went on in this simple, uncluttered way for a week. It was the
kind of week I had hoped for when I first came to Grace's, and I was
grateful.

And yet there was something that marred our happiness.

Though I didn't want to admit it, didn't even want to think about it, I was bothered by the feeling that my grandmother was hiding out, pretending to be this kind, old biddy happy to live in her old age through her books and her Bible . . . that the whole thing was some kind of sham and that neither one of us was really fooled.

I tried not to think of it. After all, it was her right to do whatever she wanted. But she had always insisted on trying to do one's best in all things. She had endorsed Gandhi as the greatest man on earth, and I had often heard her say that Dr. King was "our own Gandhi." I knew she felt that the Negro movement was the most important moral force in our country "since the Civil War."

No matter how I turned it, I couldn't understand why she wouldn't get involved, but I didn't want to bother her. I had too much respect for her to nag her about it.

And there was, too, a matter of my own survival. If I bugged her about her "moral shortcomings," she might send me home, and I feared that more than anything.

So I shut my mouth, studied, and told myself to mind my own business.

In this less-than-perfect but still fairly satisfactory way, things quietly progressed for about two weeks. I got an *A* on the *Scarlet Letter* paper and *B*s in geography and history, so I was back in the saddle again in school.

Life was fine, and I'd almost managed to put the larger questions out of my mind. Then my grandfather came home from sea.

I remember him wobbling up the front steps, his seabag thrown over his shoulder, his short sea legs almost comically bowed, his grizzled, sun-weathered face coiled in a frown. There was a scar over his left eye, a scar whitened by endless days on the bridge of freighters squinting into the sun. It was about an inch long, and it made him look fierce; it was easy to imagine him as a pirate or a smuggler. Now, though, he looked beaten, tired. He squinted at me as I read an anthology of ghost stories called *Beyond the Wall of Sleep* on the front porch, and I decided he also looked drunk. He nodded slightly, then gave me a lopsided smile.

"Hey, boy, how are you?"

G r a c e

"Hi, Cap," I said. Looking at his huge wrists and short but powerful arms, I felt small, insubstantial.

"Come over and give your old granddad a hug," he said. That surprised me. It had been years since I'd hugged him.

I lay down my book and walked over to him, feeling awkward and self-conscious. Cap dropped his seabag and gave me a squeeze. I half-expected him to crush me. Instead, I was surprised and moved by the gentleness of his touch.

What wasn't surprising was his breath, which reeked of cheap liquor. I remembered the stories of his drunken violence with my father, the fear in my dad's voice when he talked about his own boyhood, and I was a little afraid of him myself. And yet there was that tender, loving hug, the compassionate look in his eyes.

"Your grandmother in?" he said.

"No, she's up at the church. A meeting of some kind."

"Well, hell, of course she is," my grandfather said. "Last we spoke she told me you're living here with us for a while."

"That's right," I said. I dreaded that he would ask about my parents' problems and that I would have to tell him. I was ashamed, embarrassed, and frightened about what was going on at home. For most of the past two or three weeks I had successfully put them out of my mind, but one question from my grandfather would stir up my fears and worries about what recent damage my parents might have done to each other.

"You been watching after Gracie?" he said, and I breathed a sigh of relief.

"More like she's been watching after me," I said shyly.

"Yeah, well, she will do that," he said. "Like a hawk."

He smiled and rolled his eyes a little, then hoisted up his bag and went inside. I knew his pattern. He'd go upstairs, fall into bed, and sleep twelve or thirteen hours at a stretch. On board ship he barely slept at all, standing endless hours on deck watching the water, charting navigations. Once home, he collapsed, sometimes for two or three days. It wasn't at all unusual for me to come over for a weekend and still never see him.

But this day I followed him in. Suddenly, I had a great desire to talk with him. He started up the steps.

"Hey," I said. "You want some lunch?"

He turned his head and smiled down at me in his grizzled way, his seabag hanging over his shoulder.

"You the chef around here now?"

"Yeah, well, I was going to make myself a hamburger, and it's just as easy to make two."

He nodded.

"It is at that. Make it a cheeseburger, and I'll be down in a few minutes. Gotta get some of this sea grime offa me."

"Sure," I said.

I felt an inexplicable happiness. I was going to eat with my grandfather, just the two of us. What was strange about it was that up until that very moment I had no idea that I even wanted to know him at all. I liked him, admired him from afar, but the truth was, he intimidated me. He was like a man from another era, quiet, powerful . . . and the work he did seemed mysterious, romantic, like something out of a movie. Nobody else I knew had a grandfather who was a sea captain. Then I thought of the furtive look in my father's face whenever he mentioned "Cap." A furtiveness and something else, as well . . . longing, heartbreak. They'd never gotten to know each other very well.

As I flipped the burgers, a strange and lonely thought crossed my mind. For all his talk of the strain in their relations, my father missed his father . . . he needed to see his father, to talk with him. Just as I needed to talk with my dad. And none of us were getting anywhere. It was a thought that pierced me, stung me. I quickly shut it down. It was too disturbing a notion.

And there was something else as well. Maybe my grandfather knew something about my grandmother, something that would explain the mystery of her complex heart.

Cap came down twenty minutes later, his gray hair neatly brushed. He was wearing a blue T-shirt and his baggy blue navy reg pants. His black shoes were, as always, shined until you could see your reflection in them.

I poured him iced tea and gave him his cheeseburger, complete with toasted bun.

"There's condiments, too, if you want 'em," I said, pointing at the lettuce and tomato.

"Nope, like it plain. Let's just see if this young man can cook."

He smiled and took a bite of the burger. Chewed and swallowed, then nodded at me.

"Ain't half bad. Maybe I'll sign you on to serve in the galley next time I ship out."

"Hey, I could do it," I said. "You haven't ever tasted my spaghetti and my pea soup."

"Like pea soup fairly well," he said. "Grace makes it fine."

"Which is where I learned how to make it," I said. "And I'd love to ship out with you sometime."

He smiled.

"Nah, no kinda life for you. You got book smarts from what I hear. You should go to college and get a good job."

"You don't like your work?" I said.

"Okay for me," he said. "I don't know anything else."

He took another bite, then picked up a piece of tomato with his fork and laid it on his plate like a salad.

"When did you first ship out?" I asked.

"Oh, well, my dad . . . he took me out from down Mayo in a skipjack back when I was only about six. By the time I was ten I was sailing all around the bay. Me and my boyhood friends."

"Wow" was about all I could say. I tried to imagine myself sailing anywhere, and it seemed impossible.

"Was a good life down on the bay," he said. "Oyster pirating with my pals, and setting up Indian forts in the woods. Everything was fine till my daddy had his accident."

"What happened?" I wasn't eating anymore. My heart was thumping.

G r a c e

I had never expected to get into a serious talk with my grandfather. And yet, suddenly, here we were.

"Well, my daddy, his name was Robert, too, he was a great sailor, and a fine fisherman. He made money clamming, and he worked the oyster beds, and he used to bring home the finest oysters. So big you had to double-clutch 'em just to get 'em down. Anyway, he also took people out to the Chesapeake Bay on pleasure trips sometimes. Rich folks would come down to Annapolis and want to see the sights, and my daddy would take them out all around Gibson Island, places like that. One time, though, he went out there in the bay with this woman from Washington, D.C., some politician's wife, who had brought, of all things, her dog on board. That was against the rules, too, but she had a big yacht, and she said the dog could handle it. My daddy figured it would be okay. After all, the animal could swim.

"They went out in the morning, and they stayed all afternoon. Then the sky got dark, and it begun to rain. My daddy shoulda come back in, but something kept him out there. Maybe the woman, maybe his own pride . . . he always figured he could sail through any kind of weather. . . . Or maybe he figured it would just be a short blow and he could get back later. Anyway, they were having a rough enough time, the woman got sick and was scared to death, and then the dog got loose and jumped overboard. Guess he panicked, 'cause the woman said later he was drowning.

"My damn fool daddy jumped into the water to save that animal. The woman said she could see him wrestling with the dog, these huge waves maybe ten foot high towering over them. . . . They went floating up and down in the waves, the dog and my daddy, lightning crackling over their heads, the rain making them almost invisible in the dark water. Then she saw him again—he'd got his hands about the animal's waist, and using all his strength, he picked him up over his head and threw him toward the boat. Then, nobody knows what happened . . . a heart attack, another wave . . . something, because my daddy went under.

"The woman grabbed the dog and somehow managed to get him aboard. The two of them made it down the hatch to the galley and got in bed together. She said later she prayed that death would come soon and wouldn't be too painful for her damned animal. Come the next morning, the Coast Guard found her and that dog half-drowned, from where the boat had taken on water. Got 'em back to land and they were just fine. Said she was so happy she bought her dog a steak. They found my daddy two days later, washed up on Gibson Island right in the middle of some young people's beach party. And that was all she wrote."

"God," I said. "That's terrible. How old were you?"

"Ten years old," he said.

He looked at me and gave me a little smile that was more heartbreaking than any tears he might have shed.

"How did you feel?" I said.

He blinked at me as though he was shocked.

"What?"

"I mean you must have been heartbroken," I said. Then I felt self-conscious and wimpy for using a word like "heartbroken" around my grandfather.

But he got a funny twisted look on his face and nodded in agreement.

"Yeah," he said. "I guess. Had to go to work doing the things my daddy did, though. Didn't have a lot of time to think about it."

He smiled again, and I impulsively reached over and touched his shoulder. My grandfather jerked back as though I had zapped him with a live electric wire. But I managed to pat him anyway.

"You're doing good in school?" he said, as I pulled my hand back.

"So far, so good," I said.

"That's fine," he said. "Well, I feel a little tired. Guess I'll take me a nap."

"Okay," I said.

He got up slowly, nodded to me again, then turned and headed toward the stairs.

I sat at the table, stunned by what I'd learned. I had heard nothing of this and wondered why my father hadn't told me about it long before. That was his way, of course. He rarely told me anything about his own life. I knew virtually nothing about what he had done in World War II, beside the fact that he'd served in Pearl Harbor after it was bombed. I knew very little about his relationship with his father, except that it had been tense and sometimes violent . . . but now I wondered about that as well. Could this kind, sweet, and rather sad old man have been a violent drunken maniac? I supposed it was true, but it seemed like a long time ago and very far away.

Maybe I could get to know him . . .

But it wouldn't be easy. I knew he'd sleep for a long time. About an hour after he'd gone to bed, I went upstairs to get a book from my room, and I could hear him through his door, listening to his ship-to-shore radio. I suddenly realized that he never wanted to come to shore. Locked in his bedroom (read "bunk") with his radio on, he was only nominally home. Grace had told me many years ago that he was happy only aboard a ship, and now I understood that playing it this way, radio on, door locked, lying in bed (with a secret bottle?), he never had to "come home" at all.

On the third day he was home, Cap came out of the bedroom, dressed neatly in a white shirt, a dark blue tie, dress pants, and the always shined shoes. I ran into him as I was leaving the bathroom.

"How you doing, boy?" he asked.

"Fine," I said. "I'm doing fine. Going out?"

"Yep. Gotta go check up on a couple of things downtown at the Seamen's Union Hall. Ship's going out in a week or so, and I want to see if I can get me a berth."

"Oh," I said, feeling deflated. He was going away again, and I doubted if I would learn another thing from him. I started to walk past him when he tapped me lightly on the shoulder.

"You want to go down with me?" he said.

"Really?" I said.

"Sure. We can get us some lunch down there. Awww, but you probably got better things to do than hang out with a buncha old broken-down sailors."

G r a c e

"Not at all," I said. "Just let me get my clothes on."

"Fine," my grandfather said. "See you downstairs."

The Seamen's Hall was one streetcar and one bus trip away. We caught the yellow Number 8 streetcar, the last of its line, just down the street on the York Road. I remember walking down its wide aisles, aisles that felt like a spacious hallway. My grandfather sat near the window and looked out at the houses and the Boulevard Theater as I stared at the people on the streetcar. Workers, housewives, a man in a seersucker suit, with scuffed shoes . . . curiously out of place in the coming winter. Negroes, whites, two children playing peekaboo with each other, they all seemed happy, as the old yellow streetcar rolled along. In my hand was the pink transfer ticket to the bus, which I dreaded. The streetcar rocked along, pleasant, gentle, yet fast enough. The new Baltimore city buses made a horrible coughing sound as they started, and their sickening fumes always floated in the window, making me nauseated, as did the incessant rude braking of the bus. I could not understand why the city tore up the tracks, why the foul-smelling, ugly buses were replacing the streetcars. I asked my grandfather about it. He looked at me and rolled his eyes.

"Progress, son," he said. "They are putting them in 'cause they're cheaper to maintain, and they can go out to the suburbs. That and Henry A. Barnes, the traffic genius. Fella they brought in from New York. He made all the streets one way, and that doesn't work for streetcars. So you are riding on the last one."

I was astonished how much he knew about it. All my life my family had portrayed my grandfather as a kind of heathen, a natural man who knew the sea and nothing else. At home, so the myth went, he was a drunk and a fish out of water. I'd never thought of him as a man of feeling or intelligence. I had heard my father say many times, "Cap never even reads a newspaper." And yet it wasn't true, or at least it didn't seem true to me now. He had talked movingly of his own father's death, he was knowledgeable about the transportation changes in our city . . . who knew what else he might tell me?

G r a c e

We rode on down the line, and as we crossed into the Negro district, I began to see whole families sitting out on their white marble stoops. Badly clothed in the cold weather, their faces unblinking as they stared into the traffic, I wondered for the first time who they really were behind the masks. I thought of Rosa Parks and of the Reverend Gibson, and wondered for the five hundredth time why my grandmother hadn't yet embraced the civil rights movement. Again I felt that chill in my chest. What would my grandfather think of all this? I had never heard him speak of Negroes at all, but it was easy to imagine that he wouldn't like her being involved. Maybe her reluctance had something to do with him. With their marriage.

We rode up Eastern Avenue, past the cheap and ugly little shops. It seemed funny to me; my grandmother and grandfather were working-class people, but their home in Waverly was far nicer than the ones we passed on Eastern Avenue. And the people here, mostly sailors and steelworkers, who worked down at the Sparrows Point plant, were rougher looking, with sloped jaws and shapeless shirts they wore hanging out of their baggy, shiny-cloth pants. The women on the street wore tons of makeup and bright red rouge that made them look tawdry.

Even then I knew that the people I saw on Eastern Avenue were different from my family, though we were only one generation away from poverty. During the Great Depression Gracie had given piano lessons in the homes of the rich, over in Guilford, and Cap, when he was unable to catch a ship, had worked in F.D.R.'s federal parks program. But my family, especially my grandmother, had read books, had listened to great music and fought to understand it, and now as I passed by the endless poor whites loitering on the street, I gave a silent prayer of thanks to God that Gracie had been my grandmother, for without her I would have been here myself, with the lost, faceless crowd on Eastern Avenue.

The International Seamen's Union Hall was a huge dark building near the corner of Broadway and Register Avenue. The place looked dreary and depressing from the outside, but once we went in, I began to understand why my grandfather wanted to hang out there. All over the place men played checkers and dominoes, and swapped stories. As my grandfather went into the big, ramshackle place, men called to him, smiled, shook his hand.

"Hey, Captain Rob."

"'Morning, Robert."

"Hey, Cap, you gonna get to run down to the Gulf on the *Saint Esmerelda* next week?"

"Going up north, clear to Newfoundland, with a ton of coal, Cap. You oughta consider making the run."

Everywhere he went my grandfather was sought out, greeted with respect, humor, and affection.

I was amazed. The place was not only where you signed up for your next job, but it was a club, a clearinghouse for gossip, legends, stories. As we walked through the large, airy hall, gap-toothed men with leathery skin came up to my granddad and asked, "This your grandson?"

"You gonna become a sailor, Bobby?"

"Think this lad is ready for his first voyage?"

I found myself answering questions, smiling. "Yeah, I'd like to get out to sea. This summer, I'm gonna get Cap to hire me on." A little man with a broken nose smiled and looked into my face.

"Lemme tell you, you'll never go to sea with a better man than your granddad. Cap'n Rob knows every buoy in this bay, can sail the whole thing with his eyes closed, and I been with him when he's done it."

Which got a great happy laugh from my grandfather, who I suddenly realized was enjoying himself immensely.

As for me, I was so surprised by the friendliness and the camaraderie in the place that I could barely contain myself.

I was delighted by the men's obvious affection for my grandfather and thought once again of how his life had been presented to me, as a loner, no friends, only attached like a barnacle to the bow of his ship. Instead, he seemed to have a rich, full life among his sailor friends. I remembered going to my father's office once when he worked at IBM. The place was quieter than a cemetery, the camaraderie among the men nonexistent. My father had a little cubicle where he worked, and a sixty-five-year-old female assistant whose face had the look of a prune. White shirts, rep ties, short hair: you had to conform to be an IBM man. My father hated the place and lasted only a year. I vowed that day I would never take my father's path, no matter what.

My grandfather smiled and walked across the room to the registrar, who gave him a green card. "Now let's check the board and see what jobs are coming up," he said.

We walked across the room, past the tables and the men playing cards and talking. I saw one man waving his arms, obviously telling some huge lie, as a thin, sallow-faced man in denim held his stomach and laughed.

Cap and I walked to the end of the hall and looked up at the big board. First were the names of the ships—the *Excalibur,* the *Worthy,* the *Athena,* the *Cape Washington* . . .

"See, you got the names . . . then the type ships. You got your container ship, your liberty ship, your victory ship. Then you got the runs . . . foreign, coastal, which means runs sometimes all the way down to New Orleans, and then you got intercoastal, which is inland waterways . . . might be just down to Norfolk. Then you got the type jobs in the next part . . . the boatswain, maintence, master, O.S., which is ordinary seaman and wiper. Now that's one hot job."

"And you're the captain?" I asked.

"I been a pilot and a captain. See, a pilot takes the boat through all the inland waterways. The captain can't do that alone."

He shook another man's hand, and I felt an overwhelming affection and pride for him. All my life I had heard only what problems he had, and yet he could do this work, work my own father could never do . . . dangerous and hard work . . . and I thought that I now understood why my grandmother put up with him. In this world he was a man, and there was no doubt about it.

*　*　*

Things were so friendly, so chummy in the union hall that when they turned bad, I was unprepared. My grandfather was taking out a chaw of chewing tobacco from his pocket when he stopped abruptly and got a hard look on his face. His entire body stiffened, as though he were coiling himself, ready to strike. I blinked, confused, then looked to my left and saw Jerry Watkins come walking across the room. He had a couple of his pals with him, one younger, in his forties, and one Cap's age. Jerry himself was pushing sixty-five and he had a gut, but he was still big and rough, with a shock of striking white hair and a big ruddy face. He looked over at my grandfather and said nothing, but then he eyed me and gave a derisive little smile.

I felt my face redden, and I knew at once that Buddy Watkins and his brother Nelson had been laughing at me at home. Of course, they'd told Jerry about roughing me up and how my grandmother had to save me.

The whole encounter was over in half the time it takes to write about it, but it left its impression on both myself and my grandfather. I felt foolish, cowardly, and vowed that someday I'd get back at them.

"Big Jerry Watkins," Cap said. And his breath came hard.

"Jerk," I said.

"Tough guy, long as he's got his boys around," my grandfather said.

I didn't know exactly what he meant by that. I imagined he was referring to one of their legendary bar fights, but I hoped I'd never have to see one. My granddad was too old for that kind of thing, and the Watkins family, scum that they were, was capable of anything. It wouldn't have surprised me at all to see Nelson Watkins with a knife or a gun.

As we left the union hall, a big man ran up to my grandfather and the two of them hugged. He was maybe a year older than my grandfather, and he had a blowsy red face. When he turned I saw a piece of his left ear was missing.

"Hi, Rob. This young Robert?"

"Yessir," my granddad said. "Bobby, this is Terry Banks."

"Oh," I said. "I've talked to you on the phone, Mr. Banks."

Terry smiled; one of his front teeth was missing, too.

"Yeah, I guess we have at that. Rather talk to you than Grace, that's for sure."

He laughed, but Cap barely cracked a smile.

"Don't get me wrong," Banks said. "Your grandmother is a good woman. But she has a little problem with us boys having fun."

"Grace don't take much to fun," Cap said. "You doing all right, Terry?"

"Get me a ship I'll be doing better. Delores is driving me crazy. She got a new TV set, and she wants every damned thing they sell on it."

"Which is why I will never have one," my grandfather said. "They're just boxes made to sell junk, far as I can see."

He reached into his pocket and to my surprise pulled out a ten-dollar bill.

"This help you?"

"Hey, Cap, I can't take that," Banks said, making a face.

"Don't see why not," Cap said. "You buy the beer next time, okay?"

Banks smiled bashfully and took the money. He looked at me and nodded. "See a lot of your granddad in you. And that's a good thing. See you 'round, fellas."

He ambled off, an old sailor with the seaman's wobbly gait. I looked at my granddad.

"Old friend?"

"The oldest. Getting to be fewer and fewer of the old timers left."

We headed out through the big doors and walked into the suddenly chilly winds from the harbor.

"Let's go down and look at the ships," I said. I didn't want the afternoon to end.

We headed down Broadway, once one of the finest streets in old Baltimore. My mother had lived in this area of old Southeast as a child, and I remembered her telling me about the fabulous Easter Parades on Broadway, with "floats which towered to the sun." Now the blocks were inhabited by poor Negroes. Old bottles of rotgut lay broken in the street, and a few mangy dogs ran in a pack down the center grass plot, which grew wild with crabgrass.

My grandfather and I walked down past Aliceanna Street, where a boy with red hair threw a ball to an older, heavyset man who smiled down at him in a tender way that somehow crushed my heart. The sea air was strong, and I breathed in deeply.

"How long have Mr. Banks and you been friends?" I said.

My grandfather rubbed his jaw. "Reckon that would go back even before we had the union . . . long time ago."

We walked past a shop that sold Polish hot dogs. The smell of the grill was delicious, and I wanted to stop and eat, but not if it meant interrupting the story.

"Didn't plan on getting involved in no union stuff. But Terry and a couple of others did, and pretty soon there weren't no other way to go."

"You were involved in starting the Seamen's Union," I said. "But you never told me about that."

"You never asked," he said, turning toward me. There was an edge to his voice.

"Well, okay. Fair enough. I'm asking now," I said.

"Other reason I don't talk about it is it was a bad time. I mean we got a union going, but at a heavy price. You sure you want to hear all that old history?"

"Yes," I said. "All of it."

"Well, guess the best way of starting is to say that things wasn't always like you seen in there today. Guys happy to see each other, friends. Not that it's perfect now, not by a long shot. But in the beginning, it was really dog eat dog . . . this was back in 1929. In those days, there was no union."

"How'd you get jobs then?" I asked as we walked down the narrow streets toward Fells Point.

"Tell you how. Jobs was given to you by Mr. William Feeny. He was the crimp who could get you a ship or leave you standing at the dock."

"The what?" I said.

Grace

"The crimp," my grandfather said. "Crimps. That's what we called them, though I'm not sure how they come by it. They were the shipping agents who worked directly for the shipowners."

We headed down the cobblestone streets, past the No Name Tavern. Outside two old sailors sat on a parking pylon and passed a bottle of rotgut back and forth. My father stopped and pointed toward the dock.

"The crimps also owned half the bars around here, and the rooming house. You would go down to the dock to shape up—that means hanging around the crimp who had a list of the ships and jobs available. And how it worked was if you'd spent a good amount of money in the crimp's bar, he'd give you a ship. Especially if he'd extended you some credit, which he could take right out of your salary. If not, he'd just as likely pass you over."

"So it was like a monopoly," I said.

"Just about. And half the time the shipowners was in secret ownership with the crimps in the boardinghouse. The whole damned thing was rat lousy, I can tell you that. Not to mention the grub on board ship, which you wouldn't feed to your worst enemy. Food had maggots in it, and there were more rats on board than sailors. And the bunks was so small a midget woulda been crowded."

"So that was why you never slept on board ship?" I said.

"Yessir," my grandfather said, as we turned down Thames Street and saw a big Greek ship, the *Aegean,* sitting by the dock. "Was damned few guys who could sleep on those ships."

"How much did you make?" I said.

"Not much. I had a master's license so I got maybe . . . let's see— 1933, eighteen dollars a week."

"God," I said. "How did you and Gracie live?"

"Poorly," my grandfather said. "Damned poorly."

He saw the shock and dismay on my face and gave me a little smile.

"Then the union come along. The Marine Workers' Industrial Union, or M.W.I.U., started up. The owners said they were all Communists, and I suppose there was truth in it. But the guys I knew, Frank Walsh and the fella you just met, Terry Banks, they were just sailors, friends of mine, and they told me they were gonna get a union started and try and break the back of the owners. I never thought it would work, 'cause I knew some of those owners, Jim Gundy, Jake Guzman. There were as mean and hard as any man you can name. I knew right from the start there was gonna be big trouble, and I didn't want any part of it. But things happened to change my mind."

My grandfather sat down heavily on a rotted bench that looked out over the waterfront. In front of us an old tug called the *Wanda* bobbed in the water. She looked warm, secure, brave.

"Frank Walsh was like a dad to me. Ever since my own dad had died, he'd taken care of me and helped me learn all I had to know to navigate. He gave me my first berth on a ship, and he bought me drinks down at the old Wishing Well Tavern. Many a time he staked me to food or a five-spot that I'd take home to your grandmother. He was just a good mate. And that man could talk, too. . . . Funny, sometimes when I lay in bed at home, I think of him now, and his voice is as clear as a bell in my head. That happens when you get old. It's the damnedest thing. It can fool you totally. You hear a voice, and you could swear the person is alive, like old Frank . . . but he's been gone for nearly thirty years."

Then an extraordinary thing happened. My grandfather's voice broke. He was easily the toughest man I have ever met, and I had never seen much sign of emotion from him before. But now he began to sob, and I didn't know what to do or say. I stared out at the *Wanda* and tried to act as though nothing extraordinary was happening. Slowly, I moved my hand onto his shoulder. And this time he didn't jerk away.

"He was my friend, and he wasn't afraid of nothing. He talked up the union right down here on the docks. He handed out flyers, and he buttonholed guys in bars, telling them to join up. He did a lot of the latter 'cause Frank was a great whiskey drinker. One of the big owners and crimps was Grimek, Owen Grimek, and he was one tough guy himself. He didn't want any goddamned union, and he hired some boys from outta Washington, D.C. Plug uglies . . . they come around and wailed up on two of the union boys, Wally Davis and Bobby Hale. Beat the hell out of them, right down there on Thames Street."

My grandfather pointed down the street. There was an old man walking a small white dog.

"But that didn't do it. Both of them come back fighting for the union. And Frank gave interviews to the papers, naming Grimek as a scum sucker. I knew all hell was gonna break loose soon. By now the union was getting men to join. People were so damned broke they didn't care anymore. They had been pushed as far as they could go. And Billy and Terry were making speeches. So I felt I had to join or I couldn't look at my friends anymore. I came home and told your grandmother. I thought she might put up a fight about it, since we had two kids, but she just looked at me and said, "I knew you were going to do it. I've been thinking about it myself, and I've decided to come down and march with you."

"That sounds just like her," I said, and I thought of the Negroes again.

"Yeah, don't it?" my grandfather said.

"So did she march?" I said.

"She did . . . one time. But she had some problems after that. So she gave me moral support at home."

"Problems?" I said. "What kind of problems?"

My grandfather looked down at the ground, then up at me.

"Had a few of her spells," he said. "Bad ones, too. Took to bed for about three months."

"Really?" I said.

"You never seen her spells?" he said. "Can be bad. Walks in her sleep . . . bad stuff."

I started to tell him that I knew what he was talking about, but decided against it. It was clear that he didn't want to go on about it, and I knew if I pushed I might not learn about the union.

He rubbed his lined face with his old callused hand.

"Was about a week later when Frank got drunk down at the Wishing Well. I was with him for most of it, but I finally went down and fell asleep at the YMCA. They had rooms there you could pass out in if you were too drunk to make it home. The Y was started by church types trying to get sailors off the booze. Good intentions, but dull-as-hell preachers. Anyway, the guys told me the next day that Frank had left the tavern about ten to two. He was pretty well lit. He only lived up on Aliceanna Street, two blocks away, but he never made it home."

Now my grandfather stopped talking altogether and gasped for air.

"Cap," I finally said. "Are you all right?"

"Fine," he managed to say. "I'm fine. Thing is—they found Frankie floating facedown off of Pier Five. His throat had been cut from ear to ear. That's the way my best friend died."

He sobbed a little more, and I put my arm around his shoulders. I felt tears come down my own cheeks now, and I didn't give a damn who saw me.

"Guess they thought by killing Frankie it would stop us, but if they did, they had another thing coming. We buried Frankie down at Greenmount, and a big bunch of us joined up and then the fight really started. It was bloody, and it was ugly. That's how I got this."

He pointed to the scar above his eye.

"Grimek's guys gave you that?"

My grandfather shook his head.

"I wish. No, sir, I got this from the union boys themselves."

"What?" I was stunned.

"Yep. Things got kinda complicated after that. Our union went on strike, but we were never supported by the longshoremen. We tried to get them on our side, but they wouldn't go for it, because their New York leaders were all bought off by the damned owners. Now these new guys showed up, guys who were professionals, if you know what I mean, and they beat the hell out of some of our guys, and the word was they were in the pay of our so-called brother union—the longshoremen. I finally ran into it myself. I was coming back from a strike meeting, on the streetcar, down at 33rd and Greenmount right in front of the Boulevard Theater. Three guys jumped me right at the corner and hit me over the head with a lead pipe. They only got me a glancing blow, and I managed to scrape one of them across the face . . . as I was falling. He yelled like a cat . . . which startled me, and I tried to break away. But they caught me and took me back behind the Boulevard. Then they started in hitting with pipes. Hands, kicking me. As they were wailing away on me I could hear all these people laughing inside the theater. It was some old Wallace Beery movie, *Min and Bill*, I think. Real funny stuff, from the sound of it. I did my best out there. I got one of them pretty good with a right hand, but the other had a piece of a ball bat in his coat and he staved in the right side of my head. It went on like that for a while, and then I fell down in the alley and I stayed down."

"And they were guys from the New York Longshoremen's Union?"

"Yeah, bought and paid for by the owners. That's how it was. Some kids who was sneaking in the back door of the theater found me lying in my own blood. They took me over to Union Memorial, and the Chink doctor sewed me up. Those kids hadn't come along, neither one of us would be sitting here, and that's the God's truth."

I shook my head. I had a lot of romantic ideas in my head about unions from the folk songs of Pete Seeger, Joan Baez, and Bob Dylan, but I'd never heard one yet about union members beating each other's heads in.

I found myself hugging my old white-haired grandfather.

"I'm damned glad they found you," I said.

He smiled.

"That makes at least two of us," he said.

"Did you ever find out who the bastards were?" I said.

"Yeah . . . two of 'em were from out of town. The other was a kid named Dubinski, dumb Polack, would do anything for a buck. But the leader, the one I scraped across the face, him I knew."

"Who was he?" I said.

"Few days later I was up and about with a bandage on my head and one hell of a headache to boot. I seen a guy down at the hall, got a big scrape crossed his left cheek, and a couple of other bruises. He said he'd had an accident with his kids, playing 'round . . . but I knew that was three kindsa bullshit."

"Jerry Watkins," I said, breathless.

"One and the same," my grandfather said.

"Son of a bitch," I said. "And that's why you fought him at the Oriole Tavern?"

My grandfather looked surprised.

"How'd you hear about that?"

I laughed.

"My God, Cap, everyone knows about that."

He smiled slightly and rubbed his head.

"I reckon they do," he said. "But I'm not proud of it. I wouldn'tve done nothing about it out of respect for your grandmother, but he got drunk and started laughing at the union one day. . . . He made a crack about Frankie, too. I couldn't abide that."

"Jesus," I said. "The Watkins family."

"Yeah, they're bad," my grandfather said. "Say what you want, but they're just bad apples. The lot of 'em."

I felt a cold chill come, and I got up and lent my grandfather a hand.

"Let's walk back before we freeze," I said. "What happened to the union then?"

"Well, I was pretty beat up. I had headaches and couldn't get my balance just right. Never did come back all the way, neither."

I started at him in shock. So that was why he tilted from side to side when he walked. And all along I had thought it was because he was drunk or that it was just some "colorful" old salt characteristic. I felt like a fool.

"I wasn't sure I could stay with it, but Grace picked right up. She nursed me, night and day, and she come down here and she organizes the other women. I mean she was the one who did it, and they start marching for the strike, and they go right up to Grimek's home over on Bolton Hill with signs, some of them carrying babies. Man, I was worried to death, 'cause it wouldn't be beneath him or the other guys he was in with to strike down women and children. To those guys money comes before everything. I went with her a few times, and all the men admitted the girls had more courage than we did. They were out there singing union songs in front of his house and marching around with signs. Cold, rain, she and the other women were out there, and that's the damned truth."

"Did she have spells then?" I asked.

He looked at me, surprised.

"Yeah, the worst yet. She had to spend some time in the hospital."

"What hospital?"

"Out the Grove."

"Spring Grove Mental Hospital?" I said. "No . . ."

"I don't guess nobody ever told you that either," he said. "Funny, some of the things that don't get passed down."

"For how long?" I said.

"Month or so. They give her pills, and she stopped having them nightmares, but she wasn't the same after that . . . always a little afraid."

"But what could have caused them?" I said.

"You already asked me that, and I already told you I don't know," my grandfather said, and suddenly I could see a flash of his famous temper.

"You want to hear the rest of the union stuff or not?"

"Sure."

"Well, then, listen up. Seeing the women march, that gave us all a boost. And in the end, we convinced the local longshoremen to come over to our side. They broke ranks with the national union up in New York."

"Great," I said. Where was this history in public schools? Man, I thought, the Reverend Gibson is right. I could write some book reports on this stuff. A lot easier than on *Silas Marner*.

My grandfather pulled his coat up to his chin and continued, as we headed back up Broadway, past the Acropolis Bar, which featured "Real Live Greek Belly Dancers."

"We had a big overall union meeting at Saint Stanislaus Church on Aliceanna Street. It was a great day, all the guys—our union plus the local longshoremen—in one boat. But the national longshoremen's union head, Ryan, from New York, he's pissed. He comes marching all the way down here and brings some of his boys, like this neck-breaker, Chowderhead Cohen, to kick ass and convince the local guys not to break ranks. So they get here in their big, black limousine, but we had the door to Saint Stan's locked so they couldn't get in. Then when the vote was finished and we'd carried the day, voted to strike, we opened the church doors and Ryan is yelling and screaming, 'You'll be sorry! You'll regret this, you bastards!' And there's a moment when nothing happens, then all hell breaks loose. All of us swarmed Ryan and chased him and old Chowderhead back to their limo. Man, people were ripping up the streets and throwing the damned cobblestones at them. Took four squads of gendarmes to get 'em out of there, and there wasn't a damned window left in that limo as they headed back up Broadway and on to New York City where they damn well belonged."

"God, what a story," I said. I felt as though I was drunk on the excitement of history. My grandfather and grandmother's real history.

"You did it. You were part of something truly great," I said.

My grandfather smiled. But it was no great victory grin.

"Yeah, I guess . . . but I sometimes wonder if it was worth the life of my best friend. You know, at your age you're meeting new people all the time and you think you'll have a million pals, but it usually doesn't turn out that way. There's maybe two or three guys in my sixty-odd years I thought of as mates, and nobody else like Frankie. Well, that's all water over the dam, old battles that sometimes I can barely remember."

"But they matter just the same," I said. "They matter to me and to the guys who come after you."

My grandfather smiled and put his arm around me. Just for a few seconds.

"You're a fine boy," he said. "And don't let no one tell you any different."

"Thanks, Cap," I said.

"We'd best be getting home," he said. "Your grandmother will be worrying about us."

On the long, cold bus and streetcar ride back, my grandfather was quiet. It was clear both the trip and recalling those old and painful memories had tired him out, and I didn't pry anymore.

But there were questions I was dying to ask him. What other demonstrations had he and Grace been involved in? As we rolled along the pleasant old car tracks I seemed to recall my mother telling me long ago that my grandmother was involved in a factory strike of some kind. I wasn't sure what year that would have been or if it was even true. Maybe I'd invented it, as I was prone to do.

There was something else about that strike, too . . . something I'd half-heard long ago, but I couldn't remember exactly what it was. . . .

As we rolled up Greenmount Avenue on the old Number 8 streetcar, Cap fell asleep and his head lolled over on my shoulder. I started to move him back gently to his own side, but then thought better of it.

The truth was I liked his head there. I felt as though I were taking care of him. And that was fine.

As we rode along, I was overwhelmed with tender feelings for him. He was no longer just "the old salt" or my "colorful old granddad," but a real person. A person who had suffered, fought for what he believed, fought and won most of his battles with liquor, and carved out a life for himself, my grandmother, and their two kids. And now, though he might not be fully aware of it, he was giving me something precious, too . . . a history I could be proud of.

Because of the stories he'd told me, there were places in my hometown that I would never see in the same way again.

And soon we came to one of them, the Boulevard Theater at 33rd and Greenmount. I'd been to the old neighborhood movie theater dozens of times, but now I wouldn't remember the Jerry Lewis or cowboy pictures I saw there. No, instead I'd think of the alley behind the place, the alley where Jerry Watkins and his goons almost killed my grandfather.

As we went past the theater and I looked at the movie poster for *The Wackiest Ship in the Army*, I felt a cold fury run through me.

The goddamned Watkins family. How I hated them.

Bullies and creeps from three generations back. I had a fantasy of smacking Buddy's head with a rock, then I thought of Grace, of Gandhi, of his teachings . . . the moral imperative to "love one's enemies."

A good and profound philosophy, no doubt, but when it came to the Watkins family, I didn't see how I was going to pull it off.

Cap's ship

The morning sun was bright the next day, a respite from the gray cold weather we'd been having, and because I'd forgotten to adjust my blinds the night before—exhausted as I was by the emotional day with Cap—it shone brightly right into my eyes. I checked the clock. It was ten to six and I had at least another hour to sleep, so I forced myself from my aunt's warm bed and went to the window in order to let the blinds down and shut them tight. I was half-finished doing just that when my eyes focused on the garage rooftops just beyond the alley behind my grandmother's backyard.

At first glance I thought I was still asleep and dreaming one of those super realistic, down-to-the-last-and-tiniest-detail dreams that mimic reality to a maddening degree.

I shook my head, blinked, and looked around the room, then slowly turned my head and looked back out at the garage roofs.

No, it wasn't any dream.

My grandmother was sitting in the lotus position on top of her garage. She was wearing a purple-and-green sari, the one Mr. Pran had given her several months ago as a token of appreciation for all the times she'd had him to the house. Grace's hands were folded together in her lap, and she was looking up at the sun through oversized red-and-green sunglasses.

I recalled Mr. Pran teaching our family how to meditate on the living room rug.

Good Lord, I thought, that must be what she's doing.

I stared out at her in silence. She looked to me like an Indian grandmother, an eccentric silent movie star, or the perfect combination of both: a mental patient. Then I remembered Cap saying she'd had to serve time at Spring Grove. What if she was having a full-fledged breakdown? I squinted into the burning sunlight and saw something move in her lap.

It took me a second to make out what it was: Grace's cat, Scrounge, the rascal. He was happily rubbing himself against her.

The two of them looked warm and happy. Content. Mad.

I opened the window and started to yell down to her, but then I remembered that my grandfather's room was also in the back of the house and that if he heard me and saw Grace on the garage roof, there would be hell to pay.

No, I had to keep him out of it, get her to come down on her own.

I put the window back down, quickly threw on my jeans, a T-shirt, a crewneck sweater, and my Jack Purcells, then crept out of the room and hurried (tiptoeing as I went) down the steps and through the house.

I made sure the back door didn't slam as I went out into the yard. Then I leaned on the trunk of the old holly tree and looked up at the roof.

"Ahem," I half-whispered. "Grace . . ."

Nothing. She turned a little, though, and for a second I thought she'd heard me. Then I realized she was merely turning with the sun.

"Grace," I hissed again. "Hey . . ."

Now she looked down on me.

"Yes, honey," she said. "Isn't it a glorious morning?"

"Yes, it is," I said. "Is it nice up there on the roof?"

"Why don't you come up and find out?"

That was not what I had expected her to say.

"Come on," she said. "You can sit with me."

"But what if Cap sees us?" I said.

"Rob? He's asleep. If they dropped the atom bomb, it wouldn't bother him. Come on."

"Well, okay," I said. Maybe if I humored her a little, I could get her to come with me.

I went around the back of the old garages and walked up onto the weed-filled lot, which was almost even with the garage tops. Then I stepped up on the first cement block some kid had put there God knew how many years ago and pulled myself up on the rooftops. It wasn't what you would call a hard climb, but it wasn't a snap either. I wondered how my grandmother had managed it.

I walked across the Weavers', the Richardsons', and the Latrobes' garages before I got to my lotus-sitting grandmother and her now dozing, curled-up cat.

I sat down next to her, but the old tar roof was already heating up, and I quickly jumped up.

"Here," she said, moving over on the Indian rug she was using. "I can share this with you."

"Thanks," I said, sitting down.

"You're very welcome."

"Grace, do you mind if I ask what you're doing up here?"

She folded her arms and smiled pleasantly.

"I am breathing in and out."

"Oh," I said. "I kind of thought so."

My grandmother smiled, but there was pain in that smile, not happiness.

"There is a story Mr. Pran told me about an angry man who had lost his wife and his business. A monk told him if he sat by a magic stone in the lake and breathed deeply and listened intently, he would receive satori, or enlightenment. So the man sat by the spring for two years. Finally, at the end of the second year the stone spoke to him and said, 'You must forgive your enemy.' The stone said something else as well, but the man was so angry at the first part of the sentence he failed to hear the end of it. He walked away, but he felt no relief from his pain. He met the monk who had sent him there in the first place, and berated him for wasting his time. The monk smiled at him and said, 'I, too, heard the message, but I heard all of it.' The man said, 'All right, then, what was the rest?' And the monk said to him, 'Even if your enemy is dressed in your own robes.' At that the man smiled and felt satori. He went back to his village and began his life anew."

I said nothing, but I felt a strange stirring inside.

"Then are you the man?" I said to Grace.

"I'm not sure," she said. "But I'm waiting. And I think it's a nice story."

"How long have you been . . . waiting?"

"Two years, give or take a few weeks."

"Two years?" I said. "But why on the garage rooftop?"

"Why not? I'd rather it be a mountain. But I don't have time to drive out to western Maryland. This will do. Gandhi used to meditate in prison or right on the street."

"Oh," I said. I was still thinking about the story she had told me.

"Do you like the dress?" Grace said.

"Yes, very much."

"Mr. Pran gave it to me."

"I know," I said. "I was there when you got it. But on the garage roof? In Baltimore?"

"I don't know," she said. "I think I improve the roof."

"Undoubtedly. But what about the neighbors?" I said, smiling.

"The only one who's said anything is the Watkins family," Grace said. "And we don't bow to trash like them. Meditation is a wonderful thing. I thank God that I met Mr. Pran. Sometimes I think that God sent him to me . . ."

Then she stopped and looked troubled.

"What is it?" I said.

"Oh, nothing . . . just one of life's little ironies."

"I don't get it," I said.

"It's too complex to get into," she said.

"Does anybody in the family know you do this?" I said.

"I don't think so," she said. "Why should they? They'd just think I'm getting crazy in my old age, and you know what? They'd be right."

I shook my head. "Sometimes I feel as if I don't know anything anymore."

"That, my dear grandson, is a feeling that will increase as you grow older and wiser. Believe me . . . I don't know a tenth of the things I used to be dead-certain of when I was your age."

"No?" I said, bewildered.

"No. But the ones that I do know, the few I do know . . . I really believe. And one of them is that it's good to meditate on the rooftop of the garage early in the morning. It's a time when your spirit is open, and maybe God's spirit as well. And there are things I sorely need guidance on. That's the truth."

"Like the civil rights movement?" I said.

"Like mind your own business," she said. But she said it gently, then asked, "Would you like to meditate with me?"

"I don't know," I said. "The last time I got a headache."

"You have to just breathe through that. Let's try."

"Oh, boy," I said.

"Now the trick is to breathe slowly and deeply, until you slowly lose self-consciousness . . . which, by the way, could be, for you, a very good thing."

Grace was smiling again, and she folded her arms and took a deep breath.

I folded my own arms and took a deep breath.

"Do you close your eyes?" I said.

"You do if you don't have sunglasses," my grandmother said. "'Cause without them you'll be seeing sunspots all day."

"And we wouldn't want that," I said, laughing.

"No," my grandmother said. "Now breathe, close your eyes and feel the goodness of the sun . . ."

I shut my eyes and breathed deeply and smelled the tar rooftops.

I heard my grandmother breathe deeply again, and I tried it myself.

Within a few minutes our breaths were in synch and something began to happen to me. I forgot the fact that the neighbors might be watching us from their kitchens or bedrooms, I stopped thinking that any minute the police were going to come and send both of us to Spring Grove, and I felt strangely peaceful. Grace was right. The sun *was* warm and good, and I was flooded with sweet sensations. I took another breath and forgot where I was. It was uncanny, wonderful.

I wasn't on the old tar roof of the battered old garages behind my grandmother's house in Waverly. I was floating over . . . over the Ganges, and there were Indians in loincloths bathing below me, and there was Mahatma Gandhi in the river pouring holy oil over the head of one of the faithful.

Then I opened my eyes—just for a second—because though meditation was very pleasant, there was still a certain insecurity involved. Like I might fall off the garage roof and break my neck.

What I saw shocked me again. My grandmother's eyes were open, and she was looking straight ahead. But all her breezy jocularity was gone, and she seemed to be staring (as she had the night of her nightmare) at something so horrible, so terrible that it was literally frightening her out of her wits.

"Gracie," I said. "Are you okay?"

But she didn't answer. She continued to stare straight ahead. Then she began to utter a deep moan.

"*Oooooooooh, Oooooooooooh.*"

My throat got dry, and I reached over and held her hand.

"Grace," I whispered. "Hey, it's me."

"*Ooooooooh,*" she said.

"Grace," I said, louder.

She blinked and looked at me, her face full of fear.

"Honey," she said.

"Are you okay?" I asked.

"Get me out of here," she said.

"Okay."

I uncoiled myself and stood up, then slowly helped her to her feet.

"You were moaning and you looked like you were in pain," I said.

"I was. The pain was terrible," she said. "Let's go inside. I think we're done for today."

"You looked like you were seeing something, a ghost," I said. "Could you say what it was?"

She looked at me and shook her head.

"No," she said. "I couldn't say."

I was sure she was holding back. I wanted to press her to tell me, but suddenly we were interrupted by a sleepy voice from the back of her house.

My grandfather's voice:

"Grace, when you two come down from there, would you have Bobby run down to the corner and pick up some milk?"

I turned and saw my grandfather looking out the window.

"Honey, would you mind?" she said to me, giving Cap a little wave.

"Not at all," I said.

I looked up and saluted my grandfather. He gave me a snappy salute back, then closed the venetian blinds.

"You can put it on our tab at Pop's," she said. "Thanks, honey."

"You're welcome," I said as she opened the gate and walked toward the back door.

Dazed, I started down to the corner store. I was in a mild state of shock. My grandmother meditated on the garage rooftop, and my tough old grandfather knew all about it and seemed not one whit concerned.

He knew a lot more about my grandmother than he was letting on. And I suddenly thought that maybe he also knew what phantom was following her.

But I doubted I'd ever get it out of him or her.

I turned by the Bradys' house, the end house on the row with a bay window. And there in that window was one of Sue Retalliata's now-famous screen paintings of a waterfall, a blond-haired milkmaid, and some ultra-green pasture land in what looked like the mountain country of western Maryland.

I stopped still and stared at it. Grace's oldest friend, Sue, of course. Maybe my first day of meditation had given me an answer after all.

I called Sue that day, but she wasn't in. Her maid, Alma, told me she was giving a screen painting workshop and speaking at a folk arts conference in mountain country, Cumberland, Maryland. She wouldn't be back for three days. There was nothing that could be done until then.

Then I remembered Howard Murray, my Negro friend from school. We had talked about playing over at Waverly Rec many times, but I'd never actually made the call.

Now I wondered about that. Why hadn't I called him? Sure, I was busy, and a lot was going on in my life, but wasn't the plain truth that I was scared?

I condemned Grace for talking about civil rights without doing anything about it, but was I any better?

And why did I have to wait for her lead at all?

I met Howard at the Waverly Junior High Rec Center at four o'clock. I was twenty minutes early. My stomach had a serious case of butterflies. I remembered my great happiness the night before when I had finally gotten the nerve to call him, how I was sure I was doing the right thing, but now, as I waited for him to show up, I wondered where all my resolve and spirit had gone.

I felt small, scared, self-conscious. Waverly Rec Center wasn't even my own rec center. It was only five blocks from Grace's and I played there occasionally, but I didn't know many of the guys who hung out there, only Johnny Brandau, Ray Lane, and two tall blond brothers, Timmy and Billy Weaver. They were all good guys and I was sure they wouldn't mind, but there were other boys who hung out there whom I didn't know, who had long "drape" hair, as we called it back then. (Even in the '90s the ducktail "drape cut" is still the haircut of choice among many of the poor whites in Hampden and the Harford Road.) These boys were rough badasses, most of whom had recently migrated from the Deep South or nearby West Virginia. I got along with most of them. The truth was, only a few of them were really bad, but all of them wanted to look bad . . . and I was pretty sure none of them wanted to be caught liking a Negro or would help if it came to an unfair fight.

There was a tall rangy boy named Tommy Harkey who worried me, and the two horrible Harper brothers, who looked like skinny clods of dirt shoved over some muscles and sinew, and who liked to fight over anything or nothing. There was another big kid nicknamed Shelf (because his forehead looked like a concrete shelf), who lumbered about mumbling to himself. Shelf brought a switchblade knife to the court one time, and though he hadn't cut anybody with it, I didn't like the idea that he was probably going to be basket hanging and calling fouls on Howard.

And if that weren't worry enough, it occurred to me, just as Howard Murray rode up on his very cool three-speed English bicycle, that Waverly Rec was the place where Buddy and Nelson sometimes hung out. Neither of them played ball. Nelson was too old to play with kids and Buddy too muscle-bound to be any kind of basketball player, but he hung out with the Harpers, making comments and ragging on anybody who missed a shot.

As I greeted Howard and we walked into the gym, I felt my heart go into my mouth. Who was I kidding? I wasn't any battler. If anything uncool went down, all that would happen was that Howard and I would both get the hell beaten out of us . . . or worse.

I couldn't look anybody in the eye as Howard and I started warming up. Howard was a good ballplayer, a great leaper and a smart passer. I had a better outside shot, or at least I always had at school. Suddenly, I found myself with such a case of nerves that I couldn't hit a ten-footer. Then Howard smiled and started whipping me passes, and I got into the flow of the game, found my rhythm, and my jumper started falling.

I hit five in a row, then fed Howard, who made two beautiful reverse layups, and soon I didn't care when the Harpers showed up and started mumbling to themselves in the corner of the gym.

I had no doubt what they were talking about, but I took my cue from Howard himself, who remained cool, and concentrated on his shot.

A few seconds later Mouse Harper came over and started shooting with us. He wasn't a bad player, and Howard smartly set him up with a couple of good passes, which he converted into buckets. His bigger brother Butch stayed on the side, though, watching and scratching his chin stubble.

Another boy joined Harper, then Kohl, a big, heavyset guy I knew who'd developed a stutter after sniffing glue.

Indeed, he had once tried to enlist me in his favorite hobby, saying, "C-c—come on W-W-Ward, g-g-glue is h-h-harmless."

But today he seemed in an affable mood; when he got closer to me, I realized he was stoned. His eyeballs rotated in different directions.

We had warmed up for about as long as you can do that before people get anxious for a game, and I found myself anxiously looking to the door.

My prayers were answered a few minutes later. My friends Johnny Brandau and Ray Lane arrived together. They were both terrific players, and better, I knew that they had both played ball with Negroes many times at school.

Without saying a word, both of them understood that Waverly Recreation Center was undergoing a historic change. They greeted Howard with hugs, and their presence broke the tension. Nobody was going to mess with Howard Murray with them around, and I quietly let out a sigh of relief.

But, as it turned out, things got even better than that, because Lane, a huge, well-muscled but extremely athletic guy, knew Murray from school.

"Hey, Howard," Lane said. "You come over here to teach Ward how to shoot?"

"Something like that," Murray said.

G r a c e

"Got your work cut out for you," Johnny Brandau said, laughing.

"You guys are going to have to eat those words," I said.

And with that, Murray and I began playing two on two against Brandau and Lane, and something like the miraculous happened. Maybe it was the sheer relief I felt knowing that we weren't alone, or maybe the chemistry between us was a by-product of the amazing high we both felt from what we were doing. Whatever, things clicked between us. We knew where each of us was going to be, we anticipated rebounds, put back tip-ins, passed expert behind-the-back passes, ran perfect pick-and-rolls, and beat Lane and Brandau, both smooth players, by two baskets.

Afterwards, we all drank water from the fountain (the same fountain) and just hung out together in a way that felt somehow heightened and charged with excitement. Though no one said anything about it (to say something would be uncool), I think everyone realized right here and now that the Waverly Rec Center would never be the same again.

We felt so damned good, all of us, that we went back inside and played another game. That caught a couple of the kids off guard. Now Mouse Harper, who obviously hoped this whole thing was a fluke and that the nigger and his friends were gone, gave us a snarl. But Ray Lane went over to him, put his huge weightlifter's arm around him, and said, "Little Mouse, you're looking bad. You want to rumble?" All said kiddingly, of course, but Little Mouse wasn't quite as moronic as he looked. He understood the tone of things, so he just laughed and talked his usual bullshit and quickly disappeared out the door.

That's the way it went until five o'clock, with Howard Murray and I on some fantastic wavelength, making shot after shot, and everyone laughing, joking, picking up on our good vibes.

Then, as we packed our things to go, I looked at a couple of the hairhoppers, and it occurred to me that they seemed relieved as well . . . and I thought that maybe they had all secretly dreaded the day Negroes would show up and they would be forced to act like the creeps their parents expected them to be. Maybe they were damn well relieved that they had behaved better than they expected, too, and that deep down nobody wanted to be the asshole in Montgomery, Alabama, who was caught by a photographer pouring a Coke over a Negro student's head as the kid tried to get service in a lunchroom.

Try living with that picture in history books in twenty, thirty, or forty years.

"Yes, son, that's your daddy acting like a complete and total asshole, beating up on a black guy just because he wanted to eat some lunch. Hey, don't it make you feel proud?"

Outside Murray and I said good-bye to Ray and Johnny, who were heading over to Memorial Stadium—only two blocks away—to try to hustle up some end-zone Colt tickets for next Sunday's game, and there was steam coming out of our mouths, and smiles and punches on the arm, and I could tell nobody really wanted to go, because without saying anything about it, everybody knew that in our own little way we'd done something very cool. And Ray Lane said, "Hey, Howard, bring your big brother Billy over next week. I want to block his shot." And Howard laughed and said, "Hell, I do that every day," and we all laughed again and then went our separate ways.

On the way home that evening I felt like Superman. We'd done something great, and I promised myself that this was only the beginning, that I was going to be part of the movement, and I was so happy I wanted to yell, and jump in the air. I was going to read Martin Luther King's speeches and study Gandhi and get in touch with the Reverend Gibson and maybe help the Negroes in Grace's church, too, whether she did or not. Even so, I was still determined to find out what was holding her back. There had to be something, something related to those spells, and I vowed to deal with that, too, as soon as Sue got back.

All these thoughts were racing through my mind as I headed home . . . still flying from what Howard and my friends and I had pulled off at the Rec Center. Nobody would write about it in the paper, nobody would show it on TV, but it was one more place that would never be all white. I had finally done something real.

Then I came to Rado's Drugstore, the great old store on old York Road, with its green awning, white tile floor, black wire chairs, and real old-fashioned soda fountain, the place where each month I bought my sacred copy of *Mad Magazine*. As I walked past the door, Mouse, Butch Harper, and Buddy Watkins came out onto the sidewalk and blocked my path.

"Hey, hey," Buddy said. "Look who we got here, it's Martin Luther Coon."

I felt my mouth get dry, and my heart raced furiously.

"That's not funny," I said. But my voice was weak, squeaky.

"No?" Watkins said. "I thought it was funny. Didn't you, Mouse?"

"Yeah," Mouse Harper said in his paper-thin voice. "I thought it was real funny."

Buddy pushed me backward with both hands, and I fell over something and cracked the back of my head on the ground.

I groaned and looked up and saw Mouse Harper getting up from where he had kneeled down behind me. The oldest trick in the book . . . one that didn't hurt my head so much as my pride.

Buddy stood over me, his legs spraddled, and spat down in my face.

"You think it's cool to bring niggers to our rec? Do you?"

I was terrified now. I wanted to say something brave, something hard, something unforgettable like Bogart, or Alan Ladd in *Shane*, but I was close to whimpering.

"We were just playing basketball," I said weakly. And hated myself instantly for betraying my real intentions and all we had accomplished.

"Oh, they were just playing basketball?" Buddy said.

He kicked me in the leg hard. I let out a cowardly whimper.

"Come on, cut it out," I said. I hated my whining, gutless voice.

"Ooooh, stop it, you're hurting her," Mouse said.

"I'm going to hurt her ass a lot more," Buddy said, curling up his lip, "if you ever bring any niggers to that playground again. You understand? You don't even live in this neighborhood. So why doncha go back and live in Northwood with the rest of the fags?"

I said nothing but knew that he was right. I was weak—completely, depressingly weak.

"Kick his ass," Mouse Harper said.

"Nah," Buddy said. "He'll go tell his grandmother, the nigger lover, and she'll call the cops. One of these days we'll take care of her, too."

I said nothing to that either. I only wanted to scurry away, have them leave me alone.

"Remember, any more niggers and you're going to get a serious ass whipping," Buddy said.

He kicked me again in the right shin, just to emphasize his point. Then the three of them laughed at me and went back inside the drugstore.

I pulled myself up slowly. My leg was bruised and my head ached, but neither of those injuries hurt half as bad as my spirit. I began to cry, not in pain, but because of the huge disappointment I felt with myself.

Who was I to try to help the Negroes? I was worthless, not even fit to help myself.

What a sorry joke I was. I was going to help Negroes free themselves, but any couple of redneck jerks could scare me into denying everything I stood for.

I pulled myself up the steps to my grandmother's, feeling a bolt of shame tearing through me. I wished God would strike me dead. I wanted to rip my own skin from my face . . .

When my grandfather came out of the kitchen, the intensity of the shame reached an unbearable pitch. God, if he knew what I really was. He was a real man, afraid of no one. He took ships all the way to the Gulf of Mexico, he was famous for bar fights, no quarter asked and none given, he'd helped start the union. Taken beatings to do it . . . lost his best friends.

And due to some freak of nature I was his flesh and blood.

But how could that be? I was a coward, yellow. I was nothing . . . nothing at all. All talk, all bullshit.

I ignored his friendly greeting, went upstairs, shut the door, and lay in bed, curled in the fetal position, tears of self-hatred running down my face.

I was becoming a champion at self-loathing, which I now feel is probably a greater sin than physical cowardice. But back then, in my emotional whacked-out teens, every feeling I had was like a bombshell exploding inside my heart. For the next few days, when I wasn't lost in my studies, I experienced a gnawing agony that not only had I been a coward again with Buddy but that I might be one forever. In my mind he loomed larger and larger. I shut my eyes and imagined him standing over me, huge, muscled, unmovable in his wrath and stupidity and taste for violence. What chance did I have against him?

In school, Howard Murray wanted to relive our great day at the Waverly Rec, but I dodged him when he approached me, fearful that he'd find out how I'd chickened out as soon as my little bodyguard of friends had left me.

I lost myself in my studies and told myself I was now officially a wimp. I'd get a pocket protector and start collecting colored pencils. Maybe I'd get a slide rule . . . change my name to Norbert.

Because I was a Norbert in my soul. Norbert Weasel . . . the wimp . . . and not as good as an actual Norbert, because whoever he was, he was probably a genius, and I was just an average, everyday, garden-variety hypocritical coward.

I went on like that in my head for three or four days.

Then gradually, I began to talk to myself quietly. I said to myself in the calmest way I knew how that I would never chicken out with Buddy or Nelson or any of their friends again. That the next opportunity, no matter what it was, no matter how outnumbered I was, no matter if they had knives or weapons, I would fight back.

That was it. That was all there was to it. The next time.

I swore to myself I'd be brave the next time I encountered my enemies from across the street. All well and good. But what I faced next at my grandmother's was even more baffling, something that I can't fully explain even now, and something that no amount of steely resolve could prepare me for.

It was late at night, and I was sleeping fitfully in my aunt's bed when I heard something in the hallway. At first I assumed it was either my grandmother or Cap heading down the narrow hallway to the bathroom. I shut my heavy lids and started back to sleep.

But there was a small crack in the doorway—in that old crooked house none of the doors ever completely shut—and I peered through it and saw . . .

Even now I'm not at all certain what it was I did see.

A light, a bright white light, but definitely not a light from the old yellow bulbs that hung from the ceiling. No, the light seem translucent, liquid, as if it were flowing down the narrow hallway.

I blinked my eyes and shook my head. This wasn't possible.

When I looked again, it was gone.

Quickly, I jumped from my bed and eased out into the hall.

It occurred to me that maybe it was one of the Watkins boys, Buddy or Nelson. They'd gotten into the house and were up to something.

I felt myself shiver as I went out in the hallway. Two feet away from my bedroom door it was as though the temperature had suddenly dropped thirty degrees. I wrapped my arms around my body as I looked into my grandmother's room.

She was sound asleep. I could see her body rising and falling.

I turned the corner and looked into my grandfather's room. He was snoring contentedly, probably dreaming of ships on the Chesapeake.

I looked down the hallway at the bathroom door.

It was open slightly . . .

There was the light.

"Hey," I said. "Who is that?"

The light darted and became much more intense. It nearly blinded me. I threw my hands over my face—

And then, whatever it was, was gone.

I stood there in the dark, cold hallway, freezing.

My grandmother was suddenly at the door. Her long gray hair hung down her back, and she suddenly looked like a witch.

"What was it, honey?"

Grace

"I don't know," I said. "Some kind of light."

"From the street?"

"No . . . This was something else."

She looked at me for a second, then turned away, and I thought I could see shame and fear in her eyes.

"If I didn't know better, I'd have thought I'd seen a ghost," I said, half-laughing.

"Go to bed," she said. "You're overtired. You've been through a lot lately."

"Yeah, okay," I said. "I just can't believe it. I wonder what it could have been—"

"It's late," she said sharply. "Now go to bed. And let's have no more talk of ghosts."

She turned and headed back into her room.

I looked down the hallway, but there was no sign that anything had been amiss.

But I felt the coldness still and wished I'd asked my grandmother why she had been shivering . . . though I doubt she would have answered me.

Two days later, Sue Retalliata called me at home.

"Hi, honey," she said, "Are you coming over today?"

"Yes," I said. Still dazed by what I had or hadn't seen in the hallway that night, I barely remembered talking to her.

"Meet me at my studio, will you?" she said. "I've got some orders to fill."

"That's fine," I said. "It must be really exciting to be getting all this attention. Was it fun up in Cumberland?"

"Oh, yes, sweetie," Sue said. "But it was hard walking up there with this leg of mine. Those are real mountains they've got up there, let me tell you. I've got to run now. See you at one."

"Fine," I said. "See you then."

✻   ✻   ✻

G r a c e

Sue's studio was in an old warehouse, behind Read's Drugstore on 27th Street in Waverly. She shared it with a tailor named Abe Epstein, an old man with a shock of blond-white hair that fell over his ghostly face. I saw him inside, working on a buttonhole in a pool of yellow light. I waved, and he nodded back as I walked through his shop and rang the doorbell.

She hobbled down the steps, dressed in her paint-spattered smock, and then led me back upstairs to her loft. The place was cheaply furnished but she had an eye for detail that always struck me as unique. The old couch was gracefully designed and covered with a quilt she'd made herself. There was a settee and a footstool, covered in satin. The table lamps were from the '20s, and they had yellowed parchment shades.

The room had big square windows, and I suddenly saw Sue Retalliatta in a different light, not just as a friend of my grandmother's but as an artist, and a person in her own right.

Laid out on sawhorses throughout the room were screen paintings in various stages of completion, one of a white horse in a blue meadow, another of a peasant and a boy walking along a railroad. Another in the corner was unique. It depicted a woman standing on a street corner. There was a toughness to it that all the others lacked. The woman looked hard, ill-used, cheap.

"I like that one," I said, walking over to it.

"Really honey?" she said. "It's something new I'm trying. But I don't think it'll sell too well. People want these nineteenth-century nature scenes, but I got to thinking, why just paint escapist stuff? Why not paint something a little grittier? So I went outside and I looked around. That's a streetwalker a few blocks down the road. She's there every day."

"A hooker," I said, trying out a word I'd just learned on the playground.

"Oooh, you shouldn't call her that," Sue said.

I laughed, slightly embarrassed.

"What difference does it make?" I said. "I mean, we both know what she is."

"I don't know," Sue said. "I think streetwalker sounds kinder. That's all. Anyway, I doubt if anyone would want to put it in their window. So I'm just painting these for myself."

"Well, I like it," I said. "I like it a lot. It looks real. Like the city."

"Good," she said. And there was pride in her voice. "I sometimes get tired of pleasing people."

I was pleasantly surprised. I'd always thought of Sue as living to please others. But, of course, she got tired of it.

We sat down in one of her old quilt-covered chairs, and I accepted a glass of lemonade.

Her cat, Tommy, immediately jumped into my lap. I stroked him and he purred gratefully.

"Sweet old Tom," I said.

Sue smiled bashfully.

"He knows a nice person when he sees one," she said.

I smiled . . . and said nothing. I really didn't know how to begin.

"Well," Sue finally said, "I'll bet you didn't come over here to find out about screen painting."

"Not exactly," I mumbled. "This has been a crazy time for me."

"Oh, dear," she said, putting her hand to her breast. She was reverting back to her old-maid persona.

"But not all bad," I said. "I'm just finding out a lot of things . . . about my family. For example, I found out from my grandfather that he helped start the Seamen's Union in Baltimore and that both he and Gracie marched in the strike."

"You didn't know that?" Sue said. "Well, my-oh-my. I thought everyone knew that old story."

I smiled, and stroked Tommy again.

"I guess everyone did but me," I said. "And I seem to remember that my mother told me once, when I was a kid, that Grace and you took part in a strike, too."

"Oh, you don't really want to go into all that," Sue said, her hand flying nervously to her throat. "That's such ancient history now."

"Yeah, but I really want to know about it. And your part in it. You know, looking around here, Sue, I'm starting to see you in a new way, too. You're a very complicated person."

She blushed and shook her head.

"Oh, sweetie, I am not," she said.

"Right," I said. "And I'm just J. Average Teenager. Come on, I bet you could teach me a lot about the past."

She looked shy, flustered.

"I don't know if I should talk about all this, Bobby. I'm not sure I remember it all that well."

"Please," I said.

She cleared her throat and sat down on her rose-covered couch. The streetlight shone around her head.

"Well, this was way back in 1936. Grace and I worked at the Sonnenborn Plant on Paca Street. We did piecework, and, frankly, we were killing ourselves making dresses, shirts, and pajamas, all for fifty dollars a week. Those places stunk. The air was so bad in them you could hardly breathe. And the owner, old man Sonnenborn, he didn't care if we lived or died. He had a big house over in Guilford and he had three children who went to Gilman, and his wife, Elizabeth, had her horses. Meanwhile, we were all working in pure misery. Finally, there was talk about starting a union . . . a couple of organizers came in from out of town and talked to us. Well, I didn't know what I thought, but Grace was for it right away. But not long after, our management heard about the meetings, oh, yes, sirree, they did. . . . They told us the organizers were all Communists, of course, which frankly scared me to death . . . but not Grace. She went to the meetings and she read up on all the tactics that management used and she wrote pamphlets, and she and some of the other leaders defied the bosses by getting all the seamstresses to use slow-down tactics. She was terrific, I'll say. In the beginning Grace was one of the people who got our union started."

In spite of the heroic details she was relating, there was doubt and confusion in Sue's voice.

"You say Grace got you started," I said. "That makes it sound as though she dropped out."

Sue took a deep breath and got out of her chair. She limped over to the window and tapped nervously on the glass.

"Sue," I said impatiently, "what happened?"

"Grace got sick," she said. "I really can't talk about this. It's not right. There is no finer woman in the world than your grandmother and—"

"Sue," I said, "I know that. We all know that. But what kind of sick? Mentally sick?"

Now Sue looked sick.

"Well, it's not for me . . ."

"Come on. You don't have to cover for her."

"I know that," Sue said. "Don't you speak harshly to me, Bobby Ward."

She turned away, and I could see she was torn.

"I'm sorry. Really sorry. But she's my grandmother and I want to understand her. To tell you the truth, she's been having her spells again and I'm scared. Please tell me what really happened."

"I don't know all of it. I just remember that there was a big demonstration coming up, and Gracie was one of our leaders. She had helped plan it. It was going to be downtown, and it was supposed to tie up traffic. Oh, we had quite a time making up signs and giving out assignments—who would go where and how the police would react, and what we would do if they brought in their horses—at that time they still used mounted police to break up riots. It was very scary and very exciting."

"So that's it," I said.

"That's what, sweetie?"

"That's how Grace knew all about what the Reverend Gibson was talking about when he came over, the black movement in Mississippi, and what the police were going to do."

"Oh, yes, she would know all about that," Sue said. "She was like our general . . . right up until a few days before we had to have the actual demonstration. Then, suddenly, it happened."

G r a c e

I waited as Sue collected herself.

"It was at night, and I was nervous about the demonstration the next day . . . so I stayed over at your grandmother's. Rob was away in the Bahamas on a ship, and we were going to keep each other company. Well, Grace was all excited about it, answering phone calls until late at night. Then both of us were exhausted, and we went to bed. I slept in your aunt's room, but not for long."

"What happened?"

"I woke up out of a sound sleep. From Grace's room I heard this terrible moaning. I was frightened out of my wits. I got up to go see what was wrong. Then I heard a terrible bloodcurdling scream. I was shaking all over. I actually thought someone had broken into the house and was attacking her. After what had happened to Rob in the union strike, I wouldn't have put it past the owners to hire someone to murder her. I was terrified. I had never heard anything like that. Finally, I gathered up my courage and went out into the hall, and then I saw her. She was out of her bed huddled against the wall, screaming, her eyes wide open like she was seeing a ghost. I tried to wake her, but she grabbed at me, at my throat, and she was choking me. . . . I fought her but she was possessed. It was like she had the strength of a man three times her size. I screamed and fell back, and then Grace fell, too. Right on top of me. On my foot . . ."

"Your foot?" I said, stunned. "That's how you hurt your foot?"

Sue looked down at the floor.

"As God is my witness, I would never say anything bad about Grace. She taught me when I was a child, and my father was drunk and beat me, she taught me how to read, she took me places, she opened up the world to me. She did everything for me."

She was babbling on now, filled with guilt for telling me.

"Sue," I said, feeling foolish and embarrassed. "It's all right. Grace didn't know she was hurting you."

"No, of course she didn't," Sue said. "She fell on top of me, and I guess my scream and the shock of the fall woke her. She had no memory of the whole thing, and of course she was mortified when she found out what she had done. We got it bandaged up, and I went to the rally. It was a great success, too. The papers wrote us up, and it was the beginning of collective bargaining . . . for the dressmakers. But Grace, she didn't go. . . . She stayed home alone . . . said she was too sick to go. Afterwards, she told me she could never be involved in politics or protests again. She was afraid for her sanity."

"But why?" I said. "What could she have seen?"

Sue shook her head, then wrapped a ringlet around her finger.

"I don't know. I asked her, but she said that she just didn't have the stomach for public demonstrations anymore . . . that her nerves weren't up to it. God knows, I saw evidence of that. I guess that's the answer."

"No," I said. "That's crazy. That can't be it. Did you ever see her act like that again?"

"If you're asking if she's a coward, the answer is no. We were down at Ocean City once together, and there was a terrible fire. . . . This was ten years ago."

"I remember. Didn't your hotel burn?"

"That's right. The George Washington Hotel. People were panicking everywhere, but Grace was as cool as a cucumber. She helped see people out the back way and acted like she was at a picnic. Even the firemen commented on her bravery. So whatever it is that's haunting her, it has to be something big, something she can't forget."

She gave me a sly look from the side of her eyes then.

"Sue, you know, don't you?" I said. "For God's sake, tell me."

"No, you're wrong," she said. "I'm not sure of anything. Whatever it is, though, it happened before I knew her, which is her whole adult life. Maybe it happened when she was young, when she lived down in Mayo."

"Mayo," I said. "Down near Annapolis?"

"That's right," Sue said. "Grace lived down there for a while, too, in her teenage years. Maybe something happened down there. I don't know for sure, but Grace has mentioned those years from time to time in a way that made me wonder. You know how she loves to tell stories about the past.

Well, that's the one period I've always felt she kept a little bit secret. Oh, but I shouldn't tell you that. I don't know what I'm saying. You'd better go now, Bobby. And please don't tell your grandmother I was talking about her. She's my best friend in the world."

"Don't worry," I said. "This is between you and me."

I walked across the room and gave Sue a kiss on the forehead. Her skin was clammy, sweaty . . .

She knew. I was sure of it . . . but she wasn't going to tell me any more.

The next morning when I came down the steps, my grandfather stood in the living room, checking his seabag. He was dressed in his peacoat and wore his old World War II chief's hat.

"Hi, boy. Glad you're up," he said. "I'm heading back to sea today."

"Already?" I said. I hated to see him go. I had gotten closer to him than ever before, and yet there was so much more about him that I wanted to know.

"Been long enough. Got a good ship. Heading down to the Gulf of Mexico. Be gone a month or so."

"What are you hauling?" I asked, watching him stick his rain boots into the bag.

"Rubber and tin," he said. "On the way back, we'll be carrying cotton."

I smiled at him, and I felt pride swell inside of me. My grandfather did things that were essential to life. And for all his faults he was truly a man, something I doubted I'd ever be.

I walked over and gave him a hug, which he returned, rubbing his grizzled beard next to my soft cheek.

"I want you to promise me something," he said.

"Just name it," I said, with a certainty that I didn't come close to feeling.

"Take care of your grandmother," he said. "Keep an eye on her."

"Okay," I said, laughing. "But I think you and I both know that she can pretty well take care of herself."

"Usually," he said. "But not always. She sometimes gets in over her head, trying to save the whole damned world, which, believe it or not, doesn't always appreciate it."

I laughed again, and this time he did as well.

"Some folks are better left on their own," he said.

But this time he wasn't laughing. And there was a faraway look in his eye. I had the distinct impression he was about to tell me something, something crucial about himself, maybe about Grace, but suddenly there was a car horn outside the house.

"That's Terry Banks," he said. "Gotta get rolling. You keep working and be brave now. You hear me?"

I felt a flush of deep embarrassment when he said that, but I managed a smile and a nod. I watched him heading down the steps, bowlegged, wobbling, his big forearms straining with the seabag thrown over his shoulder, his peacoat collar turned up around his short, powerful neck.

From the shotgun seat he looked up at me and gave a little wave, then he was gone. I promised myself once more that when it came time to act again, I would call on the spirit of my grandfather and that no matter what happened I'd always protect Grace.

*My mother, Grace, and
my aunt Ida Louise
at an interracial picnic
in the late fifties*

That afternoon when I got home from school it was unseasonably warm, and Grace was sitting out on the porch, on the old metal glider, reading.

When she saw me, she put the book facedown. It was almost as though she didn't want me to see it.

"Reading a novel?" I said.

"Not this time," she said. "Nonfiction."

Slowly, she turned the book over. I was surprised to find an English travel guide.

"Planning a trip?" I said.

She smiled a guilty smile.

"I'm not sure," she said.

"Well, you ought to be," a voice said.

I turned around to find the Reverend Brooks coming through the door. He was carrying a glass of iced tea, which he gave to Grace.

"You ought to be very proud of your grandmother," he said to me. "She's a remarkable lady."

"I am," I said.

"Especially since she's going to be the new representative from the Women's Council to the new Methodist Church Board. As soon as the election is held next month, that is."

"That's great," I said, but my voice didn't carry much conviction. I looked over at Grace.

"When did all this happen?"

"Oh, it's been in the works for a while," Dr. Brooks said, but I felt that he was answering because she didn't want to.

I frowned, felt confused.

She cleared her throat and looked at me.

"Well, I didn't say anything about it, honey, because its not really a certainty yet. After all, there's another person who's running for the position, too. Annette Swain."

"Annette Swain?" I said. "How could anyone even consider voting for her over you?"

"Well, she has her followers," Grace said.

"But, fortunately, probably not enough of them," Dr. Brooks said. "So, young man, Grace will undoubtedly get the position. It's a very important position in the church. She'll help set the agenda for the foreseeable future . . . and the job has a few nice perks, too. Tell him, Grace."

My grandmother smiled and looked at me.

"Well, the church's international meeting is going to be held in London, England, this year," she said. "And whoever gets the job gets to . . . go . . . to represent the Eastern Regional Council for a week."

I could feel a huge smile breaking across my face.

"But that's fantastic!" I said. "You've always wanted to go there. You can visit the places in Dickens . . . see Big Ben, the Tower of London. Nobody deserves it more than you do, Gracie."

I gave her a hug, and for a second the thought of her realizing her lifelong dream made me so happy that nothing else mattered. But as I held her, Grace's body stiffened, and when I looked at her, her eyes were troubled.

"That's really great," I said again. "When will you know for sure?"

"In three or four weeks." She looked down at the porch floor. "Well, we've got a lot to discuss, Bobby. Maybe you'd better go in and get some of your schoolwork done."

G r a c e

"Yeah, I guess so," I said. "Nice to see you, Dr. Brooks."

"You, too, Bob," he said.

I went inside and started to head upstairs to my room. But I was thirsty and remembered the iced tea in the kitchen.

I walked through the kitchen and beyond to the pantry. I poured some iced tea into a jelly tumbler with black-eyed Susans painted on it.

I went back into the living room and started to go upstairs, but then for some reason I sat down in the living room, just beyond the screen window. Without half-trying I could hear Grace and Dr. Brooks's conversation, and though I felt guilty being an eavesdropper, I couldn't resist listening in.

"Grace," the Reverend Brooks said. "I want you to come and make a speech to the assembly of churches soon. Kind of a position paper telling them what direction we want our church to go in."

"I see," my grandmother said. "When would this be?"

"In two weeks," he said. "Frankly, it's very important. The truth is that though your record of service to First Methodist is superior to anyone's, you're not quite as well known to the governing body as we might like."

"You mean as well known as Annette?"

"Yes, frankly," Dr. Brooks said. "She's had certain social advantages."

My grandmother laughed.

"Annette's done very well, hasn't she? Well, that's nothing. I can be a snob, too, because I had a private tutor."

"You did?" Dr. Brooks said. "When? I thought you left school in the ninth grade."

"That's right, I did," my grandmother said. "But my mother worked as a seamstress at Greif and Brothers down on Redwood Street. It was a terrible job, sixteen-hour days, terrible working conditions . . . and she still had to bring piecework home to make enough for my family to live. My father worked at a better place, the Woodberry Mills. Eventually he got my mother a job there. We made more money, about sixty dollars a week at our best time. A union was started, the Textile Workers Union, and unlike some of the other owners in our town, the Garlands, who owned the mills, were fairly enlightened. As leaders of the union my father and mother got to know Mrs. Garland, the owner's wife. She came to our house and talked with us. She really had an interest in working people.

"Then one day my father had an accident at the mill. He was out of work for some time, and I was forced to go to work, but Mrs. Garland felt so bad about it, she got her husband to hire tutors once a week. I met with this woman, Caroline Wright. She was wonderful. She knew Mozart, she knew books, and she saw right away that I wanted to learn. She was the one who got me into reading real books, to listening to classical music. She took me and three other kids to the Baltimore Symphony for the first time."

"You were very fortunate," Dr. Brooks said, "but you were also the kind of person who took advantage of your breaks."

"It was my mother who was very smart. She was the one who pushed the idea of the tutor with the owner's wife."

I saw the Reverend Brooks get up from his chair then, and I sank down in my own. I was shocked to learn how close Grace had come to being completely uneducated, how much she and her parents had to struggle just to move our family this far along.

I felt giddy with knowledge and I would have gotten up right then and gone upstairs, but what the minister said next kept me glued to my seat:

"You know, Grace, your mother's and father's struggles are a wonderful tale. They were very smart people because they completely maximized their situation. Other people would have just been happy to make more money, but your mother saw that you could aspire to a greater world, the world of culture, and perhaps, who knows for sure, she even thought you might be able to move in that world someday."

"Actually, I do know," my grandmother said. "She always said that she hoped that I could go to college, be somebody. But that was beyond her powers, I'm afraid."

"Yes, and a pity," Dr. Brooks said, still pacing. "But just the same, now you have a real chance to get your ideas across. You can make your mark in the church and by that make a real difference in people's lives."

Though what he was saying was entirely positive and optimistic, there was a querulous tone to his voice. My grandmother must have sensed it, too, because she said nothing.

"But with this new power, this new sense of freedom, comes responsibility, Grace. A person entrusted with a position of political power must rein in his or her wilder and more radical impulses sometimes to achieve steady but smaller gains. Believe me, I know how frustrating that can be. When I started as a young minister, I wanted to make wholesale changes, changes I'd dreamed about for years, but I realized after some painful setbacks that such things aren't entirely possible. Not to resort to clichés, but Rome wasn't built in a day."

He stopped speaking and sat down. There was a long silence, then my grandmother spoke.

"What exactly do you mean?" she said.

"I think you know what I mean, Grace," the minister said. "We've talked about this matter before."

"No," Grace said. "I'm not sure I do. Why don't you say it straight out?"

There was another long silence, interrupted by the Reverend Brooks clearing his throat.

"I'm talking about this recurrent rumor I've heard that you're meeting with the Reverend Gibson and his band of radicals. That you've . . . you've thrown in your lot with them."

My grandmother gave an anguished, frustrated, and slightly mocking laugh.

"You make it sound as though I've joined John Brown's gang or become a cohort of Nat Turner," my grandmother said. "Reverend Gibson is a Methodist minister and is completely devoted to nonviolent change. And besides, I've promised him nothing."

"I know exactly what he's devoted to," Dr. Brooks said. "He's devoted to self-promotion, to upsetting established traditions in the crudest possible way. He's a loud, overbearing fraud who would cast aside anyone who disagrees with his own agenda. This is not the kind of man we want to be involved with, Grace. Oh, I admit, he has a crude kind of animal charm, and if you are out of sorts, he can sound persuasive, but believe you me he is not a solid man. Not at all. And you, in this delicate transitional time, can ill afford to become a foot soldier in his little army."

"His army?" my grandmother said, and her anguish was palpable. "I really don't think you understand what he's about. You've misjudged him and his movement, which is an arm of Dr. King's . . . not some radical, fly-by-night . . ."

Dr. Brooks was up again, and as he turned toward the window, I shrank down.

"Don't lecture me, Grace. I know the man, and I know his ambitions. He wants to be on the city council, he would like someday—and ask around if you doubt this—he wants to be mayor of Baltimore."

"So?" my grandmother said. "Weren't you and I just extolling the virtue of large ambitions? Or does that only apply to white people?"

I couldn't see Dr. Brooks's face, but from the length of the pause I knew he was furious. Finally, he spoke:

"Grace, Gibson is a politician, not a true minister. He is only using his ministerial position to start trouble, alienate white and black, and establish his own power base. The man is a demagogue, and I really can't believe you're seriously considering supporting him. Grace, you'll be sacrificing your own ambition on the altars of his, and it won't be worth the candle."

"I see," my grandmother said. "Well, if that's the way—"

But Dr. Brooks interrupted:

"Don't cut me off. Remember things once said are often impossible to unsay. I ask you, beg you, actually, to think about your upcoming election to a position of real power in the church. You have a chance now to achieve what your parents dreamed for you. To throw that away because you've been fooled by a charming con artist . . . that's crazy. There's no other way to say it. It's madness. Please consider what I'm saying."

"Well, what are you saying?" my grandmother said. "That if I help the Negro cause I don't get your endorsement?"

"I didn't say that. Don't put words in my mouth, Grace," Dr. Brooks said. "I am as much for their people's freedom as any man. But look at the way they're doing things. Look at the display they made in our church three weeks ago. Think of the damage done there, the alienation of white and black, people who got along so well before."

"Yes. Before the Negroes demanded their rights," Grace said.

"But they didn't confer with us, with me. They simply marched in and caused mayhem in God's house. That's anarchy, and there is no way the church can justify anarchy."

Now my grandmother was up out of her seat.

"No," my grandmother said. "We like order, good, old, established order . . . no matter who gets hurt."

"That's sophistry, Grace," Dr. Brooks said. "And you know it. I've prayed for those people, that they may see the light and do things in a civilized way. I'll pray for you, too, Grace."

"Thanks so much," my grandmother said, and there was thick mockery in her voice.

"Don't speak to me with that tone, Grace. I am your advocate and your friend. You should know that."

I felt like gagging when he said that. Don't fall for it, I thought to myself. Don't believe a word he says.

But suddenly the spirit was gone from Grace's voice.

"I'm sorry," my grandmother said. "I didn't mean to offend you, Wesley. I haven't lost sight of the fact that you've been my chief benefactor."

"And I still am, Grace," Dr. Brooks said. "We'll just chalk up today's unpleasantness to the strain of politics. Here's to you finally getting a post you've so long deserved."

"Thank you, Wesley," my grandmother said. Her voice was small. I could barely hear her.

"And so we understand one another?" Dr. Brooks said as he rose and walked toward the edge of the steps.

"Perfectly," Grace said.

"Good. See you in church, Grace."

My grandmother said nothing, and I shrunk about a foot deeper into the old chair. I knew that I should quickly run upstairs or at least go out into the kitchen so that when she came inside off the porch, she wouldn't know I had listened in. But suddenly I didn't care if she heard me or not.

She walked in and was nearly halfway to the dining room before she saw me.

"*Obbb,*" she said, putting her hand to her breast. "You scared me, honey."

"Really?" I said. "I used to think nothing in the world scared you."

She shut her eyes for a long time, then looked at me sadly.

"You know it's impolite to listen in on other people's conversations, Bobby."

"Yeah," I said in a surly way. "I know. I apologize. Okay?"

"Honey, sometimes the world is complex. More complex than we'd like it to be."

"Come on," I said. "People only say that to justify doing the wrong thing. Even I know that. Reverend Brooks is a racist, and if you go along with him . . ."

I couldn't finish the sentence. The idea of my grandmother being a racist was too unbearable for me.

She sighed and sat down on the piano stool. She looked tired, haggard.

"Do you have any idea why he's saying the things he is?" she said.

"'Cause he doesn't like Negroes. Or maybe he just hates change."

"No," she said. "That's not the reason. It's true that the Reverend Brooks isn't comfortable around Negroes. Few white people are . . . but that's not why he's moving so slowly. It's a matter of the membership of the church. Twenty-five people have walked out already, and many of them are people who give money to the church. Ironically, they give money to the programs for the poor that we fund, breakfasts for hungry ghetto kids, mostly black ghetto kids . . . clothing for those same kids. And the Negro scholarship fund . . ."

"Oh," I said, "I get it. The good Methodists like to give money to help the poor old darkies as long as they don't sit in their lily-white church."

"That's very harsh," my grandmother said.

"Is it? Is it as harsh as telling someone where they can sit or to stay in some garbage-filled neighborhoods? Is it as harsh as not giving them a decent education or bringing them here as . . . slaves in chains?"

I was up now, filled with anger and not a little self-righteousness. And surely, too, I was harsher with her in order to mask my own miserable cowardice.

Grace shook her head.

"No," she said. "And I wish we could make up for all those things with one stroke of the magic wand, but it won't happen that way. That's the sad truth."

"Well, maybe not," I said, heading for the door. "But if the Reverend Brooks has his way, it won't happen around here at all. Hey, but what do you care? You'll be living it up in jolly old London. Right?"

"Bobby!" she said.

I had never seen her truly, deeply mad before. The fury and hurt in her face made me breathless with shame.

But I had said it, and I meant it, and there was no use saying anything else.

Now I saw it clearly: my grandmother had sold out the civil rights movement to grab power for herself.

Before she could say another word, I stormed out of the house.

I stayed out late that night, walking up and down Greenmount Avenue, staring into the little stores in the shopping area, the Oxford Men's Shop, Thom McAn shoes, the Little Tavern, Sweeney's Bar. I felt a mixture of shame and fury. I knew I should never have spoken to Grace in that way, but I was dumbfounded at how I'd misjudged her.

She must have known about this for weeks, even before the Negroes staged their protest at the church. Of course, that was why she hadn't said anything at the meeting in Dr. Brooks's office.

She didn't want to lose any votes.

I went to the Waverly Rec and half-hoped that the Watkins brothers would be there. Maybe I could get into a fight with them and they could beat me senseless, which was what I deserved for being so damned dumb.

But they weren't around, only a couple of little kids, and I played a halfhearted couple of games of Horse with them. Then they locked up the place, and I had no place to go.

I told myself that I'd have to go home, no matter how bad it was. I certainly couldn't go on living at Grace's . . . not after the way I'd spoken to her.

Finally, sometime around eleven o'clock, I headed back to my grandmother's for what I thought would be my last night living with her.

I sneaked up the steps, half expecting my grandmother to be waiting for me in Aunt Ida's bedroom, but she was sleeping soundly.

As I crawled into bed, my head churned with pictures of Negroes at our church, Edward L. Moon and friends beating on them, and no one to help them.

Finally, though, the pictures stopped coming, and I fell into a mercifully dreamless sleep.

It was still pitch-dark when I awoke, freezing. The old heater downstairs wasn't working that well, and I scrambled across the room to my aunt's old rocker and threw on my crewneck sweater.

I was almost back in bed when I heard a high-pitched wail.

I held my breath, waited . . .

There it was again. Someone in terrible pain.

I went to the window, looked out at the moonlit backyard. The old holly tree was lit in a surreal way, and through its branches I could see the garage rooftops.

Grace

It was unbelievable. In the middle of the night, in the cold night air, Scrounge squatting in her lap, Grace sat in the lotus position on the garage rooftop. And she was moaning, rocking back and forth, like someone experiencing a terrible grief.

I pushed up the window, started to yell down to her. Then I thought better of it. I might startle her. She was very close to the edge of the roof.

Suddenly, I could make out a few words.

"I'm sorry. I'm sorry . . . Win . . . very . . . God forgive . . ."

Then she let out a piercing cry, as if someone had stuck a knife into her ribs.

I threw on my jeans, slipped into my loafers, then tore down the steps toward the backyard.

I ran to the gate and looked up on the roof, and my heart stopped.

Grace was standing up now and walking along the edge of the roof.

There was a ten-foot drop, onto cement. If she fell, she could break her arm, a leg, even her neck.

Her eyes were wide open, but she seemed to be in a trance addressing someone I couldn't see.

"Wingate . . ." she said. "You don't know . . . Wingate . . . God . . ."

Her feet were one inch from the edge. She walked along, her long robes trailing behind her . . . her gray hair blowing in the mid-night wind.

I was afraid to call out. Afraid she'd fall.

Quickly, I ran around behind the garages.

In the dark I found the old concrete block and pulled myself up. I couldn't believe Grace had come out here in the middle of the night . . .

I made it to the top and started across the roof. Grace was right on the edge.

"Gracie," I said as softly as I could. "Come this way. Come here."

But she was walking down the roof's edge now, her face ashen with fear and sorrow.

"Wingate . . . I'm here. I'm coming."

Grace

There was no time left for any more coaxing. I ran toward her, reached out . . .

And missed.

My grandmother screamed as she fell backwards off the garage roof.

Horrified, I looked down at the alley as two lights came on in the houses on either side of hers.

Mrs. Richardson looked out the window.

"My God, what happened out there?"

"Call the hospital. Grace fell off the roof," I said.

"I'll be right there," she said.

I looked down. My grandmother didn't move. She lay crumpled on the concrete.

By the time I got to her, she was moaning and moving slightly.

"Gracie," I said. "Don't move."

I knelt beside her, afraid to move her at all.

"Where does it hurt?" I said.

"My side," she said.

She started to get up.

"I don't think you should do that," I said.

"I'm so cold."

Mrs. Richardson's light went on, and she headed toward us. In her hands were a blanket and some masking tape.

"I saw her fall. Good Lord. Anything broken?" she said.

"I don't know."

"Well, help her up, Bobby, before she freezes."

I reached down and got hold of one arm, and Mrs. Richardson took the other. Grace slowly got to her feet, and together we half-dragged her into her house.

Grace lay on the couch as Mrs. Richardson and I looked at her badly bruised side.

"It's not that bad," she said. "Just a bruise, I think. Your arm must have protected your head. Aren't instincts wonderful?"

"How can you tell?" I said. "Shouldn't she be X-rayed?"

"If you want to waste the money and take an unnecessary trip to the hospital," she said. "If her ribs are broken, which I don't think they are, there's nothing you can do anyway. Rib injuries heal in their own sweet time."

I must have given Mrs. Richardson a slightly doubtful look, because she laughed at me.

"You're wondering how this old bag knows," she said.

"I wouldn't put it that way," I said.

"Well, sweetie, it so happens I served in the Red Cross in World War II, in Europe. Now, Grace, what on earth were you doing out there meditating at this hour?"

"I don't know," Grace said, giving me a look to keep my mouth shut. "The spirit just got ahold of me."

"Spirit and a fifty-five-mile-an-hour wind," Mrs. Richardson said. "Now you drink some hot chocolate and take some aspirin, and we're going to take a look at you tomorrow. Okay?"

"Okay, Emma," Grace said. "Thanks for coming over."

"God, yes," I said. "I couldn't have made it without you."

Mrs. Richardson smiled and shook her head.

"That's what neighbors are for, honey," she said. "Now let's help your grandmother up to her bed and all of us get some sleep."

After I tucked Grace in, I went to my own bed, and for the first time in a long while I offered up a little prayer.

"Thanks, God, for saving my grandmother. And whatever's torturing her, please let me help her. I love her a lot, Lord, and couldn't bear it if . . ."

I couldn't go on.

Up until then I had thought that whatever was bothering Grace was mysterious. But because I felt that she was basically indestructible, I wasn't deeply concerned.

Now I knew that her demons were dangerous. She could have easily been injured tonight . . . or worse.

What would happen the next time?

And there was something else, too. Tossing and turning in my bed, I wondered for the very first time if my beloved grandmother Grace wasn't losing her mind. After all, she'd been hospitalized before. What if this was the final straw?

In the morning I called our family physician, Dr. Lloyd Saylor. Without going into the whys and wherefores I told him that Grace had suffered a fall and that we needed to see him. A round little man with endless energy and a wonderful Buddha-like disposition, Dr. Saylor offered at once to come around and make a house call. At first he said he couldn't make it until the end of the day, but when I mentioned that Grace was in quite a bit of discomfort and that the bruise on her side was huge and ugly, he said he'd be around at twelve. I realized that he was giving up his lunch and offered to bring her to his office in a cab, but he wouldn't hear of it.

"I've taken care of you, your father, and your grandmother," he said with a laugh. "Besides, I need to lose a little weight anyway."

I told him I'd see him at twelve o'clock and went up to tell Grace.

"He's making a house call?" she said. "That's too much. I'm not dying. *Ohhhhh.*"

She grimaced and I took her hand.

"You okay?"

"Yes. Good old Dr. Saylor," she said. "You know a lot of doctors nowadays won't make house calls."

I sighed.

"They say they don't have time." She laughed. "Maybe if they ate some more fish sticks, they'd save enough time to come see their patients again."

I laughed. It was like her to joke to make me stop worrying about her.

I held her hand tightly.

"You need an aspirin?"

"Lord, no. I've had three. That's my limit. Besides, it only hurts on one side."

I nodded and felt like a creep.

"You know what's strange," Grace said. "I remember going up on the roof. But I must have been dreaming, because it seemed like there was someone there, helping me up."

"Who?"

She shook her head.

"I'm . . . not sure," she said.

"But you have an idea."

"No . . . I mean. Well, that's crazy."

There was something fragile in her eyes. I felt she was on the cusp of telling me something terribly important.

"Who or what is Wingate?" I said.

Her eyes opened wide in fear.

"Where did you hear that?"

"You were yelling that on the roof. 'Win——gate . . . I'm coming.' "

She turned away from me, onto her bad side. I saw her shudder in pain.

"That's nothing," she said. "Nonsense from a dream."

"Some people believe in dreams. Even Jesus."

She turned back and looked at me angrily.

"It's nothing," she said. "Now let me sleep. Please."

She turned back away from me and shut her eyes. I let go of her hand and left the room.

Wingate. As soon as she was well enough, I was going to press her on that name. There was something there. I was certain of it.

Dr. Saylor said that when she was better, Grace should schedule an X-ray down at nearby Union Memorial Hospital, but he doubted that her ribs were broken. He applied a little tape, gave her some pain pills, and told her she was very, very lucky.

G r a c e

As he was leaving he turned back to her and said, "Grace Ward, I never tell you what to do, but maybe you ought to start meditating on lower ground."

Then he walked out of the room.

"Good Lord, he knows, too," she said. "Doesn't anyone have anything better to do than spread gossip about me?"

But I could tell she was kind of happy about it. Though she pretended to be totally modest, the truth was that Grace enjoyed being thought a little outrageous.

I brought her some lemonade and told her I was going to call Cap and tell him what had happened. But she forbade me to do it.

"He'll just rush home here and go crazy hanging around. That will drive me crazy, and I'll feel even lousier than I already do."

"Well, you've got to just lie around until you feel better."

"So they tell me," she said. "But I'll bet you I'm out of this bed in two days."

"No," I said. "You really need bed rest."

"Bed rest is highly overrated," she said. "Get up, get going, and forget about your wounds. That's what makes a person heal."

I just sighed. On this kind of thing there was no arguing with her.

Then it occurred to me that in all the commotion I had never said what I needed to tell her.

"Grace," I stumbled. "The other night . . . those things I said to you . . . they were awful."

"Yes, they were," she said. "No one speaks to me that way."

"I know. I know," I said. "Listen, please. What you do about the civil rights movement is your business . . . okay? I mean, who am I to tell you how to live your life?"

"You're my grandson, that's who," she said, her eyes narrowing in pain.

"Okay. But I just want you to know that I—"

"Quiet! Gosh you go on a lot. Now listen to me, 'cause I'm feeling lousy and I'm only going to say this once. Here is the deal. You were impo-

Grace

lite, overbearing, self-righteous . . . a totally unearned self-righteousness, by the way . . ."

"I know, Grace. I couldn't agree more."

"*Shhh.* I'm talking now. Show some respect."

I nodded as I sank farther and farther into the chair. This was going to be worse than I had expected.

"And the thing that is positively the most annoying factor to me," she said, "is that you were right."

"Huh?"

"You were deeply and annoyingly right. And I've decided now . . . I know what to do, which way to go."

"You do?" I was flabbergasted.

"Yes, and I've already done it. Dr. Josiah Gibson and his contingent from African Methodist and Sean Hunter and his contingent from dear old First Methodist will be here on a week from Sunday at one o'clock for dinner and a serious discussion group on nonviolent action. Do you think you can make it?"

"You know it," I said. "But that's in ten days. You'll still be—"

"I'll be fine," she said. "This is the first time I've known what to do in years. But obviously I'll need your help with the food and preparations."

"Of course," I said. I must have been smiling like an idiot, because she waved her hand as if she was going to hit me.

"Don't gloat," she said. "It's unchristian."

"Sorry," I said. "One thing, though. What about Dr. Brooks and your trip to England?"

"He'll just have to live with it," Grace said. "And as for England, I've been there many times with Mr. Dickens as my guide. Now get out of here and go play some basketball up at the Waverly Rec with Howard Murray."

"You knew about that?"

"Of course. It's the talk of the neighborhood. I figure if you can pull that off, maybe I can dig up a little courage myself."

"You can't do this because of me," I said. "What if you have another spell?"

"I'm not doing it because of you," she said. "Don't get that idea. I'm doing it because I need to for my own soul. But if you inspired me a little, that's okay, isn't it?"

"I guess so," I said. "But I'm not that brave."

"Bull," she said. "You don't even know how tough you are. So relax."

I tried smiling, and after patting her on the head I left the room.

But that didn't stop me from worrying. I didn't want to be her inspiration. What if it was all too much for her and she had a spell? A fatal spell? If I was her inspiration, then wouldn't it be on my head?

I took a long walk and thought on it. Life was so complex. What one person did purely for his own reasons could affect someone else in a way that the first person never dreamed of.

I had gone from really wanting to get my grandmother engaged in the civil rights movement to practically wanting to talk her out of it.

Finally, I offered up a little prayer, and suddenly I felt clear about it.

I had to take what Grace said at face value. She was doing what she wanted, what she really felt she needed to do . . . and it was up to me to swallow my own doubts and to support her.

And, I reminded myself, thinking of some of our less-than-evolved neighbors, to protect her if it came to that.

*A*ny secret and guilty hope that Grace or I had that the contingent of Negroes would come unnoticed by the neighborhood ended abruptly when the Reverend Josiah T. Gibson and his group arrived in a big black Lincoln, replete with running board and white-walled tires.

As the minister got out from behind the driver's seat, three other well-dressed Negroes—two men and a spectacular-looking tall and very dark woman—opened the doors, and the little block of Singer Avenue was amazed.

Grace and I stood on the front porch, she dressed in a pink taffeta dress, seashell brooch, and white shoes, me in a navy blue jacket, rep tie, and loafers.

Dr. Gibson fairly bounded up the cement front steps, covered the little walkway with two big steps, and came up the final three wooden stairs with enough thunder to shake the whole front porch.

"Mrs. Ward," he said. "You look exceptionally beautiful today."

"And you look very dashing yourself, Dr. Gibson," she said.

With that said, Dr. Gibson and my grandmother proceeded to give each other a very natural and spontaneous hug of affection. And as they did, I heard the chorus from the street whooping out the universal adolescent mockery—"*Whoaaaaaa!*"

G r a c e

I turned and looked down at them.

Sherry Butler was hanging on a taillight, along with her latest paramour, some tall balding guy named Mick, with a pot belly and an Oriole cap. She and Mick were passing a bottle of Richard's Wild Irish Rose back and forth, and laughing, as they pointed at the porch.

And just behind them were the Watkins brothers, Nelson and Buddy. They were leaning on their own porch rail, their big red faces contorted in dismay and disbelief.

I felt my stomach turn, and there was the copper taste of fear in the back of my throat.

I remembered what I had promised myself and my grandfather.

But inside I felt sick as I watched the Watkins brothers come down off the porch and drift over to the curb, where Nelson took the bottle out of Mick's stubby hands without even looking at him.

"Well, look at that," Nelson said loudly, squinting up at us. "Mrs. Ward and the nigger must be real old friends."

That got a big laugh out of Sherry, Buddy, Mick, and a couple of the other hillbilly neighbors from down the block whose names I didn't know, but I recognized them as pals of the Watkins brothers.

I was furious at the comment, and though I was scared, I suddenly wanted to strike back at them.

The Reverend Gibson must have sensed my mood because he took me by the shoulder and turned me toward one of the other people in his group.

"Hello, young Robert. Allow me to introduce my associates from African Methodist."

I turned and shook hands with the two Negro men and the long, willowy woman, but I barely got their names because out of the corner of my eye I was still checking the street. And listening to what sounded like the bleating of goats and pigs:

"Look at 'at up at Grace Ward's . . . niggers in big cars."

"Yeah, and wearing suits, too."

"Dress 'em up anyway you want, and they're still monkeys."

"I don't even beleef it. Right here inna neighborhood, for Christ's sake."

"It ain't right, Nelson. You gonna just let 'em take over or what?"

The last line almost made me laugh. The problem was that it wasn't really funny. To these imbeciles, any Negro's appearance in the neighborhood for any reason was tantamount to Negroes taking over the world.

I shook hands with the tall dark woman, but my nerves were jangling.

"*Hiiiii, Bobby,*" Buddy Watkins now yelled up at me in his most mocking high-pitched voice. "Having some of your friends over for lunch?"

That bit of wit got all the rest of them on the street chattering and laughing.

Now my grandmother put one hand on my shoulder, and I turned toward her.

"You simply have to ignore them," she said. "Remember why we are here. Nonviolent protest."

"Okay," I said. But I didn't feel nonviolent. I felt jacked up, scared, and at the same time anxious to do something, anything, before the little mob did it to us first.

At that moment two more cars drove up the street, a bright shiny Chevy and a maroon Buick. More T-shirted neighbors piled out into the street now, and I saw the Harper brothers down at the corner hanging on the lamppost, watching like hunched buzzards. Both of them looked goofy-eyed and dangerous.

As Sean Hunter and the six other Negroes—all of the men dressed in suits and the women in tasteful Sunday dresses—got out of their cars, the Harpers started making apelike noises, scratching themselves on their ribs, and dancing up and down.

"*Chhhheeeeeeeeee, cheeeeeeeee, cheeeeeeee.*"

I felt such fury and hatred for them, such intense pain for the Negroes who walked up my grandmother's street, that I suddenly remembered an old hunting rifle Cap had stored away in the attic. Time was he had used it every season to hunt rabbits and geese down on the Chesapeake Bay. Now that he was older, he didn't use it much anymore, but he had always taken extraordinarily good care of it, and I even recalled where the shells were—in an old rolltop desk.

He had even taught me once, a couple of years ago when Grace was not home, how to load and shoot it.

If they charged us, what were we supposed to do? I thought of what my grandmother had read me of Gandhi, and I knew what was expected. If attacked, we were supposed to offer nonviolent resistance—form a human chain, let them beat us, just as the people of India did when the British beat them with steel-shank lathis.

Die if necessary.

Not that I thought it was going to come to that. But I thought about that gun nonetheless. I was fifteen and didn't want to die or get hurt, and beyond that I especially didn't want my grandmother to suffer at the hands of moronic assholes like the Watkins brothers.

And suddenly it occurred to me again just how disciplined and courageous the blacks and the young whites who were doing voter registration work in the Deep South were. They faced scenes ten times as bad as this every day, yet they held their ground and didn't fight back. They were the true heroes and heroines of my generation, without question, and I felt an awe for them that day, which I've never lost.

As I watched the street action becoming more and more menacing, I felt an amazing kinship with people in the Student Non-Violent Coordinating Committee (SNCC), but at the same time I felt something growing in myself, and it was a far cry from nonviolence.

As I fantasized about blasting away, Hollywood marine–style, on my redneck neighbors, Sean Hunter and the six other young Negroes from First Methodist came up to the porch and politely introduced themselves to my grandmother and me, all smiles and very cool, as if this was a typical day on the street.

I remembered my own cowardice, and I felt a wave of self-disgust and shame wash over me so powerful that it nearly made me physically ill.

"I've seen you up at church," Sean said. He didn't even sound nervous. It was as though he had utterly tuned out our charming neighbors.

"Yeah," I said, feeling haywire, not at all sure of what I was saying. "What you guys are doing, that takes guts."

"Not really," Sean said. "Not when you think of what people are doing every day down south, brother."

"That's true, I guess," I said.

The clatter on the street was rising now. Emboldened by cheap booze, Sherry Butler was yelling "Jigaboos!" and doing some parody of Aunt Jemina dancing with her fat, drunken boyfriend.

"No place like home," I said as we went inside.

"Don't let them get to you," Sean said. "They're scared to death. All of them."

He smiled at me again, and I didn't know what to say. His coolness under fire, the coolness of all of them, amazed me. I knew, as surely as I've known anything, that if it came to a fight, Dr. Gibson and Sean Hunter and the two well-built young Negroes with him could knock the hell out of the Watkins family and their moronic minions.

But there was no question of its coming to that, because the Negroes had already been tested, and they came at all this from some mysterious position of inner strength and faith in their mission.

I, on the other hand, felt jumbled, confused, alternately terrified and furious.

For now as we sat down in the living room and got ready for the meeting, I could hear Buddy Watkins yelling both Grace's name and my own.

"Bobby Ward is a chick-chick-chickie . . . and Grace Ward is a nigger lover."

I felt a violent hatred rising up in me. I looked around, but my grandmother had gone into the kitchen to get some refreshments. The two factions of Negroes were acquainting themselves with each other, shaking hands and making small talk.

The call from the street came again, Buddy's voice:

"Grace Ward is a nigger lover. The Wards are all pussy assholes."

I took a deep breath and shut my eyes.

When I opened them again, my eyes lighted on a book by Gandhi that Grace had left out for our guests to leaf through. I picked it up and held it so tightly that sweat from my hands dripped onto the pages.

Finally I opened the cover and was puzzled by what I saw. There on the flyleaf where my grandmother invariably wrote her name and address was another notation:

W. W., Mayo County.

Adrenaline coursing through me, I opened it and mindlessly flipped the pages, trying to keep my rapidly disappearing cool.

And again I heard Buddy and Nelson yelling at me from the street below, this time in unison:

"Bobby loves the niggers."

They were challenging me personally.

I knew precisely what I had to do. Be together. Be impervious. Cool.

I stared down at the book. Maybe, I thought crazily, maybe I had seen this book for a reason. Maybe if I opened it and read a transcendental quotation or two from Gandhi, the prince of peace, I, too, would gain control of myself.

Desperately, I flipped through the book, and soon I found a quote . . . but what it offered me was not solace. Gandhi's exact words were:

"Nonviolence is not a cover for cowardice, but it is the supreme virtue of the brave. Cowardice is wholly inconsistent with nonviolence. Nonviolence presupposes ability to strike."

I looked down at those passionate, thoughtful words, and I heard myself make a bleating noise, more like a donkey braying than a laugh. My stomach curled up inside of me. I knew that any attempt to appear nonviolent was for me purely bogus, that in my tormented and twisted heart I had secretly hoped nonviolence would bail me out of having to fight back against the Buddys of this world.

Hey, guys, I would battle the racist jerks, but I'm nonviolent.

Standing there among the Negroes, some, like Sean Hunter, only a year or two older than me, I realized how pathetically lame I was. The Negroes in Grace's room were cool because they were nonviolent out of strength. I was frightened and dreamed of violence because I was a coward.

G r a c e

And outside I heard the taunts again:

"Ward is a chicken shit. Grace Ward is a nigger lover."

I felt my face burn with hatred.

Slowly, as the Negroes all sat down and the Reverend Gibson and Grace made ready to explain what the new coalition hoped to accomplish, I let myself out the screen door and went on the porch.

I was so jumbled with fear, hatred, self-loathing, and fury that I couldn't see the street clearly. Indeed, Singer Avenue looked unreal to me, not black macadam but instead a melting black river of tar, which was guarded by wolves and weasels. And behind me I could hear the Reverend Gibson's powerful voice through the window as he said, "My friends, we are here today at our friend Grace Ward's house to make a plan, a nonviolent plan, which will accomplish our goal of successfully integrating the First Methodist Church. Our protest will be, in the words of Dr. Martin Luther King, a protest not of hatred, not of desire for revenge, but one of love. For only love can conquer hatred, ignorance, and fear."

I heard all this in some strange fog . . . as though Dr. Gibson was in some movie that was playing inside . . . a pretty movie, a movie about love and the ultimate dignity of man.

Only just now, outside on the street, it didn't make any sense. There was another movie going on. A movie about how little we all cared for one another, how close the street people were to the apes we all descended from.

Again I heard the voices from the street, mocking me, my family, the Negroes inside the house:

"Grace Ward is a nosy old bitch."

I thought of Jerry Watkins and his three goons beating my grandfather in the alley behind the Boulevard Theater all those years ago.

I thought of Buddy pushing me over Harper's back down at Rado's Drugstore, of the way they laughed at me like I was less than nothing . . .

I heard Buddy call my grandmother a nigger lover . . . nigger lover . . . nigger lover . . .

And then, amazingly, and against my will, I heard my own voice scream down into the street at Buddy:

"You come out in the middle of the street and say that again, you asshole."

Suddenly, Singer Avenue became deathly quiet. I checked my own emotions—for signs of fear, the quivering hand, the feeling of dread, bubbles popping in my chest, the desire to turn and run . . .

But I felt none of those things.

I was no longer afraid of any of them.

I had Cap inside of me and, God help me, Grace, too.

Buddy Watkins looked around at his friends. At Shirley, who sucked on her wine; at staggeringly drunk Mick, who looked confused; at slit-eyed, bad-skin Nelson who was watching his little brother with a morbid curiosity in his eyes.

"What did you say, Ward?" Buddy yelled.

"I said come out in the middle of the street and say something about my grandmother, you stupid, ugly, son of a bitch."

I had no idea where these words were coming from. They seemed to be emanating in some deep, dark place in my soul, because they were not merely words at all. They were the condition of my consciousness. I was ready for him, no matter what happened. I hated him totally and absolutely. And, God help me, I wanted to destroy him.

Buddy must have sensed it, too, because his walk to the center of the street took him longer than I would have expected. He wasn't exactly frightened—God knows he had never had any reason to be afraid of me—but there was something tentative in his stride now. And a little hitch in his walk, a hint of indecision and confusion. I could sense it all the way up on the porch. He was thinking, But this isn't the way it's supposed to go. Ward isn't supposed to yell back.

My God, I thought, he is actually unsure of himself. Maybe even scared.

But it was only for a second. His history of dominating me went back too far for him to really feel any significant fear. I saw him suck in his breath and smile up at me. Now, standing there in the very center of Singer Avenue, he shaded his eyes with his big right hand and crowed:

"You're a chicken shit, and your grandmother fucks niggers."

I waited for a brief second, feeling an insane pressure building in me. Then I let out a cry, a crazed, lunatic battle cry:

"*Ahhhhhhhhhhhhhhhh!*"

And I tore down the three wooden porch steps, picked up speed on the top sidewalk, then ignored the cement steps altogether and instead made a running, flying leap down Grace's grass hill, crossed the pavement, and ran into the street, barely keeping my footing.

I kept right on running and screaming until I slammed my head into Buddy Watkins's stomach.

He gave out a loud groan and fell straight backward, his head bouncing on the concrete as I landed on top of him.

It was only a second before I came to my senses. Good Lord, what had I done?

If he ever got up, he was going to kill me.

Okay, then, that's easy: he must never, ever get up.

I threw myself on his chest as he looked up at me, his blue face and pop eyes reflecting the agony of fighting for air.

I took no pity on him.

I hated him, and I wanted to kill him.

In full sight of his big brother, Nelson, who looked so astonished at what had transpired that he did nothing at all to help him, I grabbed Buddy's ears and began to smash his head on the street. And each time it hit, I screamed:

"You got something to say now, Buddy?" Bash.

"You want to tell me something about my family now?" Bash.

"How come, Buddy?" Bash.

Buddy Watkins was crying, screaming, in total terror . . . and I was gone . . . mad, insane. All the frustrations and agonies of my parents' crack-up, Grace's confusions, and my own cowardice were being wiped out in one violent act.

Or so I thought . . . if I thought anything at all.

But suddenly I felt someone pulling at me.

"Son, son, this isn't the way. No, Rob, no . . ."

I turned and to my horror felt the huge hands of the Reverend Gibson pulling me off Buddy. Behind him was Grace, her mouth hanging wide open, and behind her, up the steps, on the lawn and on the porch were the Negroes who had come to my grandmother's house for their nonviolent protest meeting.

Dazed and half-crazy, I let Dr. Gibson pull me away from Buddy, who was bleeding from his mouth and from the back of his head.

For a second I panicked, thinking I had killed him. But he made it to all fours, then crawled across the street toward Nelson, who looked down at him with disgust and disbelief.

Dr. Gibson led me slowly back toward Grace's house now. I felt confused, exhausted . . .

Who was that who had run down the hill like a madman?

It couldn't have been me. I was a nice, bookish boy, sweet-natured and thoughtful.

But the look of huge disappointment on Grace's face told me that it was none other than myself.

"How could you?" she said. "How could you?"

I had never seen her so furious, so humiliated. I thought for a second that she would do the unthinkable and slap me.

"You . . . you go right up to the bathroom and clean yourself up, mister," she said to me through pressed lips. "And you stay there until I come and talk to you."

"I'm sorry," I said. "I don't know what happened. He was saying things about you and . . ."

"Go!" she said. "And be quick about it."

I went. Quickly.

It would be a lie to say that I felt no pride in attacking Buddy Watkins. Indeed, it was probably a signal moment in my life. For despite all the proclamations of the new sensitive man, physical courage is the dream of every man I've ever met, no matter how intellectual, no matter how artistic, no matter how weak or strong, no matter how committed to nonviolence. No man can bear to think himself a coward, especially when matters of honor are on the line.

I knew all this at age fifteen, knew it intuitively, and yet I also aspired to a higher goal, the goal of nonviolence, because I also understood the wisdom of what Gandhi wrote:

"It is the law of love that rules mankind. Had violence, i.e., hate, ruled us, we should have become extinct long ago."

This I also knew at fifteen, and I learned its true spirit in the person I loved and admired most, Grace.

As I sat in her bathroom, wiping the dirt and grime from my face and cleaning my scraped-up knees, I felt cheated. I had heard other boys brag about the day they overcame fear, the day of their coming-of-age, and I wanted to revel in what I had done to my enemy. (And he was my enemy, of that I had no doubt.) Not only that, but I had done it for a righteous cause, my own good name and that of my grandmother and not the least to avenge what he had said about Negroes, whom I considered far and away higher and greater people in every way than the Watkins brothers and their white-trash neighbors.

But my victory was hollow.

I knew as I sat there listening to the meeting dying down that I had revealed myself to be nothing more than a self-indulgent white man. I had humiliated my grandmother, and embarrassed and maybe even endangered the valiant Negroes who had dared come to this cracker neighborhood . . . and all to prove my own dubious manhood.

And so instead of reveling in my day of glory, the day every good and sensitive boy secretly dreams of, "the day I bashed the bully," I sat in my grandmother's room and wept.

Tears rolled down my cheeks in an unending flow, and I felt such a mass of adrenaline and confusion and pride and self-disgust and, most of all, shame for embarrassing Grace—who had, I knew, overcome a huge mental block of her own to commit to the Reverend Gibson and Sean Hunter—that I felt almost more tortured than I had before I made my crazy dash down the hill.

"'Think with a pure mind, live right,'" Grace once quoted the Buddha to me. But what *was* right?

I knew the answer to that question . . . knew it all too well. The answer was that I would never know. All was confusion and anarchy in my soul.

Finally, the last person left, and then I heard my tired, bruised, and humiliated grandmother coming slowly up the steps toward me.

Tears streamed down my face.

I didn't know how to face her. I knew that she hated me now, that she was the last adult who had cared for me, and that when she opened that door, she was going to tell me that she was through with me, that I had disappointed her just as I had disappointed my parents.

I was alone in the world, and what's more I was so confused, so incapable of doing the right thing, that I deserved to be alone.

My grandmother opened the door and stared at me.

I looked up at her and started to cry again, and then felt like a fool. I was too old to cry, too sensitive, too weak . . .

"I'm sorry, Grace," I said. "I don't blame you if you hate me."

She shook her head and stared through me.

"What on earth came over you?"

"I don't know . . . I knew exactly what I was supposed to do, and I was going to do it, but then something happened inside me. . . . I couldn't control it . . . it was like a runaway train . . . and I . . ."

I cried again.

"I'm just no good," I said. "No matter what I do, it's wrong."

I slumped down on the side of the tub, and my grandmother stood above me.

She handed me a towel.

"Wipe off your face," she said.

I did it, and sucked in my breath.

"I'll go home tonight," I said. "I'm sorry. I'm just no damned good."

"That's not true at all, honey," she said.

"Oh, yes, it is. You . . . you're good. You take your time, you make up your mind, and then you do the right thing."

I looked up at Grace, and she smiled down at me.

"And why do you think I'm like that?" she asked.

"I don't know," I said. "You've always been that way, I guess. I mean I know you have faults and all that . . . but really, I think it comes down to the fact that you're good and I'm a mess. . . . I don't even do the right thing when I know what it is."

There was some self-pity in what I said, but on the whole I felt that I was being sincere. I was lost. And I saw no way out of the confusion.

Grace must have sensed it, too, for she smiled slightly.

"You're a very good and kind person," she said. "And you're very wrong about me."

"Oh, no, I'm not," I said. "Everyone knows how good you are. Dad told me you're the best person he's ever known. Sue, too . . ."

"They're prejudiced." She laughed. "No, the truth is not very glorious, I'm afraid. I know what people think about me. I'm a saint. I'm Baltimore's answer to Eleanor Roosevelt. But all that proves is how successful I've been in creating an image for myself."

I started to disagree with her, but something stopped me. It occurred to me that I'd been having those very same doubts about her myself.

Just a few days before in church, Grace had failed to back Sean Hunter. I remembered accusing her of forsaking civil rights so she could grab power and get her trip to England.

I thought of the absolute weirdness on the garage rooftops.

"Come downstairs," she said. "I think it's time you heard the truth."

I got up slowly and followed her. I felt my throat grow dry. After all we'd both been through lately, I didn't know if I could stand any more truth.

Grace at 19

*G*race sat under her antique reading lamp, and I sat across the room in the big green overstuffed chair.

She put her tired feet up on the satin footstool Sue had made for her and began to talk. Her voice was firm, but there was a strain in it, as though she had finally willed herself to tell me something, though at great personal cost.

"This all happened in a very different world," she said. "The past . . . when I was only a year older than you, sixteen."

She cleared her throat and went on:

"It all began in the summer of 1920 when my family and I were living over on Fairmont Avenue. My father and mother worked at Hampden-Woodberry Mills off the Falls Road. Together they were working many hours, but they were doing fine. As you may have heard when you were so busy eavesdropping on Dr. Brooks and me the other day, I had a tutor for a while."

"I'm sorry about that," I said.

Grace raised her eyebrows, then continued:

"Anyway, this story really begins when my father was laid off, for drinking. I know I told Dr. Brooks that my father had been injured, and it was true. He'd hurt his arm in a press, but it was because he was drunk. Shortly after, my mother took sick, probably from overwork trying to keep the family together, so I was forced to go to work in the mills. It was a hard job, very hard, and I hated it. Sewing, working twelve hours a day . . . just terrible. And yet the tutor I had, Caroline Wright, was a wonderful woman, far better than anyone I'd encountered in the public school system. She encouraged me, taught me math and English. . . . I still remember the books she got me to read that year as if it was yesterday . . . Sinclair Lewis's *Main Street* and F. Scott Fitzgerald's *This Side of Paradise* and Edith Wharton's *The Age of Innocence*, and they all had a tremendous effect on me. I mean they were very different books, of course, but all three of them were very critical of middle-class society . . . the stifling and boring compromises people made so they could be part of the herd. You've talked to me a lot about conformity . . . and how much you hate it . . . and believe you me, I understand only too well, dear, because in those days I was sure I would have to conform to ever fit in. And I hated it, too. You best believe, I didn't plan on becoming some housewife who gives up her dreams and ends up like a female version of George Babbitt. And there were other things going on then as well . . . terrible things that seemed to me to be the real price of conformity. There were the A. Mitchell Palmer raids on so-called Communists. My father read about them every day from the *Sun* to us. Palmer was the U.S. attorney general, and he spent all his time 'exposing Communists.'"

"I've read about him in history," I said. "He reminded me of Senator McCarthy."

"Exactly the same kind of animal," my grandmother said. "A hypocrite and a grandstander. He constantly warned us all that the country was going Red . . . which couldn't have been any more absurd in 1920. Though I was always taught to be charitable and to love my neighbor, the truth is I hated him and all he stood for . . . and he wasn't the only one. This was also the time when Sacco and Vanzetti were being railroaded for a holdup in Boston. Of course, they both had airtight alibis, but in those days, anyone who appeared to be a Red was automatically suspicious. And so they were arrested. . . . There was a great outrage about it in progressive circles. And my tutor, Caroline, was *very* much in those circles. Of course she was circumspect about it all. She had gotten her job through one of the richest

G r a c e

women in Baltimore, and she didn't want to be tagged a Socialist herself . . . but there was a real affection between us, and once I expressed my own feelings of outrage about the unfairness of the world, Caroline let down her guard and began to teach me history in a totally new way. And believe you me, it wasn't history as taught in Baltimore schools. She taught me how the Indians had befriended the original Pilgrims, only to be slaughtered by them. She taught me how J. P. Morgan swindled and smashed his enemies on the way to creating his great fortune. And she taught me how women had been systematically taught not to think about any of these things or even of their own rights. She was an ardent admirer of Susan B. Anthony and the suffragettes. You must remember this was 1920, the year women got the right to vote, and there was a great to-do about it, oh, yes indeed. The very first demonstrations of any kind at the White House were held by women. Bet you didn't know that."

"I didn't," I said, smiling.

"Well, my dear grandson, all this was as exciting to me as what's going in our country now is to you. You best believe it. And finally, Caroline taught me about what she called the worst crime committed by any people—slavery, and the subjugation, organized murder, and destruction of the Negro races."

My grandmother stopped then, shook her head, and shut her eyes.

"As you get older, honey, your body falls apart, and you forget where you put your glasses and the darn house keys, but the past becomes so clear. You can see it, hear the voices of people you haven't seen in years . . . just like they were standing by your side."

She smiled and opened her eyes. And looked at me sharply.

"Like you, I was eager and idealistic . . . and what my tutor taught me shook my whole being. I was shocked, horrified . . . and when I learned about these inequities I wanted to strike them from the earth. If poor people had to suffer, like my own parents had suffered, then there should be no more millionaires. If anyone touched another Indian's land, I would have him jailed for a hundred years. And, needless to say, if anyone said women couldn't vote, they were idiots, my sworn and total enemies. Never was one to go halfway. But most of all, I was affected by what Caroline told me about Negroes. She was a great teacher, had an ability to make history live. She told me of the slave narratives she'd read. . . . I don't know if you're familiar with them . . ."

Somewhat guiltily, I shook my head.

"Well, you should be, honey," Grace said. "You'll never fully understand what's going on now until you understand what terrible things Negroes have had to go up against from the first days they were brought to this country in chains. They were beaten, hung, shot, their bodies cut in two. And, I'm sad to say, things like this happened right here in good old Maryland, too. Their children were taken from them and sold, and if they protested, they were murdered. When I learned about such infamy, my heart went out to those people, and I promised Caroline and myself that if ever I had a chance to help even one of them, I would do it, no matter what.

"It was such an exciting time for me. That year, Caroline and I lived in our own little dream world. Though I worked hard at the mill, I was in a constant state of intellectual excitement at learning what I took to be the whole truth and nothing but. She even began to teach me mythology, some of which I had learned from my mother . . . but this was different. Caroline had gone to New York and attended salons in Greenwich Village, and there she'd met people who studied the secret meanings of symbols and what she called 'poetic reality.' Soon I was reading poets and understanding myths and legends in a whole new way. I loved it all, ate it right up, I'll tell you. I felt that at every session with her I was on the brink of something new, impossibly exciting. But even so, my schedule got me run-down. It was all too much for a girl of my age, sixteen. Endless work and endless study and not much sleep in between. Finally, I took sick, very sick, with a strep throat first and then, because it wasn't treated properly, I came down with rheumatic fever. It was touch and go for a while. I had spiking fevers of a hundred and five, and terrible, terrible pains in my joints . . . especially in my arms . . . truly unbearable. What was worse was that my parents were themselves sick, my mother with a serious case of pneumonia and my father . . . well, my father was sick from drink. Anyway, my parents had one

Grace

other child, my brother, Bill, whom you've never met, because as soon as he could get about on his own, at age sixteen, he ran away to live in Texas and never returned. I hear from him once every year, at Christmas. But he was a boy, the only boy, so he was the one my parents pinned their hopes on."

"That's terrible," I said. I couldn't imagine anyone having such an attitude about a daughter, especially not my brilliant and wonderful grandmother.

"I know it sounds harsh, honey, but you have to understand the times we lived in back then. This was before antibiotics, and families often lost children. It was a fact of life, and so people had to pin their hopes on the strongest. But my parents loved me and tried to do what was best for me. Which is why they decided to send me to my father's brother's place in Mayo County for a year or so. My mother had very romantic nineteenth-century ideas about the simplicity of country life and good country air. If anything could do it, the country would cure me from disease. So I was sent down to Mayo to live with my aunt and uncle."

"So you left home, too?" I said, stunned.

My grandmother smiled.

"Did you think you were the only person who ever moved in with a relative, honey?"

I managed a laugh. But truthfully, it was a little disturbing to me. Even my angst wasn't unique.

My grandmother sighed and went on.

"Now, I liked Mayo just fine in the summer. It was a beautiful little town on the Chesapeake, backwoodsy and picturesque. On a peninsula of the South River about forty-five miles below Annapolis. In the summer it was wonderful, with the fields and the water and the animals . . . and the shellfish—crabs, mussels, oysters. . . . Truthfully, it was like a little paradise.

"But it was very backwards socially . . . and having just discovered the world through Caroline's eyes, I didn't want to go there one bit. The thought of that dull little town in the cold winter . . . no movies, no stores, no Caroline . . . I cried for a week when I learned of my parents' plans. But it was no use . . . they had made up their minds. So I said good-bye to them

and to my dear tutor, and my father took me and my pile of books down to Mayo to my aunt and uncle, Vern and Sally, to live with them."

"That must have been very hard for you," I said. "I just can't imagine your parents shipping you out like that."

"I had a little trouble believing it myself. And my aunt and uncle weren't exactly the kind of people who doted on children. Vern sold fish in a market in Annapolis, and Sally kept some chickens. They seemed like decent, hardworking people, but they never had much to say. Their place was just a small, white-board cottage with a little front porch and small front yard, surrounded by an old picket fence. Fine in the summer when you could walk down to the South River and jump right in. But in the gray freezing winter with all the snow and rain I felt as trapped as some animal in those woods. There was nothing to do but go to school, do my homework and my chores, listen to the radio for an hour, and go to bed. And what a school. It was like I'd been sent back to the Stone Age. Mayo High was a white building, a five-room place, with very few supplies and ancient textbooks, and our teacher, Mr. Simmons, was a nasty and bitter man who wore the high starched collar and bow tie of the era. He had a trim little mustache that I'm sure he thought was sophisticated but actually made him look like a prude. He had a stern authoritarian manner, and he reveled in the eradication of the Indians, which, of course, he called the 'taming of the West.' I remember even now how his lectures always included lines about 'the necessity of subjugating the savages.' He compared wiping out the native population with the Palmer raids of the day. But he wasn't critical of it—he loved Mitchell Palmer.

"He also made cracks about women getting the right to vote, and worst of all, he taught us that slavery wasn't so bad, saying that 'indeed many of the slaves were happier and better cared for on the plantations than they would have been left on their own.' Needless to say, all of this was extremely repugnant to me. Lord, I disliked that man. And what got me even hotter was the fact that the class, especially three boys, J.J. Randall, Bailey Calhoun, and Lee Harrison, thought Mr. Simmons the world's greatest wit. They greeted every one of his stupid and offensive jokes about Ne-

G r a c e

groes or the stupidity of women with great gales of laughter. I decided right then and there that I would not sit still for it. I might have been banished to the nineteenth century, but I wasn't going gently. I began to speak up in class. When Mr. Simmons taught us that slavery was kind and compassionate, I would cite chapter and verse about hangings and stabbings and rapes. When he talked about the treachery of the Indians, I would mention how they were helpful to the Pilgrims who then showed their gratitude by betraying their trust and killing as many as they could. And courtesy of Caroline Wright, I had names and dates to back up my arguments."

I smiled as Grace went on. It was so much like her.

"Of course, none of this sat well with Mr. Simmons. His face puckered up and his cheeks got red. I thought his head was going to blow up, which would have suited me just fine. He had never been challenged before . . . and he didn't quite know what to make of me. He told me to hush my mouth, said that 'this is Mayo County, where the teachers teach and the students listen.' That bit of sophistry was met with hoots and hollers from the king of the local hillbillies, J.J. Randall. He was a big, good-looking boy, but he was stupid and mean, and it became immediately apparent to me that he absolutely hated Negroes and also hated me for defending them. I found out that his father was a rich man who owned a marina and a lot of land in the area, and was even on the Annapolis city council for a while."

"I hate him already," I said.

"Oh, you would have," Grace said. "He was very much like Buddy Watkins, only with just enough brains to think he knew something about life, and a rich father who could buy him whatever he wanted. He even had a car, a new Ford, in which he drove his two pals and several of the local girls. All of them assumed his attitude about me, and I found myself just about totally alone. Lord, I was miserable and unhappy, but I was also angry, and I kept up a steady barrage against Mr. Simmons, so much so that he called in my aunt and uncle to 'discuss my problems.' They were horrified. They had assumed I was this nice, polite, and sickly little church girl and that I would never open my mouth. Uncle Vern told me I had to 'cease and desist sharing my opinions in class.' My aunt Sally claimed that she was 'coming down with sick headaches,' she was so upset. They begged me to be quiet, and I felt bad for their sakes and tried, too . . . for a while."

"Didn't anyone in the class side with you?" I said.

"I'm getting to that," my grandmother said. "Yes, there was one girl, Bonnie Grady. She was from a more progressive family, and she and I became the two musketeers, thank the good Lord, because without her friendship I would have gone crazy down there. Bonnie didn't say much . . . unlike me she didn't have a big mouth, but she was a very kind and very serious girl, and also unlike me, she believed that actions spoke louder than words. She had joined a group who went to what they called Nigger Row on the outskirts of town."

I felt my face redden when my grandmother said "nigger." It was considered far worse than any curse word by my family, and I had never heard her or anyone else in our family say it before.

She looked at me and shook her head.

"The place was known as Dave's Corners, too, but only the Negroes called it that. Even my own aunt and uncle said 'Nigger Row.' As if that was a perfectly acceptable name for a place. Mayo, Annapolis, Nigger Row . . . to these good country people, all one and the same. I was furious about that, too. But to get back to Bonnie, she took clothes and food over to the Negroes every couple of weeks, and she had gotten to know some of them and even gone to a few services at the Negro church. One winter afternoon when we were taking a walk by the frozen-over South River, two things happened, things that at the time seemed like nothing much . . . but they changed my life forever. First, Bonnie told me that she had heard the most remarkable preacher at the Negro church. He was a brilliant speaker, both intelligent and highly emotional. He had talked about love, she said . . . love as forgiveness and consolation in the world. . . . She said he had an almost hypnotic control over his audience.

"Well, I was immediately interested in this person, you can count on that. And when I heard his name, well . . . I just had to meet with him. It was like no name I had ever heard of before . . . Wingate Washington."

As she said the name I thought of the night she had first had one of her spells. That was the name she had cried out, 'Wingate . . . Noooo.' Then I remembered the inscription in her book on Gandhi. W. W., Mayo County . . .

"Quite a name," I said. "What was the first most interesting thing about him?"

"He was sixteen."

"And preaching?"

"Yes . . . Of course, he wasn't an ordained preacher. But the Negro community has often had child preachers. Anyway, I was dying to meet him. And Bonnie just laughed and said, 'The feeling's mutual. I've told him about you, and he wants to meet you, too.' Now you must remember in those days Negroes and white people did not mix socially. It was all right if you were giving charity to Negroes, but socializing because you wanted to know a Negro . . . well, that was unthinkable. After all, why would anyone want to know a Negro? Lord have mercy. So Bonnie showed a lot of courage talking this way . . . and her courage made me bolder. She said she would try to set the meeting up . . . but that it was dangerous for everyone involved and it might be best if I disguised the meeting as part of the charity visits. The only problem with that was that her group had just made a visit and wasn't due to go again for a month. That was far too long for me, so I begged her to see if we could do it sooner. I had never really talked with any Negroes, and the prospect of meeting a teenage preacher . . . well, that was terribly exciting."

"What was the other thing that happened?" I said.

Grace seemed lost in a fog.

"I'm sorry. I've lost my way. What?"

"The second thing. You said two things happened that day that changed your life."

"Oh, of course," she said. "Well, this other one is rather important, I think. . . . Bonnie and I continued to walk and talk. The river was frozen white, glistening in the sun. . . . It was incredibly beautiful. The whiteness of the snow-laden trees, the crisp coldness of the day . . . and then to complete the picture I looked up the river, and suddenly I saw the most incredible sight—a single solitary skater cutting and slashing his way over the ice, heading toward us. I'd never seen anything quite like him. Bonnie and I stood there watching with our mouths open at the beauty and power of this man skating toward us. He was strong-legged, well muscled. He had on a plaid shirt, britches, and a brown watchman's cap, and he fairly soared over the ice. It was thrilling to see him, and as he got closer I could make out that he was so very handsome . . . ruggedly handsome, in a way that took my breath away. I hoped, said a little prayer, that he would come closer . . . for I knew there was something about him. I was young and blossoming, and my heart made this huge pounding sound in my ears. I badly wanted to see him up close . . . but he came to the center of the river, waved to us twice, then turned and headed north, the direction from which he'd come."

"Who was he?" I said.

She smiled.

"Can't you guess?"

"Cap?"

She smiled affectionately, and suddenly I was shocked to see that though they'd been through a million battles, she still loved him. I mean romantically. She had a dreamy, sexual look on her face . . . which surprised and shocked me. I had always assumed that they were . . . well, my grandparents, that that was their relationship not only to me but to each other. Now I realized how narrow and childish my view had been.

"What happened?" I said. "How did you two get together?"

"My, you are in a hurry," my grandmother said. "Listen, it's taken me a lifetime to tell this story, so you'll just have to be a little more patient if you want to hear it all."

"I'm sorry," I said.

"It's okay," Grace said. "I forgive you. You're just suffering from an advanced case of 'young.'"

We both laughed at that (her more than me). Then she cleared her throat, stretched her arms, sighed, and began again.

G r a c e

"I went to sleep that night with crazy images in my head. A young black preacher, in a black suit, skating over a river of glass. . . . It was a strange time, a time in which I felt as though I was lost inside a dream even after I was awake. There have been only a few times like that in my life, times in which I felt that something incredible was just about to happen . . . and the tension was all but unbearable. I knew, like I've never known anything else in my life, that a huge change was coming. Suddenly, I felt that I had been sent to Mayo for a purpose, a great and good purpose . . . and I couldn't wait to see what it would be.

"But meanwhile, J.J. Randall and his friends were driving me half to distraction in school. I had defied Mr. Simmons in class again, and the boys would not stop teasing me. Before school, at recess . . . they bothered me with their 'nigger lover' talk. I remember praying to God to deliver me from my own hatred of them.

"Since my only friend was Bonnie, and she was often busy with her own life, I found myself hanging around the house a lot. My aunt and uncle had a radio, which thankfully sometimes picked up classical music from Washington, D.C., so I listened to that. But there was so little else to do, I decided to try and draw my relatives out. It occurred to me that maybe they were just shy, that underneath they might really be interesting people. So one night at dinner I didn't let them off the hook with their usual 'pass the potatos' talk. I told them all about school, how I was doing better in class . . . which they were thankful for . . . and then I dropped the bomb. I told them that my real problems were that I truly believed that Negroes were as good as white people and that as Christians we had a moral obligation to stand up for them. Well, you never saw such a reaction. The two of them stopped chewing and just stared at each other for a second. I thought my uncle Vern was about to choke to death. Then, after what seemed like an eternity, they resumed eating, as though I'd said nothing whatsoever. But I didn't want to let it go at that . . . no, sir.

" 'Listen Uncle Vern,' I said. 'I really do want to know what you think about this? Am I wrong?'

"He looked like he had a sudden attack of gas.

" 'Each has to think his own way,' he mumbled.

" 'Yes, that's all well and good,' I said, smiling with all my charm, 'but I'm very confused on the subject. I mean if my elders won't tell me what they think, how am I to know what's right?'

"My uncle looked powerfully disturbed.

" 'Mr. Simmons thinks that the idea of equality between the races is a Communist plot,' I said. And this time I couldn't help but laugh.

" 'Don't know that he's wrong,' my uncle said.

"Now it was my turn to be shocked. I had actually thought that underneath my aunt and uncle's straitlaced social conventions they were probably more liberal than they made out. My, was that ever wrong.

"My aunt spoke up then, sweetly and determinedly.

" ' My dear,' she said in her kindest voice, 'absolutely no good can come from the mongrelization of the races.'

" 'The what?' I said. Oh, they had me good and angry now.

" 'You heard what she said,' my uncle said. 'You want to know how we feel—well, that's it.'

" 'That's crazy,' I said. 'You sound like members of the Ku Klux Klan.'

"They looked at each other again, a look that sent fear straight through me.

" 'The Klan has its good points,' my aunt said.

" 'I cannot believe that I am hearing this,' I said. 'Burning and torturing and killing innocent people.'

"My uncle suddenly pounded his big fist on the table.

" 'Some races are meant to serve,' he said. 'That's their place in the scheme of things and when they are told time and time again that they must remember this, and then still willfully rise up and try to usurp the natural order . . . well, then, things, ugly and unfortunate things, will happen to them.'

"I was crying now. I simply could not believe that I was hearing such talk. . . . I barely knew what I was saying . . .

" 'Are you a member of the Klan?' I asked.

"'No, I am not,' he said. 'And I don't condone what they do, but I understand their reactions . . .'

"'Oh, you do,' I said. 'How charitable and truly Christian of you . . . of you both!'

"I pushed my chair away so hard I tipped it over, and then I stormed up the steps and slammed the door behind me as hard as I could.

"I fell on my bed and felt as though I were going mad. My own family . . . thinking such horrid things. I wanted to go home at once, and to hell with the country and its perfect air.

"Yessir, I was ready to leave that night, to walk back in the snow if I had to . . . but I thought of how tired, how sick my parents were, and how I would miss a whole year of school . . . and I decided that I would finish the semester, then leave.

"To her credit, my aunt came up to my room and talked to me. She told me that she was sorry my uncle had lost his temper, that he was tired, and things had been difficult for him and that in reality he would never hurt a soul . . . he just liked to hear himself talk . . . that kind of thing. I let her calm me down . . . but my mind was set. As soon as I could I would leave. Of that there was no question at all.

"And I would have, too . . . if things had turned out differently."

My grandmother sighed and rubbed her neck.

"This stiffness . . . that's what old age is, Bobby . . . everything stiffening . . . including your spirit if you aren't careful. You remember that."

"I will," I said.

"Now, let me see, where was I? Oh, yes . . . after that pleasant dinner I barely spoke to my relatives. I had decided they were the enemy, too. My only ally was Bonnie, and the only thing I liked in school was that they had a music teacher. She was a volunteer from the community named Marjorie Chase, an old maid, but she was very nice and a fine teacher. She was teaching me piano one day after school, and I was doing pretty well at it. The only problem was that I missed my ride and had to walk home in the dark. On this particular day it was cold and rainy, so it had gotten very dark early . . . and I wrapped my scarf around my neck and buttoned up my coat, and headed down the path through the woods. I hadn't gone far when I heard the sounds of something trampling through the trees to the right of the path. At first I thought it was my imagination, and I went on walking. But then I stopped quickly, and I heard someone take a few more steps before stopping, too. My blood ran cold, and it had nothing to do with the weather. There was someone there . . . and I was pretty darn sure I knew who it was. J.J. Randall. His taunts had become increasingly threatening, and now he was trying to scare me to death. I kept walking straight ahead, and with each footstep I could hear the echoing step in the trees. Then I thought, maybe . . . maybe he wasn't just going to scare me. Maybe he was really going to hurt me. But I managed to keep my head. I told myself that I was not going to be beaten by someone so damned ignorant and hateful, that whatever it took, I was going to protect myself. I looked up ahead and saw a bend in the road. There was about a hundred yards from that bend to the main road. If he was going to do anything to me, it would have to be before I got there . . . so I had to act soon. I picked up my pace. When I got fifteen yards or so from the bend in the road, I broke into a run. I was fast, and I knew that running on the path, I'd get there quicker than J.J., because he had to dodge trees and brush in the near dark. I went around the corner fast, then ducked in behind some pines. I searched the ground and in a few seconds found what I needed, a tree limb. I picked it up, crouched, and waited. I heard him coming through the trees fast. I'd surprised him, but he was making up for lost time. Then I saw him come around the curve. I didn't wait. I knew if I let him strike first, I was finished. I jumped out from behind my tree and swung the tree limb hard. I hit him right in the chest, hard, and he moaned and fell back on the ground. I jumped out over him, holding the tree limb like a war club. . . . If he tried to get up, I was going to bash him again.

"'Whatsa matter, J.J.!' I yelled. 'Cat got your tongue?'

"Then I managed to make out his face. It wasn't J.J. Randall at all. To my total surprise and horror I looked down and saw a short, thin, delicate-featured Negro boy of around my own age."

"'O Lord, forgive me,' I said.

"I dropped the branch and knelt by his side. His eyes were closed, and he was making a terrible sound.

" 'Oh, God, I'm so sorry,' I said. 'Please, talk to me.'

"Slowly his eyes opened. The largest, most luminous, and most intelligent brown eyes I've ever seen. He looked at me and then gave this strange little laugh. More like a gagging sound than a laugh.

"He said: 'I heard you were a remarkable person, but I had no idea . . . just how remarkable.'

"And that, my dear grandson, is how I first met Wingate Washington. He had followed me from school and was waiting for me to get far enough away so that he might introduce himself. But he was afraid to come out, fearful that I might not want to meet him after all; afraid, too, that someone might see us. I looked down at his wide, slightly hooked nose, his large, beautiful mouth. His features were outsized, just as his head was for his body. He looked in some ways like a black pixie, I thought, not like any other Negro I'd seen or any white either. He was, I knew from talking to him only a few minutes, an altogether remarkable person. After I'd made my apologies and we saw that he had only a large welt on his chest, that he could breathe, he wanted to make no more of it.

" 'Let's pretend it never happened,' he said. 'I want to talk with you . . . but I've picked a bad time. You have to get home and . . .'

" 'No, I don't,' I said.

" 'Won't your uncle worry?'

" 'Him? I seriously doubt it. I'll just tell him my piano lesson went longer than I expected. We can talk here . . . if you like.'

" 'No, not here,' he said. 'Would you trust me enough to go somewhere with me?'

" 'Yes, I would,' I said.

"I said it just exactly like that, right off. I don't know what it was . . . but I felt . . . no, I knew that I could trust him perfectly. I knew it . . . even after all the stories I'd heard all my life of Negro boys raping white women. I had never really believed them anyway, and I knew that Wingate would never hurt me in any way.

"I went with him that second . . . in the dark, walking next to him through the woods. I had never done anything so bold in my life. Soon I had no idea where we were at all. Some place to the north of my uncle's home, not far from the coast, because I could smell the sea, but that was all I could say. And then we came to a little culvert, where I stumbled over a log and he reached out and took my hand. I grabbed his, and there we were walking hand in hand through the dark woods.

" 'You must be careful here,' he said. 'Lots of fallen trees to trip over.'

"I held on to him for dear life, and we scrambled over a ledge . . . and came up a hill, and suddenly, there we were at the door of an abandoned cabin. An old place with a sagging roof. But the door was still on its hinges, and we went inside.

"Of course, it was pitch-dark, and for the first time I felt afraid. What was I doing here with this stranger? But within seconds he'd lit a lantern and I saw what he'd done to the room. He'd built a little table and two chairs from saplings. There was a cross on the table, made from driftwood . . . a cross he'd carved and sanded. And on the wall there was a picture of a Negro woman and a man . . . older people . . . I guessed they were his parents. The little lantern flared and made the place seem suddenly cozy, intimate.

" 'This cabin is over a hundred years old,' he said. He looked at me, and there was pride and a certain arrogance in his smooth, deep voice.

" 'It's like your own little hideaway,' I said.

"He smiled with one side of his mouth, again a curious, pixieish smile. As if he had a secret and might or might not share it with me.

" 'Did you do all this yourself?'

" 'Yes. I come here to be alone. A retreat.'

" 'It's wonderful.'

"He looked up, and that's when I saw the hole in the roof and the winter moon shining down on us.

" 'And if the weather's clear, you don't even need a lantern.'

"I walked over and looked up through the rooftop and saw the cloudy winter moon.

" 'Amazing,' I said.

" 'Bonnie tells me you're a wonderful person,' he said.

" 'Oh, God—Bonnie,' I said. I was blushing.

" 'So be wonderful,' he said.

" 'You first,' I shot back.

"We both laughed then. And it occurred to me that under his bluster he was as nervous as I was.

" 'I hear you're a preacher,' I said.

" 'Guilty as charged,' he said. Then he gave me a curious smile.

" 'And I hear you know history,' he said. 'I'll trade you my sermons for your knowledge.'

" 'I'd get the best end of that bargain,' I said. 'Because I know very little history.'

" 'Then you know a little more than me,' he said. 'I have a cousin in Harlem . . . my cousin Sonny. He has written me letters, and poetry. He's said that in Harlem, educated Negro men and women write poems and essays and novels.'

" 'Yes, I've heard about that,' I said. 'I had a teacher in Baltimore named Caroline. She even gave me a magazine from Harlem, called *The Messenger*.'

"His eyes sparkled in the lamplight.

" 'You've read it?' he said, leaning across the table.

" 'I've got one of them with me at my uncle's.'

" 'Really? Can I see it?'

" 'Of course,' I said.

"He smiled for the briefest of seconds. Then he got an intensely serious look in those big eyes and stared at me so intently I felt that he was literally photographing my heart. People will tell you they long for someone to know them deeply, intimately . . . but when it's happening, it's not an entirely comfortable sensation, believe you me. I felt shy, awkward, nearly naked in front of him. It was as though we were fated to meet, and that scared me, because if it was true, then something cataclysmic was going to happen, and though I'd always prayed for something to happen, really happen with my life, now that it was, I didn't know if I could stand it.

"We stared at each other for a long time. It was strange. He could do that, just stare at you and make you feel connected to him. I felt that I couldn't bear the intensity of his gaze, and yet if he stopped looking at me, I'd be lost. I don't remember exactly what we said that night . . . nothing, really. He had already said all he needed to say to me. I wanted to know him and find out everything about him, and he made me feel that I was the most important person on earth."

She stopped then. I said nothing, and she got up and walked to the window and looked out, but I felt that she wasn't seeing anything out there at all . . . certainly not Singer Avenue. She was back at Mayo, thinking of her own past, lost in that cabin with the hole in the roof under the chill winter moon, and for that matter, so was I. I felt that whatever had happened there between them would be of the deepest significance to me as well. I thought of what she'd said, of "waiting for something to happen," and it occurred to me that this was a pretty good description of my own life . . . waiting and waiting for something . . . and now, now was my time just as that time had been hers. And that somehow, too, they were the same time.

My Father's rendering of Mayo

We met in secret maybe six times over the next few weeks, and we kept the bargain we'd made that first night. I told him the history I'd learned from Caroline Wright, and he told me about his experiences growing up in Mayo, his mother and father's hard life, working various jobs in the county, barely staying out of the street. He also told me about having a vision at the age of thirteen. He'd been walking across the iced-over South River when suddenly he heard a sharp noise. He looked down and before he knew it, the ice was cracking beneath his feet. He watched himself falling into the water . . . and he knew he was going to die. The water was cold, freezing cold, and he couldn't pull himself out. And then it happened.

"'I felt something picking me up,' he said, 'as though I was as light as a feather. I hovered over the ice for a second, then the same force that had dished me out laid me down on the solid ice. I knew then that I had been saved for some reason . . . and the reason was to tell my people of God's glory.'

"Well, I listened to this with a doubting heart. When I questioned him about it, he admitted that he was barely conscious from the cold, and so I suggested that perhaps he had somehow pulled himself out. But he simply smiled and said softly:

"'You don't believe in signs or omens or miracles?'"

G r a c e

" 'I don't know.'

" 'But you say you're a religious person. A Methodist. What about the star of Bethlehem? Don't you believe that it signaled Christ's birth?'

"I laughed nervously when he said that. I had sung the hymns and heard the stories of Jesus' birth all my life, and if someone had asked me, I would have said that of course they were true. But when Wingate asked me to examine the individual parts of the story, like the star of Bethlehem, when he asked me if I really believed that a star shone over Jesus' manger, lighting the way for the Three Wise Men, I realized that I wasn't sure. That for me, the story was emotionally true, like a legend might be . . . but real, absolutely real? I realized for the first time that I wasn't at all sure I believed it. Not like he was sure, that was for certain.

"He wouldn't let me off the hook, though.

" 'You must believe in it,' he said. 'We must take it on faith . . . and my faith is strong.'

" 'Well, so is mine,' I said, reassuring him. But inside I wondered . . . how strong?

"That was a tricky moment, and it worried me. But not at first. There was such joy between us, the joy of true friends discovering each other, of like souls . . . the kind of joy you can only know with people when you are both very young. It's hard to put it into words. . . . 'Sympathy' doesn't really express it. 'Companions' is too weak. . . . It was something so mysterious, so compelling that it seemed wondrous, something nearly perfect . . . but also at times ominous, as though whatever it was that compelled us to see each other was almost beyond any rational description."

She stopped again, struggling to find the words.

"I bet I know what you're thinking . . . that all this is just an old woman's old-fashioned way of saying we were attracted to each other . . . but neither one of us could admit it."

I felt my face redden. Sometimes Grace credited me with a prescience I didn't have. In fact, though, this time she was partially right. I had begun to think of a notion somewhat along those lines, though it was scarcely a true thought. I was, after all, fifteen years old, and if the idea of my grandmother having sex with my grandfather was a fairly radical notion, the thought of her having sex with a Negro in 1920 . . . well, that was almost unthinkable. Still . . .

"Well, if that's what you're thinking," she said, "and I can see by your sudden sunburn that it is, you're dead wrong. First of all, I had those feelings, Bobby, but they weren't for Wingate. They were for that strange, muscular, yet amazingly graceful skater I'd seen skating on that cold day on the South River. But I hadn't been able to find out much about him . . . except that he was older than me and he'd already quit school, and Bonnie said that one of the girls she knew thought maybe he was a Bayman . . . a crabber.

"And second, having a friendship with Wingate was radical enough. And Wingate never gave any indication that he wanted any other kind of relationship.

"In fact, he told me several times that he admired Gandhi for his chastity . . . as I did. We were, after all, young idealists and very much in love with the idea of purity.

"So, my friendship with Wingate grew. We were able to talk to each other in a way that I'd never talked with another person before. . . . I showed him *The Messenger* I had with me, the magazine by A. Philip Randolph, who later organized the railroad porters. Wingate was thrilled. He said that his cousin Sonny was supposed to send him copies but had never gotten around to it. He loved the magazine, read it over and over, and we discussed the rise of his people. He felt that the world was entering a new era, that men and women would see things clearly, that they needed to relearn basic things . . . trust, love, and most of all the love of the earth through Christ.

"One afternoon while we were eating a basketful of crabs in the woods, he leaped up on a tree stump and said:

" 'Look at the trees and see the face of God. Look at the animals and feel God's glory. White people put their trust in machines . . . but it's a false trust.'

"I smiled at him. I was in love with his passion . . . but he frowned at me.

" 'Do you know the twentieth psalm?'

"I was embarrassed to say that I didn't. He looked down at me from the stump and quoted:

" ' "Some trust in chariots and some in horses, but we will remember the name of the Lord our God." '

"I loved that line . . . 'Some trust in chariots.' He was referring to World War I, which had crushed so many people's spirits but, he said, not the Negroes'.

"He laughed and told me that Negroes had already been crushed so many times that they had an advantage now over whites. They knew how to survive disaster, while white people were experiencing it as a race for the very first time. He said that everything pointed to the Negro's rise . . . the brilliance of the culture and politics he'd heard about up in Harlem, the Negroes' sense that they had to unite as a people . . .

"And he knew that he was destined to play a part in it all. He wasn't sure what it would be, but he knew that God would send him a sign, just as he had before.

" 'What kind of sign?' I asked. Once again I was uncomfortable with such talk.

" 'I don't know,' he said. 'It might come in the form of an animal, it might come in the form of a storm. A leaf, a rock . . . I'll just know when I know.'

" 'Where did you first hear about signs?' I asked. 'The Bible?'

"He nodded, then added, 'And from my grandfather, Moses Washington.'

"Then he told me the saga of this grandfather who'd raised him when his own father disappeared and his mother had died. Moses was a country preacher and as far as I could tell a rambler, storyteller, and gambler.

"Moses believed in signs, symbols. Some came from the Bible, some from local folklore. If Moses saw a crab on Monday, it meant that he would have bounteous fishing and hunting all week. If he heard an owl hoot three times in the morning, he believed that the day would bring rain. If he saw a shooting star, he knew that money was coming his way.

" 'Grandaddy was a two-faced man,' he said. 'He was a preacher but he was also a gambling man. And he could throw some mean dice.'

" 'Ah, I see. Your grandaddy was Janus,' I said.

"Wingate looked at me and shook his head.

"I explained to him that Janus was the gatekeeper in mythology, something my mother had taught me.

"Wingate was fascinated. I explained to him that Janus had two heads that signaled change . . . that the gatekeeper ushered in a kind of change.

"That sent Wingate off in a new direction. He wanted to know more . . . no, not more, everything about myths and legends. Though I was no expert in mythology, I told Wingate all I knew of such things, but he was insatiable. Finally, I went to the little country library in Mayo and found an old book on mythology. I met Wingate in our cabin, and we turned on the lamp and began reading it.

"And there in our little cabin in the sandy woods outside of Mayo, by candlelight, things that I might have smirked at in the past suddenly took on a new meaning. And Wingate's belief in such things, his absolute faith that we were learning the hidden reality, the true meaning of the universe, was like a drug to me. The more we met, the more we studied, the more I came to believe . . .

"I remember one night we were sitting under the stars. I'd told my poor exhausted aunt I was attending a school play, and Wingate looked at the magazine *The Messenger* and started laughing.

" 'What is it?' I asked.

" '*The Messenger* . . . Hermes,' he said. 'And Iris . . . the messenger of the Gods. The River Styx . . . that could be the South River . . . the river of death.'

" 'Or of rebirth, in your case.'

"He smiled and came over and hugged me. I put my arm around him, and we looked up at Cassiopeia and the Big Dipper, and the world seemed full of magic and meanings. And I felt such love and affection for my friend . . .

"And yet, even then, there was something underneath that threatened to mar our happiness. Oddly, I think it was the same thing that made our friendship so unique . . . Wingate's passion.

"It was true that we set each other's minds on fire, but there was something about his eagerness, his endless passion for knowledge that frightened me. He was like a man who has been in the desert for three years, barely surviving on whatever moisture he can squeeze from succulents, and then all at once he's seated at a banquet with the finest wines, and he drinks too much at once and makes himself drunk.

"I feared that he lacked judgment, that we could take this belief in magic too far. . . . I even tried to tell him that on occasion, but he would say, 'Yes, yes, of course . . . Not a good idea to take anything too far . . . yes.'

"But it was obvious he was only saying this to please me. He hated arguments between us as badly as I did . . . and so I didn't press him.

"Besides, I understood his hunger. He was in love with life and learning, and I wanted to be carried away myself . . . even though I had my doubts.

"I loved our secret world.

"The fact that it *was* secret made it all the more intense, magical. I felt that I would do almost anything to protect it. For the first time in my life, I became adept at lying. Lord . . . it's true, so help me. It was so unlike me, against everything I had been taught. . . . And yet I felt that Wingate and I made up our own higher honesty . . . black and white. Even in the mythology books we found references to black and white . . . the underworld and the outer world. The combination of the two made a whole. I felt that I had found a friend with whom I could say or do anything and that I had opened up inside to the world around me in a way that was unimaginable only a few months ago.

"And so I began lying to my aunt and uncle about late meetings at new clubs I was joining in school. They were delighted that I was becoming part of the social scene, that I wasn't always complaining . . . and I have to admit I gloried in deceiving them. They were, after all, still the enemy, apologists for the Ku Klux Klan, and so I felt it was practically my duty to lie to them.

G r a c e

"What could they possibly understand of the magic we felt when we were together?

"I remember one day I was riding my uncle's old bicycle down the little path by the bay. The spring had finally come and Mayo was in bloom, which made it far different from the place it was in the gloom of winter. It was truly lovely, and I was pedaling fast, feeling the wind in my hair, thinking of Wingate, wishing he was here with me. Then I shut my eyes and pedaled blind for a few seconds, hoping that Wingate would be with me to share this perfect moment, and when I opened them again, it was like I'd willed it to happen. He was actually there . . . riding beside me on his own beat-up old bike . . . and I was so astonished that it took my breath away."

Grace must have seen me make a face because she waved her hands.

"I know what you're thinking. It was a coincidence that I'm turning into some kind of mystical moment. . . . Well, whether it was fated, like Wingate thought it was, or mere coincidence, it was still wonderful. I got used to the idea that we shared a common understanding of the world, of what we knew about history, of books and of nature. I found out that he knew every plant, every tree in Mayo . . . dogwood and pine and poplar, gum tree and pin oak . . . and he was a great fisherman as well . . . though we went out on the river only twice, both times after dark, when I told my aunt I was at Bonnie's house. We went out on the old Rhodes River and caught bass and haddock.

"And cooked them over a fire right outside the cabin.

"Our talk wound around again and again . . . religion, mythology, the ultimate rise of the Negro, which I now totally believed in, and Harlem. For Wingate, Harlem was less a real place than a dreamscape. He showed me letters from his cousin Sonny, describing poetry readings he'd been to, where he'd heard Countee Cullen and Langston Hughes and Zora Neale Hurston read from their works, and there were rent parties Sonny had attended in which some of the greatest jazz musicians of all time played, even Louis Armstrong. Some afternoons when we walked in the woods, Wingate would describe in detail what it must be like there, and I could just picture the black women in their long dresses, the dignified young poets reading their work . . . the musicians playing. . . . Those were the kinds of sermons he preached to me as we walked through the trees . . . and down by the river. And I loved every minute of it.

"Of course, we didn't agree on everything. We had some dandy arguments, let me tell you, about music especially. I loved Mozart above all else, and he argued for Bach. He had heard Bach on the radio . . . on the 'Saturday Afternoon Symphony,' the same one I listened to from Washington. But it was impossible for me to believe that anyone, especially my soulmate, could prefer Bach to Mozart. I was about to go home in a funk when he looked at me and said, 'Isn't this sad. We're arguing about music that we can't even listen to together.' And the truth of that overwhelmed my anger. We were fighting about music we could never share, because we weren't allowed to be seen together. The only place we could be together was the woods, or on the river at night, or in our cabin. . . . And so I told him that we couldn't let that happen to us . . . that we absolutely had the right to listen to music together . . . and that we would listen to the 'Saturday Afternoon Symphony' on the radio within two weeks. He didn't believe it, but I swore it was going to happen . . . and it did.

"Now it so happened that my aunt and uncle had cousins in Annapolis named the Weavers . . . very nice people I'd met once or twice. During the next week I told relatives that I really wanted to go see them, that I loved going to Annapolis, that my life would be over if I didn't get to see the Weavers on Saturday. I must have driven them both crazy, and I'm sure they thought I'd near lost my mind. But they were so happy that I had conformed, they didn't want to do anything that would set me back again, so they set up a day trip to Annapolis. The great day arrived, and I suddenly came down with a stomachache. It was hard to get my aunt and uncle to go without me, but I insisted on it. Oh, I was so noble, quite the martyr. But in the end I convinced them that they needed the trip more than I did anyway, that the Weavers would be deeply disappointed after going to so much trouble, and finally, at eleven o'clock, off they went. Five minutes after they left the house, I went flying on my bike to the cabin and met Wingate, and though he thought I was crazy, we went pedaling through the woods as fast as we could toward my aunt and uncle's house. There was only one other house near them, a family of poor whites named the Sattersons, and we had to hide our bikes in the woods . . . cover them with leaves, and then sneak to the house. Mrs. Satterson was outside, a great fat woman in a dress with pink camelias on it. She was putting her equally plump children's clothes on the line, and we had to sneak through the woods, going from tree to tree, both of us giggling like crazy, though if we'd been caught, it wasn't going to be funny . . . but we made it. Suddenly, we were there. Inside my aunt and uncle's house. Wingate was nervous, jumpy, and so was I. But I was also enjoying our subterfuge. If they had known that a Negro was in their house, listening to a symphony . . . this was my secret revenge on them.

"I made us both ham-and-cheese sandwiches, poured glasses of lemonade, and then we went into the living room and turned on the old radio. And there it was . . . the announcer with the deep classical voice saying, 'Today's presentation will be Beethoven's Fourth.' We looked at each other and laughed out loud. We sat together on the old overstuffed couch, listening to the great music together . . . and at some point I felt his head fall over in my lap, and I stroked his hair, and he smiled up at me, and it was perfect. Just perfect."

She sighed and shook her head.

"And when it was over, Wingate had tears in his eyes, and he said to me that this was one of the finest days of his life . . . perhaps the finest ever . . . and I agreed. There could be, for me, nothing higher than this, to be in such complete accord with a friend. . . . I wanted it to last forever. I was about to tell him that, too, when suddenly we heard a car in the driveway.

"'It can't be them!' I said. 'They'll be gone for hours.'

"I looked up and out at the driveway, and my heart fell into my stomach. It was Alma Marshall, Aunt Sally's friend. She was a widow and often got lonely and just dropped in. Worse, she felt no need to knock at all . . . and I wondered if I'd even bothered to lock the front door.

"'In here,' I called out.

Grace

"I pushed Wingate into the back pantry and went to the front door as she knocked for the third time.

"'Grace,' she said. 'What's the door doing locked?'

"'I didn't realize it was,' I said.

"'Well, where's Sally?' she said.

"'Gone to Annapolis,' I said, my voice cracking. 'I would have gone, too, but I got sick.'

"'Oh, you poor thing,' she said. 'Let me come in and keep you company.'

"I nearly panicked when she said that.

"'I would, Alma,' I said. 'But it's catching, I'm afraid. Stomach sickness. I wouldn't want to get you sick.'

"That cleared her out fairly quickly, but when I got back to the pantry, Wingate was sweating. He looked frustrated, even furious.

"'It's okay,' I said. 'She's gone.'

"'No, it's not okay,' he said, flopping into a chair at the kitchen table and rubbing his neck. 'It's not okay that we have to live like this. That we have to sneak around like . . . like criminals just to listen to music together.'

"'I know. I hate it, too.'

"Wingate looked down at the floor and then stared directly at me.

"'I might as well tell you now. I've been thinking hard about leaving for Harlem. I could go live with Sonny until I find a job.'

"I was absolutely crushed. I couldn't stand the thought of his going.

"I gave no thought at all to why he wanted to go—the sheer impossibility of someone so brilliant living in such a limited place as Mayo. I simply thought of myself. I felt that I couldn't bear life without him. And suddenly, I hated Harlem with all my soul.

"'Why?' I said, though I knew perfectly well why.

"'Why?' he said. 'Grace, I can't be seen with you. I can't even listen to music without tricking your uncle. . . . I have to get away. And . . . I have no right to ask this, but I wish you'd come with me.'

"'That's crazy,' I said. I was furious, upset. 'I can't go to Harlem.'

185

" 'Why not? You love the same things I do. There are plenty of white women there. It would be an education for both of us.'

" 'But I can't just leave,' I said lamely. 'And I don't really understand why you want to.'

"He raised one eyebrow, as he often did when he found something I'd said impossible to believe. 'How can you not understand?'

" 'I'll tell you how,' I said. 'Because your people don't need you in Harlem. They need you here. Here is where you can make a difference. Here is where you can become great. You can preach and you can reach people. Here among your own country people. Think of it, Wingate: if you leave, who will help them?'

"He said nothing but stared down at the table. He took everything I said with the greatest seriousness.

"Finally he spoke:

" 'It's so odd that you say that. I've thought those same things myself, Grace. I've prayed on this for weeks. And I asked God to give me a sign. Now that you've said this . . . I'll think on it again. But I want you to know that I'm inclined to leave.'

"I was ready to burst into tears.

" 'Go ahead then,' I said. 'Why wait? You should leave now, this very night.'

" 'Don't be like that,' he said. 'I can't bear it if you're mad at me.'

" 'Really?' I said. 'It seems like you scarcely care what I think at all.'

"And even as I said it I knew suddenly that I was wrong. That he might very well be better off if he went away.

"He was deeply upset by what I'd said. I'd hurt him, but I didn't care. I wanted to hurt him as badly as he was going to hurt me by leaving.

" 'Grace,' he said, coming around to my side of the table and looking down at me. 'Please . . .'

"But I wouldn't relent. All I could think of was myself. Alone in Mayo.

" 'Do whatever you want,' I said. 'If you want to leave me, if you want to leave the people who need you, go up there and enjoy yourself.'

"I walked over and opened the back door for him.

" 'Grace, don't be like this. It wouldn't be about me enjoying myself. I'd learn, grow . . .'

" 'Don't tell me that,' I said. 'You just want to go up there to be part of the social scene. Drink and listen to music and meet women.'

" 'No,' he said, but he looked flustered. Of course that was part of it . . . as it should have been. But I wasn't going to let him off the hook.

" 'Grace, don't be this way,' he said, his voice cracking.

" 'I'm not being anyway at all. It's you who are . . .'

"Then I burst into tears and ran into the living room. I cried bitterly, feeling deeply sorry for myself, and when I got back, he had gone."

Grace stopped and sucked in her breath. She looked tired; her body sagged.

"I didn't see him for a week after that. I was crazy. Of course, part of me felt terrible for the way I had behaved. But I didn't feel bad enough to go see him or to take it back. I spent the week feeling sorry for myself, trying to prepare for his departure. Finally, one day in school Bonnie came up to me. She told me Wingate wanted to meet me that afternoon at the cabin. With her I pretended that it was nothing out of the ordinary, but I was excited the entire day.

"It was nearly dark when I got to the cabin. Wingate was already there. He was sitting at the makeshift table, his hands crossed. He looked so serious it frightened me. He got up and came to me and held both my hands.

" 'Grace, I've thought about this,' he said. 'I've prayed on it and turned it every way. And then, yesterday, it came to me . . . I knew.'

" 'And what will you do?' I said. I was certain he was leaving.

"He walked under the hole in the ceiling, and the moon shone down on him so that he seemed to radiate.

" 'All my life I have looked for signs. For portents like the star of Bethlehem, like comets, like a limb pointed in a certain direction, tracks in the sand . . . sounds only I can hear. The legacy of my grandfather.'

"He looked at me intensely, then went on:

" 'It's funny,' he said. 'I've been looking to the heavens, praying to the stars above us, looking in the trees and on the earth . . . and the true sign has been here right in front of me all along.'

" 'Really? What is it?'

"He smiled and pointed at me.

" 'You,' he said, staring into me. 'You're the sign. You were sent to me to make me see.'

" 'Wait,' I said. I felt flattered, moved, embarrassed all at once.

" 'I have been waiting all my life,' he said. 'You know we both feel there's something that guides our friendship but stands outside it. Well, now I'm sure what it is. It's God's will that you came into my life. You came here to Mayo so that I would know which way to go. And now because of you, dear friend, I do know which path to take. I've even started heading down it.'

" 'What do you mean?' I said.

" 'Pastor Phillips,' he said. 'He runs a mission in town. He's been after me to come and help him, and I've been resisting because I was going to leave. But since you have helped me see my way, I've gone to him and it's settled. I'm going to assist him. Right here in town. We're going to get things going here. And I have you, my dear friend, to thank for helping me see the right path.'

"We embraced then. Of course I smiled and said that was wonderful, but inside I was full of doubts. The idea that I was sent by God . . . that I had delivered God's word . . . well, that was only true if God worked in truly mysterious ways and delivered His message through a young, jealous, and confused girl who was totally selfish. I tried to tell Wingate that, too, but it was no use. He had prayed and he had heard his prayers answered, and nothing I could say now could change a thing. I asked him then about Pastor Phillips . . . and he looked at me and said, 'He's a brilliant man. I think he's a great idealist. He wants to help organize Negro people, and he's started to make some headway.'

"Organize? In Mayo? I felt such a fear for him when he said that, and such a terrible premonition that I could barely speak.

" 'You aren't going to go preaching revolution in Mayo, are you?' I said, laughing a little, as though it was funny.

" 'Don't be afraid,' he said. 'We're going to preach the truth. I talked to Reverend Phillips last night, and he said an amazing thing to me. He said, "Christianity isn't just about Jesus on the Cross but real jobs for the hungry." They've done it in other places, so maybe we should try it here. Real Christian protest. "Don't buy where you can't work." You see, you were right, Grace. . . . Harlem can wait. My mission and my calling are here.'

"I must have given him the most sickly smile I've ever given anyone as I congratulated him on his decision. And all I could think of was, He's doing this because of me. He's changing his whole life because of me.

"He hugged me again and said, 'I love you, Grace Ward,' and all I could do was hug him back, without saying a word, because I felt such total confusion. First of all fear and then, too, a kind of sickening and frightening responsibility for his safety."

Cap at 19

Since I'd met Wingate I'd let things slide. I had a lot of
schoolwork to make up, and so I buried myself in my work. I
tried to talk to Bonnie about all this, but she was busy so
there was no one I could confide in. After reading and writing for long
stretches, I'd go on walks down by the South River. It was so beautiful
there. All the swamp grass was in bloom, and the flowers and trees gave off
an amazing perfume. I walked, trying to remember facts for history and science class . . . and occasionally thinking of Wingate. One day it occurred to
me . . . maybe it was the flowers and some cherry trees that inspired me . . .
I don't know anymore . . . you lose so much as you get older. Anyway, I had
this thought that maybe Wingate was right, that it was God who was guid-
ing us, and that what I had really gained from all this was that I had actually
met someone who, unlike myself, truly believed in God."

I must have looked shocked when she said this, because Grace shook
her head.

"Wait," she said. "Of course, I believed in God in my own way, the
quiet, humble way that we Methodists do. We believe in kindness and good
works and being humble . . . like Christ himself was . . . except I often wondered if that was true. Read John 2: 'He drove them out of the temple and
the sheep, and the oxen; and poured out the changers' money, and overthrew
the tables; and said unto them that sold doves, "Take these things hence;

190

make not my father's house an house of merchandise.'" And only a few verses before that, Jesus turns water into wine. All these things, violence and miracles, make citified Methodists very queasy. So in true Methodist fashion, rather than debate these matters, we simply choose to ignore them. Deep down, I think we feel that any religion that emphasizes the more sensational side of Jesus is lower-class. It's the kind of thing we associate with Southern Baptists. Hillbillies. Buddy Watkins's people. But now I'd met someone I respected and loved deeply as a friend, and he believed in signs, miracles. God help me, he believed *I* was a sign for him. And I had had enough of those feelings myself around him . . . feelings that we were fated to meet. How ironic it was that I had come to this little place and had the most important relationship of my life. Perhaps Wingate knew something my own lukewarm experience of religion didn't encompass. And I respected him for being able to embrace what he felt, like an Old Testament prophet. And I knew in my heart that he was more serious about changing the world, more serious about all we had studied and talked about, and finally that he was more serious about God than myself, which made me see how shallow my faith really was.

"I thought about all these things for days, walking through the woods near my uncle's place. Ironically, even though Wingate hadn't left, I saw less and less of him. He had gone to work for the mission, and he had long hours. I promised to get down there soon, to spend the day with him, but I had schoolwork to catch up on. And to be honest, I felt jealous of the church itself. I had talked him into staying here purely for selfish reasons . . . I wanted our little communion of saints to go on undisturbed, just as before. Now, though, he was working for the poor, and he was always busy. I knew he was doing good, but what of me? I was now more alone than ever.

"I took more long walks alone, trying to sort out my feelings. One afternoon I was walking down by the South River. Spring had finally come, and the trees were budding, the river was roaring by, and the sun was shining. It was a glorious day, and I looked out at the sparkling water and saw *him* rowing. The skater. I felt my mouth get dry and my stomach turn. . . . It was definitely him, and he saw me and rowed toward the spot. I was so excited, all I could say was, 'You . . . the ice skater.' And he looked at me and said, 'The girl on the shore. I won't tell you how many times I've rowed by here looking for you. Would you like to go for a row?' I didn't say another word but got into the boat. And as we rowed out into the water, Rob and I . . . I was speechless, and we rowed by the oaks on the shore and the bluffs and back into an inlet where the banks were covered with blue-green moss, and by the time we got home I was seriously smitten. Lord . . . it seems like yesterday.

"I can see why," I said, laughing.

"Can you, honey? Even now?" my grandmother said.

"Yes," I said. "I feel I'm just getting to know Cap . . . but I can see how when he was young he must have been handsome. . . . He's still good-looking and strong."

My grandmother smiled and looked at me.

"He's still so cute," she said.

I felt my heart tighten when she said that. It was so sweet and sentimental and heartbreaking.

"Well," she said, "I was crazy about your grandfather, believe you me. Young people today think they invented sex. Surprise, it's not true. I knew then that Rob and I would never have the kind of meeting of the minds and soul that Wingate and I did . . . but it didn't seem to matter much."

She stopped and looked breathless just recalling their courtship.

"Well," I said, trying to fend off my own worries about this story and her part in it, "you were a young girl and you were falling in love, right?"

"Yes," she said. "But I allowed those feelings to provide an excuse for me to avoid my responsibilities to Wingate."

"But what could you do?" I said. Suddenly, I realized that I didn't want her to go on. My stomach was in knots.

"I don't know what I could have actually done," she said "But I believe that when you have a friend and that friend acts on what you instructed him to do, then you have a responsibility to him."

"Yes," I said. "But is it your fault that he took what you said in a moment of anger or jealousy and interpreted it as the word of God?"

"I don't know," she said, shaking her head. "You're asking me the question I've asked myself for forty years . . ."

"Tell me what happened," I said, though I knew it wasn't going to be good.

"Well, I spent every day of the next few weeks with Rob. He *was* a Bayman, I discovered. He lived near Annapolis and had quit school when his father had drowned. You know that story, though . . . right?"

"Yes," I said. "Cap told me the other day."

"I'm glad. There's so much you don't know about him. In so many ways he was . . . is a wonderful man. But he was so much more wonderful before the drinking took hold of him. He was fearless and capable and so masculine. . . . He could take a boat anywhere, through any kind of water, and I knew that we'd be fine. I loved him and was drawn to him, but I also admired him."

We were both quiet when she said that. I had felt much the same thing when Cap and I had gone downtown together. Though he was old and worn out from his hard life and from booze, it was easy to see the man he'd been.

"Anyway, I acted shamefully . . . in regard to Wingate. It wasn't that I didn't want to see him, but I was fearful and jealous and a little ashamed. I mean we had talked about God, and helping the poor and destiny and all the rest, and he was actually doing it . . . while I stayed in a school that was meaningless to me. Oh, Lord, I was confused. I just didn't want to think about it anymore. So I let school and Rob become my life for a time. Wingate sent me a message through Bonnie that he was working with the Reverend Phillips and that he was preaching at the Baptist church, and that he and Dr. Phillips were starting to make a difference in the neighborhood. He told her that he was happy . . . but missed me terribly, and that I should come see him soon.

"I told Bonnie I would . . . as soon as tests were over.

"But Lord help me, I didn't do it. . . . I was enjoying myself too much on a completely different level, sailing and taking walks and being overwhelmed by your grandfather, and I didn't want that to end . . . or even to be interrupted. Not for all the ideals in the world.

"And then I heard something, something I'd dreaded from the day Wingate had announced he was going to work in town. Rob and I were getting ice cream at a place called Murphey's . . . an old-fashioned ice cream parlor in town, and sitting at the counter were J.J. Randall, Lee Harrison, and a couple of their local girlfriends. To tell you the truth I rather enjoyed the fact that they were there, because when I was with Rob, they wouldn't dare say a thing about me. J.J. knew Rob was tougher than any of them and that if he said a word against me, he'd have his block knocked off. They were chattering on about sports and clothes and the prom that was coming up . . . and then Randall said, 'Did any of you hear about the little nigger who's preaching down there at their mission?' I looked up from the booth we were sitting in. It was like someone had slapped me in the face. Of course, J.J. was aiming all this at me, but he wouldn't dare look in my direction, the coward. Instead, he said, 'Yeah, he's making quite a name for himself. Preaching all kinds of nigger propaganda . . . from what I hear. I'm thinking we all oughta go down there and hear him sometime. Maybe he could explain Jesus to us.' And all of them said, 'Yeah, right!' and laughed in this horrible way, a real hater's laugh. I was so upset that I told Rob I wanted to go home at once. He hadn't really heard any of this. He was busy eating and paid no attention to those boys, so he had no idea why I wanted to go. He thought maybe I was sick . . . which was right. . . . I was sick at heart, and I knew I had to go see Wingate at once.

"Two days later, I went down to the Negro section of town and found the little mission on Front Street. On the outside someone had painted in neat red letters 'The Temple of Hope Non-Denominational Church, Reverend Garret Phillips. Assistant Minister, Wingate Washington.' I couldn't help but smile a little. To think he was now somebody in the world . . . maybe it was going to be all right. . . . I knocked at the door, and it fell open. I found myself in a very pleasant little room, with about ten chairs facing a homemade altar. I had to smile at that altar, because it was made partly from driftwood. The cross, too, on the wall was carved from trees, and the figure of the Savior was Wingate's as well. I couldn't help but notice, too, that his work had improved. He was always skilled with his hands, but there was a subtlety and power to the carving now. I stood there admiring it . . . when suddenly he came through the back door.

"You've come at last," he said.

"I turned, and I was so glad to see him that I nearly began to cry. He was wearing laymen's clothes, but he was dressed in black, and he wore a white tie.

" 'How are you, Grace?' he said, and there was such warmth and sweetness in his face that I embraced him at once.

" 'Fine,' I said. 'And you?'

" 'Excellent. Do you like our little church?'

" 'It's beautiful,' I said.

" 'I'd introduce you to the Reverend, but he's out making sick calls now. Come in the back room . . . that's our rectory, nothing to speak of . . . but we've got a fine backyard. We're doing a little work out there now.'

"I followed him through the little rectory. Like the church it was clean and neat, but Wingate was right . . . the real prize of the place was the backyard, which was surprisingly large. There were rosebushes and a decent-sized plot of grass and an elm tree. There were three other Negroes, two men and a woman, working in the yard. The woman was tending the roses, and the two men were nailing the fence. They barely looked at me.

" 'We're mending the old fence,' Wingate said. 'Then we're going to bring camp chairs out back, and I'll preach here.'

"When I heard the word 'preach,' I must have given a start because he got a grave look on his face.

" 'All right,' he said. 'I know that look. This isn't just a social call, is it?'

" 'No,' I said. 'I came to warn you.'

"He knelt down and picked up the saw and began cutting a length of board. I saw he was having some difficulty, so I held it for him. He sawed through it with long, powerful strokes.

" 'Warn me about what?' he said.

" 'Your speeches are reaching more than the Negro community.'

" 'Good,' he said stubbornly. 'I intend them to.'

"I sighed and shook my head.

" 'You ought to come hear me sometime,' he said. 'I'm even managing to include some of the history of our people in the sermons. Not to mention mythology, signs. The very history that my good friend Grace taught me.'

" 'I've heard about that, too. Doesn't it occur to you that you're in danger?'

" 'No,' he said, smiling at me. 'We dumb Negroes aren't smart enough to recognize danger.'

"I frowned and shook my head.

" 'Now you're being unkind,' I said.

"He sawed the wood again, then looked at me sincerely."

" 'I'm sorry,' he said, 'but that's kind of an insulting question, don't you think?'

" 'Is it?' I said. 'You don't act like you recognize it.'

" 'I choose not to,' he said. 'Listen, I'm not alone. That's what I've found. Do you remember how excited I was when you first showed me the door into history?'

" 'Of course.'

" 'Well, now I've started to teach other people the same things you taught me, and I see the looks on their faces. . . . Not all of them, of course, only a few so far . . . but people are starting to get it, to understand what's been done to them. And when I see that wonder at becoming conscious—when I see that, I don't care about danger. I don't care about anything as small as myself.'

"I heard him say all this as if I were in a fog. Because on the way down to see him, I had convinced myself exactly how it was going to be. I would charm him, and he would be sensible and listen. And somehow, we would become as we were before, the two of us against the world. But now . . .

now, almost before we had begun, it was over. I knew I wasn't going to get anywhere with him. So, in spite of my best intentions, I felt furious with him all over again. He had his own people, his own friends, a community, and he had left me as surely as if he had gone to Harlem.

"I was jealous of his new friends, his responsibilities. I felt abandoned . . . but I was also really worried for him. He didn't know J.J. Randall and his crowd. Or what they might do.

" 'Well, maybe you don't care about yourself,' I said. 'But I do. And these people I heard . . . they're bad . . . they're ugly, and you're frightening them.'

" 'Good,' he said as he stopped sawing. 'Good. If they're frightened, maybe they know a little bit of what a colored man feels every single day.'

"I felt like crying all over again. Crying and beating him on the chest. Now I understood he was way beyond me, though it didn't occur to me that I had also grown away from him by dating Rob. I only thought of myself.

"Then he suddenly said:

" 'Look, I've got something to show you. The most remarkable thing.'

"He reached into his vest pocket, pulled out a letter, and put it in my hand. It was from A. Philip Randolph himself. Wingate had written to him at *The Messenger*, and Randolph had replied. I don't recall precisely what the letter said, but there were words of encouragement for Wingate's work. Wingate was ecstatic and wanted me to share those feelings with him, but I couldn't do it. I felt utterly betrayed, and underneath I was terrified for him. I knew that nothing I could say could compare to a letter from a man as great as Randolph. And so instead of sharing his happiness with him, I said, 'That's all well and good, but does the great Mr. Randolph know you're only a kid?'

"That stung Wingate to the core. I knew it the moment I said it, but things once spoken . . .

"He looked at me and said, 'My age has nothing to do with anything. Which I thought you understood.'

"He started working again. I wanted to cry, I felt so confused. . . . I mumbled something about being sorry. But now he was hurt and proud, and he wouldn't hear of it. I didn't want to make a scene, so I turned to go.

"But something inside me wouldn't let me leave it there. I turned back and said to him:

" 'Please, can we go inside for a second?'

" 'Why?' he said. 'Do you want to insult me in private now that you've done it in public?'

" 'Please,' I said.

"Reluctantly, he put down the saw, got up, and followed me into the rectory. I paced around the room, thinking, I've got to say something that will cut through all the confusion, all the twisted arguments I've made before. Something decisive. Something he couldn't escape from.

"Finally, I looked at him and said, 'Listen, Wingate, listen to me, please. I'm nobody . . . I'm not special or wonderful, and I'm not . . . I'm certainly not some emissary from God. I'm just a regular girl from Baltimore, Maryland, and when I told you to work here in this town instead of going to Harlem, I was just thinking of myself. I knew I'd miss you, and I didn't want to be here in godforsaken Mayo all alone.'

" 'Stop,' he said. He'd shut his eyes as though what I was saying was too much for him to bear. I knew I was hurting him, but I couldn't stop now. I knew this was my last chance.

" 'Wingate,' I said. 'You hear voices and see signs everywhere, but have you ever considered the fact that . . . they're just in your head because of your granddaddy, and because you're poetic and imaginative and talented?'

" 'No,' he said. 'That's not true. You don't really believe that.'

" 'But I do,' I said, tears coming down my cheeks now. 'I do believe it. It's all inside you, because you're wonderful. Talented. But these things . . . shooting stars and animals that are talismans and all the rest of it, they don't really exist. . . . The star of Bethlehem, the gods and goddesses . . . it's all superstition, fantasy. Make-believe. Things people had to believe in to explain away their fears before we had reason and science.'

"He put his hands to his ears, his face contorted.

" 'No,' he said. 'Stop! Now!'

"His face was wrenched in pain . . . but I had to finish.

" 'Listen to me,' I said. 'Tell me the truth. Haven't you thought . . . I mean when you're alone, in the middle of the night . . . haven't you thought that you're risking your life for nothing? For fantasies?'

"His face changed then. He didn't look stricken any longer but furious. He stared at me then with an anger I'd never seen in him or anyone else before. His eyes widened and his nostrils flared, and he raised his hand above me in a fist.

" 'Get out!' he shouted. 'Get out of my church!'

"I knew I had hurt him beyond all repair . . . but still I felt compelled to make him see.

" 'No, I won't. . . . You have to listen. We're both just kids . . . that's all. Kids. We should be having fun, discovering the world . . . not sacrificing our lives for some impossible ideals. Come with me. We'll go back to Baltimore. You shouldn't be doing any of this.'

"Slowly, with the greatest of effort to control himself, he brought his hand down to his side and unclenched his fist.

" 'I can't speak for you,' he said. 'But I'm a man doing my people's and my Father's work. You . . . you have forsaken our friendship, and, worse, you have lost sight of all that really matters. Or maybe you never cared. Maybe it was always just an entertainment to you. The progressive white girl with her bright but primitive little Negro friend.'

"I don't know what happened. I just snapped. That's when I slapped him in the face.

"He didn't move but stood there staring through me.

" 'Now we finally get to it,' he said. 'When your Nigrah don't please, you gots to whip him into line.'

" 'God, I'm sorry. So sorry.'

"He didn't move a muscle. But the look on his face told me that I was now classified with all the other white people who had hurt him and his people. I was now the enemy."

" 'Get out of my church,' he said. 'Don't ever come back.'

"I turned and stumbled through the door of the rectory, knocking over chairs on my way to the street.

"During the next week, I felt as though I was living under water. Everything that happened between Wingate and me was like a dream. Did he ever really exist at all? Or had I invented him and the whole story just to get through my exile in Mayo? I now know that this feeling of unreality is like being in shock. I cared for and admired him so much, and the pain of what had happened to our friendship and my selfish part in its breakup were so painful. . . . Well, I simply retreated into fantasy."

Grace fidgeted in her chair, ran her hand nervously up and down her jaw. I wanted to say something, something that would relieve her anguish, but I could think of nothing.

"I was lost, so in need of a rudder . . . that I leaned heavily on Rob. He was strong. . . . I couldn't really talk to him about Wingate, but what was there to say? I retreated into everydayness . . . studying, meeting Rob after school. I tried to talk to Bonnie about it all . . . but she seemed distant, unapproachable. Then one day when I finally cornered her and made her talk about it, she told me the truth. She wasn't afraid *for* Wingate anymore. She was afraid *of* him.

"She told me that she was certain he was preaching Negro violence against whites . . . armed revolution.

"I told her that was ridiculous, absurd. But I was unable to convince her.

"Nothing scared me more than that. Bonnie was the most liberal person I knew down there. If she felt that way . . . what must the others feel?

"I lay in bed worrying about him . . . knowing there was nothing I could do. I tried to lose myself in my love for Rob. We were inseparable at that time . . . we went rowing and we hiked . . . and we began to make plans to be married. Sometimes I feel that we made plans all too fast and all because of my own fears, just because I wanted permanence, no matter what the cost."

Grace took a deep breath and stared down into the carpet.

"One night Rob talked me into going to the school football game at Annapolis. I was, as you already know, Bobby, no football fan, but I was trying very hard to escape back into what I imagined Everygirl would want in life. So I went and huddled with Rob and watched as he and some other boys passed a flask around. I even pretended to drink some of it . . . that's how normal I wanted to be.

"After the game we went out to the parking lot, and Rob began to drink more. . . . He and his friends were laughing and sort of wrestling around. It made me nervous, frightened. I wanted to leave but he was having fun, so I stood around smiling, pretending it was all okay with me.

"Then I saw J.J. Randall, Lee Harrison, and Bailey Calhoun. They were just a few cars away from us, and they were really drunk. They were yelling and laughing because we'd won the game . . . and they were getting loud and mean. I told Rob I wanted to go, but they'd drifted over near us and I saw that Bailey had a jug of p.g.a., pure grain alcohol . . . the strongest stuff around, strong enough to knock down a racehorse. They offered Rob a pull off the bottle. I was sick when he took it . . . but I didn't say anything. I figured we'd leave soon enough . . . and maybe it was a good thing that they were trying to be friendly. Some of the other kids were going down to the waterfront to take a sail, and I said, 'Rob, can we go?' but he wanted one more drink . . . and one more after that . . . and then when they were very drunk, Randall turned toward me and said half-kiddingly:

" 'Heard about your friend Wingate Washington? He's been preaching Bolshevism, telling all the niggers they should band together.'

"I looked over at him and felt such a deep revulsion that it turned my stomach.

" 'That's a lie,' I said.

" 'Oh, no, it ain't,' Randall said. 'That Washington thinks who he is, sure enough.'

"Now Lee Harrison looked at me. His fat face was distorted with drunkenness. Ordinarily he wouldn't have said a thing because of Rob, but he had drunk plenty of courage.

"'The son-of-a-bitch nigger,' he said. 'Out there in plain sight, running down the white man.'

"I felt fear running up my spine. I looked over at Rob, who was heading back to me, laughing.

"'We oughta teach him a lesson,' Bailey Calhoun said.

"'Oughta lynch him,' Lee Harrison said.

"I walked right into them when I heard that.

"'You say that again, and I'll . . . I'll kill you myself,' I said.

"Of course, all that got me was a huge round of laughter from all of them. And then J.J. said:

"'Way she always take up for that nigger boy, you'd think she was sweet on him or something.'

"I didn't have to beat him up after that. Rob heard him, walked over, and hit him so hard that he knocked J.J. over the back end of his car. Two of his teeth were lying on the ground next to him. I was so scared. I said, 'Let's go . . . before something terrible happens!' I just wanted to get out of there. I had never seen anyone hit so hard. . . . Rob looked at them all and said, 'Anyone else got a problem needs attending to?' None of them said a word, of course, but as we started to leave, I heard one of them say, 'All that damned nigger's fault. We oughta get that son of a bitch.'

"We took Rob's old car down to the beach, but I couldn't forget what they'd said. Of course, they'd said things like it a hundred times before, but tonight . . . there was more anger behind their words. And stronger alcohol. I kept asking Rob, 'Would they do it? Would they really go after him?' but he just laughed and said, 'Those three? They couldn't beat an egg. . . . That's just drunk talk. You saw how tough Randall is, didn't you?'

"That made me feel better. I told myself that it was going to be okay. They'd get drunk and pass out . . . and I let Rob take me out in the boat. It was a rich man's skipjack . . . a lovely boat. Rob took the man and his friends out fishing. He knew where all the best spots were, so he got to use the boat as a reward. Rob was teaching me how to trim the sails. I let myself relax a little, and we sailed out into the Chesapeake Bay under a full moon. Rob lent me his coat—in those days he could be so gallant—and I snuggled in his arms. We'd been out about an hour when I turned and looked back toward land and saw the fire, a raging wildfire in the trees. I began to scream, for I knew beyond any doubt that they'd done it. . . . They'd gone and burned out Wingate.

"By the time we got to the church, the place was already smoldering embers. . . . The town's little fire department—one pathetic truck—had come and done the best they could, but it was no use. The church had burned down. There was a wagon from the coroner's office there . . . and they were taking away two bodies. They had sheets laid across their faces. When I saw that, I broke away from Rob and raced toward the ambulance.

" 'Who is it?' I said. 'Tell me.'

" 'A man and a boy,' the fireman said.

"Then I did a shocking thing. I pulled the sheet right off the smaller of the two corpses.

" 'Are you out of your mind, ma'am?' the doctors said.

"I looked down at that poor, blackened body. A boy of thirteen, only a few years younger than Wingate. I felt sick, but I also felt relieved. Then I turned and saw an older Negro man with a clerical collar. I figured it was the Reverend Phillips and quickly went to him. I introduced myself and told him I was a friend of Wingate's. I asked him if he'd been here when it happened.

"The Reverend was a huge man with the sleepiest eyes. He looked down at me, and I felt that he knew all of my sins and was judging me. If God is black, he must look like Dr. Phillips.

" 'Somebody threw a bomb through the front window,' he said. 'Wingate was coming out of the rectory, and he was blown back. I think he was injured, but he went out in the street after them. Crazy fool child, he ran after them. They drove away, and he went after them on his old bicycle.'

" 'Oh, God!' I said.

"I turned to Rob and told him that we had to go after Wingate. He looked at me as if I was mad, but he got back in his old Ford and we headed out, down the road.

G r a c e

"It was dark, and there were no lights on those old country roads. Hard to see. We drove for four, five miles. Then I saw something on the side of the road. I told Rob to stop at once, and then I jumped out and ran to it. The bicycle. And next to it there was a trail of blood on the sandy grass. I ran into the woods . . . in the dark, Rob calling after me from the car. Finally, he ran in, too, but he couldn't find me, and I kept running, falling over logs and roots, running through branches that scraped my face. I didn't care. I kept going.

"It took me a while in the dark, but I finally got there. To our old cabin. I'd run all the way, and I could barely breathe. I'd lost Rob in the underbrush, and I suddenly wished he was here. Slowly, I opened the door, not even daring to hope.

"He was up against the far wall, under the spot where the roof was ripped away. He looked up at the shining full moon, and he stared at me as I bent over him.

"He was covered with blood. Blood running down his neck, and there was a slash in his side . . . I could see ribs, and beyond that intestines.

" 'Oh, God!' I said. 'What have they done to you?'

"I held his head in my lap. He looked at me and traced his bloody finger down my face.

" 'My angel,' he said.

" 'You have to rest,' I said.

" 'Don't worry,' he said. 'I'm almost there. Almost.'

"He tried to laugh but coughed, and I tore away my blouse and wiped the blood from his lips.

" 'I've got to get you back,' I said.

" 'Back to what?' he said. 'What we had . . . that was the best world . . . that was the only world. Why did you cast me out?'

" 'I don't know,' I said. 'I'm sorry. God forgive me.'

" 'It was so good here,' he said.

" 'Yes,' I said. 'I love you.'

"He used all his effort and sat up, looking up through the trees at the moon.

" 'Did you ever believe me?' he asked. 'I have to know. Did you ever believe me . . . that I had a mission, or were you just slumming?'

" 'I believed you,' I said. 'I believed you. I swear it.'

There was no use hiding it anymore. I cried, and my whole body was wracked with sobs. He began to cough and spat up more blood.

" 'You did?' he said. 'Really?'

" 'Yes,' I said. 'Really.'

"His huge, expressive eyes opened wide then, and he looked straight into my face.

" 'Damn your soul,' he said.

"Then he fell back and died.

"Rob found me holding his body, and together we got him back to town."

Grace's head dropped, and she put her hands over her face.

"Those words have haunted me all my life," she said.

"God," I said.

My grandmother rocked back and forth in the chair, staring straight ahead, her face waxen, as though she herself were a corpse.

"It was a perfect day for his funeral. There were over a hundred people there. Mostly, but not all, Negroes.

"Of course it came out that I'd been with him when he died. My aunt and uncle were horrified. They tried to question me one day, but I screamed at them so loudly they ended up calling the doctor, and I had to be given a shot to make me sleep.

"I walked all the way from our house to the graveyard. About four miles.

"I half-expected to cry all the way there, but I couldn't. I felt a remorse and sorrow too deep for tears. All that kept going through my head was, 'If I had just let him go to Harlem, but I kept him here.' "

Her voice cracked now, and I felt that I had to try.

"Grace," I said. "You helped him find who he really was. What you said was right . . ."

She shook her head.

"No. I was a young girl, and I wanted him around to . . . to . . . amuse me. If he'd left, I'd have been lonely. And when I thought about it later, I had to admit that deep down when we had played our games in the woods, and he saw signs of the spirit in a bird's call or in a tree limb being broken a certain way, I didn't really believe him. Not literally. Which wouldn't have been so bad, except I said I did. I told him what he wanted to hear . . . that he was a leader, that he was a visionary. But in the end, I was just talking, you understand? It was like an exciting game. The problem was, he was really listening. What I told him out of vanity cost him his life."

"No," I said. "That's not so. He was a leader . . . so he led. And maybe he was a little bit crazy. You say yourself that he had all these visions and things before you ever came around. He would have probably gotten into trouble whether he met you or not."

Grace nodded wearily.

"My dear, sweet grandson, don't you think I've gone through all these arguments myself? Even if it were so, if he had gone to Harlem, he would have gotten seasoned, matured . . . and then if he had come back to Mayo, he would have had experience, he would have known how to deal with people. But he trusted me, and I betrayed him. That's the long and short of it. To say anything else is to cheapen it, to tell more lies."

She looked so weary, so tired . . .

"I remember the funeral like it was yesterday. A hundred people there, the church overflowing with those who came to take one last look at him. I walked in the line, and I felt they all knew, they all knew that somehow I was his Judas. I thought of Rob hitting J.J. Randall . . . was that the final insult to those boys? And why, why didn't I go warn him? I knew that things could get out of hand. But I let Rob talk me out of it. Why? Do you know how many thousands of times I have asked myself that question?"

She was pacing nervously, rubbing her hands on the front of her dress, as though she was trying to wipe off Wingate's blood.

"I finally went to see him lying there in that cherry wood casket. He looked so small, so young . . . just a child . . . and I thought he'd been like a comet, blazing brilliantly, then gone to ash. I kissed him on the top of his forehead and went out. There was a service, but I didn't stay for it. I didn't want to hear someone else's version of Wingate Washington. I knew him. Better than I have known any living person. I knew him and I loved him and I helped get him killed."

She stopped and looked at me, her eyes filled with what looked like an unbearable sorrow and grief.

"You didn't," I said. "You didn't. You were just a kid yourself. You were mixed up. You couldn't know what he would do when you told him to stay. You couldn't know that those boys would kill him. Maybe it wasn't even them. How do you know it was?"

"I know . . . they laughed about it. Rob even talked about beating a confession out of them, and I almost let him do it. But in the end, I knew that was wrong . . . and I stopped him."

She shook her head.

"They were never charged. They got away with it. One of them, Cal-houn, is still alive. The other two drank themselves to an early death."

There was a long silence. She had gone into a place in the world that I hadn't even known existed. Finally, I managed to speak.

"Now I understand," I said. "And I thought it was about your trip to England. I'm sorry."

"That's all right, honey."

"And last week . . . the fall from the garage. That's what these 'spells' of yours have been about all these years?"

She nodded. "Yes, honey, I'm afraid so."

"But you told me you weren't sure what they were."

"A white lie," she said. "I was . . . I am ashamed of all that happened. I could barely admit it to myself . . . so how could I tell you?"

"What is it you see in your spells?"

Grace took a long breath.

"Wingate," she said. "That's the other reason I didn't tell you . . ."

"I don't understand. You dream of Wingate?"

She gave an embarrassed laugh.

"No, I'm afraid I haven't yet told you the complete truth. You see, I don't think I'm dreaming. When he comes to me, I mean. I think you saw him, too. That night."

Now it was my turn to get out of the chair. I paced around, trying to absorb what she was saying.

"You mean a ghost? Wingate's ghost? Are you telling me that's what I saw that night in the hallway?"

"I'm afraid so, honey. Yes. What else could it be?"

"I don't know. A trick of light. The moon through the blinds. Or maybe we ate one too many crab cakes."

"At first I thought it was a dream, but it's been a long time and I'm usually awake enough to kind of know what's going on."

Naturally, I leaped on that:

"But you're not sure. Which means it could be a dream."

"Yes, I guess . . . but I feel his hand on mine. I felt him lead me to the garage."

"But that's crazy. Ghosts only exist in stories and the movies."

"Well, there is one other explanation," Grace said. "I could be stark raving mad."

I felt a chill go through me when she said that. It was the exact thought I'd had only a few days ago.

"I don't know anything about madness. Only maybe Dad . . . in the bathroom."

I stopped then. We'd never discussed my father.

"It's all right," she said. "You haven't betrayed any confidences. I wish . . . Lord, I wish I could help him."

"But when Dad gets like that, it seems like craziness. You're calm and collected. You sit there and tell me you've seen a ghost and . . . you sound sane."

"I suppose so," she said. "But do I act sane when it happens?"

She had me there.

"At my worst moments, I've even thought, Bobby, that I've passed on my madness to your father. I felt so terrible about it that I secretly went to a psychiatrist a few years back."

"You did?" Grace lying on a psychiatrist's couch? It seemed impossible.

"He told me that what your father had was something else entirely. He thought I had invented a ghost to torture myself for my guilt about Wingate's death."

I stopped pacing then.

"That sounds right to me," I said, "except for one thing—I saw something, too. And if you get involved with civil rights now, aren't you putting yourself in danger all over again?"

"Yes, I am."

"Well, then why?" I asked. "Why now?"

"Because I had a sign," she said. "A sign from God."

I felt a terrible sensation creeping over me.

"What is it?"

"You," she said. "God sent me you to get me involved again. That must be it."

"No," I said. "You can't say that to me. That makes me like Wingate."

"I know," she said, and she was smiling. "It's all come full circle. Now let me ask you something. Did you really think you could escape your troubles by moving in with me?"

I said nothing for a long time. I was scared by what she had just said. Finally, though, her look compelled me to answer.

"I guess I did," I said.

"It's all right," she said. But you may as well learn now that life is trouble, life is difficult, and the choices we make often backfire and lead to pain. And sometimes when a good person is struck dead early in life from a heart attack or cancer . . . or polio . . . life seems unfair. But the surest way I know of guaranteeing pain in your life is to pretend to an innocence you no longer possess. I've thought about it long and hard, and I've finally understood that's what I was doing with Wingate. He may have been confused, and he may or may not have seen visions, but in his own way, the way that was right for him, he was becoming a man . . . and I was angry at him for leaving our little world of innocence and sweetness. Wingate understood Jesus when he said, 'When I was a child, I spoketh as a child but when I became a man, I put away childish things.' My problem was that I was having a temper tantrum, the tantrum of a child who wants to return to an innocent state and is furious she must give up that innocence. But once innocence is gone, there's no going back to it, Bobby. Better that you embrace the real world that is full of real dangers and real rewards, real pain and real joy."

I was overwhelmed by all she had told me. Much of it, I confess, washed over me, and it wasn't until a good deal later that I understood it all. But there were two things I recognized even then. First, I had come to her house to try to extend my own childhood. Instead, I had found nothing but complexity and challenges.

And second, that her young life seemed to be repeating itself in mine. And I didn't want that kind of responsibility.

"Look," I said, "you can't tell me that I'm a sign from God. . . . What if . . . what if something happens to you when we go on a demonstration? Then I'll be guilty for my whole life just as you have been."

She smiled at me.

"Listen, Bobby, you'll have to take your chances out there on the street, and so will I. I have my own free will, and you have no responsibility at all for me. No more or less than you have for any other person in the world. We must behave as though we are all brothers and sisters . . . and when we don't we're wrong. I happen to feel that your coming to live here is a sign . . . but it's my feeling, not yours. And you aren't responsible for it. I risk what I risk because I must."

"That's very fancy," I said, "but I have to tell you that it still makes me very uncomfortable. Can't you just say that you're going out there to help the Negroes achieve equality because it's the right thing to do and that's the end of it?"

"Bobby, you're not a child anymore," Grace said. "You must learn to both tell and hear the truth. And, honey bun, it ain't always what you want to hear."

She smiled at me and opened her arms. And there was nothing to do but hug her . . . but it wasn't the same kind of hug I'd given and received in the old days: the warm, reassuring kid hug, which made me feel that indeed everything was going to be fine.

No, it was a troubled hug, a doubtful hug . . . maybe what you'd have to call my first adult hug.

I wish I could tell you that I liked it . . . that I felt good about what I'd learned that day, that the truth had set me free . . . but that wouldn't be true.

No, truth had disturbed me greatly, and no hug or kiss or fairy tale was going to make it all go away.

My grandmother, the wise and wonderfully complex woman that she was, could always sense my moods, and she put her hand on my cheek.

"One more thing," she said. "What you did to Buddy Watkins today?"

"I'm really sorry about that," I said.

But she put her finger over my lips.

"Don't be. It was wrong, but as long as you did it, I'm glad you really knocked him for a loop. I've always wanted to see somebody do that to that kid. Nice going."

She smiled, then pulled away. I stood there, dazed, shaking my head.

Grace at 23

*F*our days later, Grace, the Reverend Gibson, and Sean
Hunter met with Dr. Brooks at his rectory. Of course, I was dying
to go as well, but there was no way a kid was going to be at that
meeting. Instead, I did my part by inviting Howard Murray, his brother,
and two other friends to play basketball with Ray Lane, Johnny Brandau,
and me at the Waverly gym. They all showed up, and we ended up in a five-
on-five full-court game that included white Waverly rednecks, North Avenue Negroes, and two Jewish kids from northwest Baltimore. The Harper
brothers were there and Buddy Watkins walked in, and neither of them said
a word. As for the other white kids, I noticed they all wanted Howard and
his brother on his side . . . because they wanted to win. From that day on,
and all through the '60s, Waverly Rec was interracial . . . and not a shot
was fired.

Meanwhile, at First Methodist Church, Dr. Gibson, Sean Hunter, and
my grandmother walked into the Reverend Brooks's office ready to lay out a
list of their "concerns" . . . but Brooks had his own strategy, a preemptive
strike designed to take the teeth out of the coalition's demands.

He sat behind the desk, smiling, and offered everyone tea, which they
in their wisdom accepted. Then Dr. Brooks said that he had thought it
through and talked it over with several church board members, and they all
agreed the church was living in the past and that Negroes should now sit

wherever they wanted on Sundays or any other day. He was prepared to re-
lease an announcement to that effect and to mention it in his sermon on
Sunday.

He seemed very pleased at his own efforts. It was then that Sean
Hunter spoke. He said that while this was all well and good, he wanted
much more. He wanted the First Methodist Church and the Reverend
Brooks to make statements that racism is wrong and that the church supported civil rights in spirit and in practice. And to illustrate what he meant,
Sean Hunter asked Dr. Brooks to walk with Dr. Gibson and seven other
groups of blacks and whites two weeks from now, when they would demonstrate at none other than my own parents' shopping place, the brand-
spanking-new Eastgate Shopping Center.

Grace told me later that Brooks seemed shocked by the demands. He
felt standing up for Negroes' rights to sit where they wanted in church was
practically a revolutionary act. But to actually go out there and walk with
Negroes, and go to jail with Negroes . . . well, this was not the kind of
thing he had gotten into the Methodist ministry for.

He turned a bright red and looked at Grace for some kind of support.

"Grace," he said, his voice cracking. "Do you intend to . . . uh . . .
demonstrate?"

"Yes," she said. "And I expect to get arrested as well. The time has
come for Christians to act like Christians and stand up for their beliefs.
These people sitting here are my brothers and sisters in Christ, just as
they're yours. . . . We can't turn our backs on their struggle and really call
ourselves Christians."

"Well said, sister Grace," Dr. Gibson added in his booming voice.
"Let all of us who call ourselves Methodists stand up and be counted."

After a very long time staring at the whorls in his desk, Dr. Brooks
said, "Well, of course, in theory I am with you. But I don't work as an individual. I have people to see and to talk to about this."

Dr. Gibson smiled at him and put a huge hand across the desk, which
Dr. Brooks at first shrank from, but then finally grasped.

"Then let the talk begin, Dr. Brooks," Dr. Gibson said. "And let the words you say be true and in the spirit of freedom. Remember, Jesus Christ was not a shrinking lamb, sir, He was a powerful force. He threw the moneylenders out of the temple. He fought and He died for our sins. . . . Some say that He was a revolutionary."

My grandmother gave him a very skeptical look when he said that . . . but as we came to know later, once Dr. Gibson got hold of a favorite metaphor, he let it work for him.

At the end of that meeting, Dr. Brooks was covered in sweat. Laughing as hard as I'd ever seen her, Grace told me that evening she doubted if he had ever been in such a closed space with so many Negroes. He was terrified.

Unfortunately, that wasn't the only emotion he felt. Two days after the meeting, he called my grandmother on the phone, which I happened to answer.

"Hello, Bob, this is Dr. Brooks . . . uh, Wesley. No need for us to be so formal all the time. Is Grace at home?"

"Yes, I'll get her."

"Fine."

She was in the pantry, getting dinner ready. There was the smell of chicken gravy coming from the kitchen. I'd been hungry, but now I felt my stomach turn.

"It's the Reverend Brooks," I said.

She nodded and sat down slowly in the old phone nook.

"Hello? Yes, I'm fine . . ."

There was a long pause as she listened. I saw her sigh and put her hand up to her head.

"I see," she said at last.

Another long pause. She pushed back a strand of her iron-gray hair.

"Yes, I see. Of course . . . I understand your decision. Of course . . . I'll abide by it. Good-bye."

I stood there looking at her, my heart racing.

"Annette Swain will be representing the church in England this summer," she said.

"But that's so unfair," I said.

"Yes," she said. "It is."

"But isn't there a vote?"

"A board vote. And Dr. Brooks's endorsement means everything."

"That creep," I said. "He shouldn't be allowed to be a minister at all."

"Bobby," she said. "Don't talk that way."

"But . . ."

"He has his reasons. But he *is* going to say something about civil rights in the sermon. And we're going to be handing out pamphlets about the demonstration at Eastgate Shopping Center. So we march on."

I went to her and put my arm around her shoulders.

"I don't understand. If he allowed all that, why isn't he supporting you?"

"Because," she said, "I embarrassed him by going into his office with Dr. Gibson and confronting him. This is personal, I'm afraid."

"Revenge," I said. "Very Christian."

"No," she said. "But very human."

In the following week, I readied myself for my first demonstration. My grandmother and I went to a special training session at Dunbar High School, a long way from Grace's house in the black section of town. Three nights in a row we drove there in her old Studebaker, down the York Road, turned right at 33rd, and headed across town to Dunbar. There we met with over fifty other activists and learned the principles of nonviolence. We learned how to think of our goals, why it was important to sing (to inspire others and to block out our own fears), how to avoid injuries to your body if being hit (double up to protect ribs, hands over face to avoid injuries to the eyes).

And ironically, given my experience with Buddy, we were broken into groups and taught how to respond to taunting. I remember a huge black man in a blue Baltimore Colts windbreaker standing one inch from me, screaming:

"What's your problem, nigger lover?

"You're worse than any nigger, white boy . . .

"We're gonna string you up first, boy."

I felt a fury as he screamed at me and an intense embarrassment. Though it was only play-acting, I think I felt one hundredth of what Negroes must feel every day of their lives. And it sickened me. But I knew, or at least I was pretty sure, I would stand up to it.

But I was more worried for Grace. I winced as a middle-aged white woman screamed directly in her face:

"What are you doing here, you old bitch?

"You love niggers, lady? You ready to die for them?"

I saw Grace stick out her jaw, trying to look defiant, unafraid, but to be honest, she looked fragile, like she very well might crumble . . . and I suddenly doubted her again. Maybe she was simply too old for this kind of action, or maybe . . . maybe the truth was that she had always been a parlor liberal, that she lacked the physical courage it took to get down and dirty in the streets.

And, of course, I thought about her saying that my coming to her was a sign from God. . . . Man, to be honest, I appreciated her attempt to make me grow up, but I didn't need that. And I was angry at her for laying it on me. Just as she must have been at Wingate.

I tried to tell myself that the difference was that I wasn't going to abandon her. I was going to be out there with her.

But what would happen if she crumbled out there on the line? She might put other people at risk, and I knew she would never be able to see herself in the same light again.

And I would never be able to see her in the same heroic light again.

More important, if she couldn't handle it, I would have to defend her, which was strictly forbidden. But what would I do if someone pushed or kicked her?

I suddenly understood that nonviolence was so much more than mere physical bravery. I had to be brave enough to not strike back if I was hit, and brave enough to let her get hit, trampled, blasted with high-pressure hoses . . . whatever the cops used.

During a break in the training, I walked over to the high school gym bleachers, deep in thought. How could I allow anyone to hurt her? She sat down next to me, small, fragile. Her arms looked like sticks.

"What is it?" she said.

"I don't know," I said.

"You don't know if you want to do this?"

Her sweet face was open, not judging me harshly.

"No, that's not it. I don't know if you should do this."

Now her eyes narrowed, and she stared at me intently.

"Why?" she said. "Do you think I won't hold up?"

"No," I lied. "It's not that at all. I love you, and I don't want you to be hurt."

She squeezed my wrist.

"I can do this," she said. "Believe me."

I stared at her, my heart racing, my mind filled with fear and doubt.

"Okay," I said. "Of course you can."

They must have been waiting for us all night, because we didn't get back to Grace's until after eleven o'clock. She pulled her Stude into the parking space, and we traipsed up the steps toward the bright, inviting lights of her house, both of us exhausted.

But we never made it. Suddenly I felt someone pull me back, and I landed on the sidewalk. I looked up, confused, bleary-eyed, and saw Nelson Watkins standing above me. Buddy stood just behind him. They both had on black T-shirts, black Levi's, and black garrison belts. All the better to hide themselves in the dark.

"Look who's coming home late," Nelson said. "Out with your nigger friends?"

Buddy Watkins quickly ran up the hill and blocked Grace's way to the porch.

"Mrs. Ward, the nigger's friend," he said.

"You touch my grandmother, Buddy, and I'll kill you," I said. I meant it, too. Once again, I could feel it rising in me, something primitive, ugly . . . violent.

There was a terrible silence after I said that. With six-foot-two, ex-con Nelson there, I wasn't going to kill anybody, and we all knew it.

"Tough guy. Well, listen, tough guy, we're sick of you and your nigger friends in our neighborhood," Nelson said. He laughed as he hovered over me. "I'm thinking that we should teach you a lesson."

"Go ahead then," I said. "But leave my grandmother out of it."

"Don't see how we can do that," Nelson said. "She's the one who brung all the trouble down onna neighborhood."

"You'd better not touch her," I said.

Nelson looked up at Grace, who stood there staring at us. Then she spoke, coolly and calmly.

"No," she said. "You go ahead, Nelson Watkins. You do whatever you want to us."

I swallowed hard. Oh, man, now was not the time to try out our new nonviolent tactics.

"Go ahead," my grandmother said. "But I'm telling you now that it won't make any difference. No matter what you do . . . my grandson and I are committed to civil rights. And to nonviolence."

"Huh?" Nelson said. "I don't get it."

My grandmother smiled and looked at him again.

"Well, would you like to kick me?" she said. "Or would you like to scratch out my eyes?"

Oh, sweet Jesus, I thought . . .

"Hey, you crazy or what?" Nelson said.

"Maybe you could just jump on me," Grace said. "You're big boys, and I'm sure you'd get a kick out of that."

"Hey, wait a minute, she's making you look like a chump, Nelson," Buddy said.

My grandmother turned to Buddy.

"Here I am," she said. "Go ahead and do whatever you want, Buddy."

"You think I won't?" Buddy said. "You think I won't?"

"No, I'm sure you will, Buddy. Hitting a woman is just the kind of thing you'd be good at. So go right ahead."

Buddy lifted his fist, and Nelson walked up the steps toward my grandmother.

"We'll do it," he said. "We'll make you wish you'd never been born, you old bag."

"So go ahead then," Grace said.

She took off her glasses and stood still as the two of them converged on her.

"You're making us do it," Buddy said. "You're making us hit you."

"And we're gonna," Nelson said.

"Well, get on with it," my grandmother said. "For bullies, you two are certainly slow at this kind of thing."

They looked at each other, then down at me.

"What are you gonna do if we hit your grandmother?" Buddy said.

"Me, I'm gonna watch," I said. "I think it would be real interesting to see what kind of punch you use. Uppercut or right cross."

Nelson looked at Buddy, and the two of them suddenly seemed mightily confused.

"It's a trick," Nelson said. "Gotta be."

"Maybe old Rob's home," Buddy said, looking up at the house.

"Maybe old Rob's just waiting for us to hit her, and then he's gonna come out with a shotgun."

"'Cause one thing I know for sure," Nelson said. "Grace Ward may believe in nonviolence, but old Rob believes in a good ass whipping."

I looked at Buddy, and suddenly my tongue got the best of me.

"I don't need old Rob to kick your ass, Buddy. But today is freebie day. You go right ahead and hit me and my grandmother . . . and nothing much is gonna happen to you."

Buddy looked at me, and his eyes kind of crossed.

"Much," he said. "You hear that? 'Much'?"

"I heard it," Nelson said. "You two think we're gonna fall for that stuff. Know what I bet . . . I bet they have ten niggers in the house right now, ten niggers and old Rob, waiting to come out and get us."

"Boo," my grandmother said.

Both Nelson and Buddy jumped back, as if a firecracker had gone off in front of them.

They began to back away from the porch, heading for their house across the street . . . looking around behind them as they went, as if afraid that Negroes might be strategically placed behind parked cars.

"You can't fool us, Grace Ward," Nelson said.

"Whole house full of niggers," Buddy Watkins said.

"Plus old Rob," Nelson said.

"Imagine trying to set us up," Nelson said. "She thinks we're idiots or something."

"Well, it didn't work," Buddy said. "'Cause the Watkins brothers ain't a couple of damned fools."

They headed up into the house and slammed the door. The last thing I heard was the satisfying click of the deadbolt lock.

I looked up at my grandmother, and both of us burst into laughter.

"Gracie, that was stone beautiful," I said.

"You're right," she said. "It was. Now let's get a little sleep. We've got a demonstration to attend."

It was more than a little strange to be standing in the Eastgate Shopping Center with fifteen demonstrators and my grandmother outside the very store—the Food Fair—that I shopped in with my parents, the store we discovered the wonders of Mrs. Paul's Fresh Frozen Fish Sticks. Now as I walked around in a circle holding up my sign, "Negroes Can't Work Here," I looked up and saw Grace with her sign as well, "Freedom for All or Freedom for None." As we all began to sing "We Shall Overcome," I looked at the store my family and everyone else in our neighborhood had considered the very essence of modernity, and I realized that only the packaging was new. Oh, the place was all polished chrome and neon lighting, but underneath they were the same old American institutions—good for white people only. In that way the Food Fair was very old-fashioned. As old-fashioned as slavery itself, and I felt a great pride in my grandmother and some in myself, too, walking out there . . . standing up for the rights of our Negro brothers and sisters, but also for something else as well.

Standing up for justice. Standing up for honesty. America's honesty, and purity of vision. And standing up for my own best self . . .

For all the bright packaging in the world cannot make up for a bad conscience . . . which is, I realized, what I had before I acted on my beliefs. And all the moralizing and self-justification in the world doesn't make you feel as good as doing one simple thing honestly.

The right thing.

Not the TV dinner but the real dinner.

Not the fish stick but the fish.

Not just talk but righteous action. The right action.

And it seemed to me then, just before the paddy wagons came to take us to jail, that things weren't as deeply complex as I had thought.

Yes, moralists and sophisticates will tell you that all is irony and that modern life is so complex, so deeply confusing that a man or a woman, even given his or her best intentions, can't really know what's right.

To that Grace said, "Bunk!" She was tortured by her own past, a past in which she hadn't acted on her own best instincts.

But now she was through with that, and I wasn't afraid for her anymore. I understood most of what she had said. If she wanted to interpret things in a religious way, that was fine.

The important thing was that we had done it, we had acted on our beliefs, and I think I knew that day, much more than the day I ran down the hill to whack Buddy, that I was becoming a man.

And as the Baltimore police assisted my grandmother and me into the paddy wagon (the truth is they were decent guys, definitely not Bull Connor, the racist sheriff from Alabama), I felt a tremendous happiness flood my soul. It was a new feeling, the feeling of acting in a righteous way, of overcoming fears and doubts by doing the right thing. Yet as we rode along, singing together, it was a familiar feeling, too, and as we pulled into the parking lot at the city jail, I realized what it was: the old warmth of inclusion . . . the feeling I'd had in my younger days on Grace's front porch when I was surrounded by my family, and we'd see the bright lights of Memorial Stadium shining down on us almost like some celestial halo, a feeling that I thought I would never have again because my family was splitting up and my grandmother seemed not to be the woman I thought she was, and I was most definitely not anywhere close to becoming a man.

And yet here in the paddy wagon with complete strangers, most of them Negroes from a very different Baltimore, a very different America, I felt a new home, one that I knew would sustain me as a man, just as the world of my family had sustained me as a child.

The difference, I thought, as the Baltimore police took me inside for fingerprinting, was that this new family was one of my choosing. I no longer had to be protected by it; on the contrary, I had to work to protect it from those who wanted to tear it apart.

My new family was people like Grace, people in all their glorious imperfection, who nonetheless tried to live decently, people who stood up for people less fortunate than themselves, who fought to preserve real art in a world of phony art hustlers, people who battled to keep a true democratic spirit in a world that sometimes seemed to be all about fish sticks and not at all about fish.

And for that I thank Grace, who taught me that staring endlessly into self is a losing game, a deadly game, that the glorification of self above all deadens the very life one needs to nurture a true self. That social protest is not only our right but in this world of sham and willed ignorance and immense bad faith . . . our responsibility.

All this I learned from Grace and from Cap, too, and from the brave and selfless leaders of the Negro civil rights movement. They were my heroes then, and all these years later they remain my heroes: King, Abernathy, Moses, Rosa Parks . . . and my old friend Howard, who integrated a basketball court and never said a word about it.

G r a c e

Heroes large and small . . . bravery with a purpose. Rebels with a cause. Inclusion in this family is one that will feed your soul. As it fed mine. And as it fed Grace's, who sang the loudest and most off-key from her jail cell, driving her guards a little mad. They were very happy when we were bailed out the next day.

Dr. Gibson gave us a ride home and told us that the demonstrations would continue at other sights, that pressure would be kept on Eastgate . . . and that so far it was working. They'd lost about a third of their shoppers at both Food Fair and the Hecht Company, and the owners were close to making a deal.

He let us out and said he'd be in touch soon.

Though her spirits were soaring, Grace suddenly looked very, very tired, and as I waved good-bye to the Reverend Gibson, I turned and helped her up the steps toward her porch.

"You need a good long nap," I said.

"I'll get to bed," she said. "I've got some church work to attend to first. You go ahead, honey."

I could only laugh. When had she ever admitted she was tired?

I had things to do, too. I called home and told my mother where we'd been.

"You been where, hon?" she said.

"In jail, Mom," I said. "With Grace."

"Oh, my God, hon," my mother said. "What did you two do?"

"Nothing," I said. "Just demonstrated with the NAACP down at Eastgate Shopping Center."

"With Negroes?" she said.

"That's pretty much who's in the NAACP, Mom," I said.

"Well, did they hurt you?"

"Who, the cops?"

"No, the Negroes."

"No, Mom," I said. "I was with them. They are trying to fully integrate the Eastgate Shopping Center."

"My, my," she said. "What next? . . . Well, I'd tell your father, but he's not living here much these days."

"No?" I said.

"I'm afraid not. It's kind of lonely here. I wish you'd come home. I miss you."

"Yeah," I said. "And I miss you, too. I'll be home tomorrow."

"Good," my mother said. "We'll be all right. You can tell me all about the Negroes. I hope your grandmother didn't have one of her spells in jail."

"She didn't," I said. "I don't think she's going to be having them much anymore."

"Really? How come?"

"It's a long story, Mom. Maybe I'll tell it to you someday. Or better yet, maybe Grace will."

"Good. You coming home tomorrow then?"

"Yeah," I said. "Gotta go do some schoolwork. Love you, Mom."

"Me, too, honey. And that's good, what you did with the Negroes. Somebody ought to cut out the crap and let 'em live right. You'd think that Baltimore was Germany, the way we treat people sometimes."

"You got it, Mom," I said. "See you later."

I hung up and lay back on my bed, half drifting off. But I felt good, satisfied . . . and brave. Not pumped up, not movie-hero brave . . . but brave. Solid.

Then I fell into a deep, long sleep.

That would be the end of my tale . . . of the days I lived with Grace and the things I learned from her . . . except for one last little curve, the one I will never fully understand.

I almost hesitate to write it because it seems so strange, but in the name of honesty, I think I must.

I slept most of that day, only waking up around dinner to eat some of Grace's wonderful pea soup. By six o'clock she looked exhausted, and though she complained she had some more church duties to see to, calls

to make about some upcoming charity function, she finally let me talk her
into going upstairs to "rest for a while." I knew that once she hit the bed
she was going to be out for twelve hours, which was precisely what she
needed.

I brought her robe and warm pajamas, and combed her long hair for
her, and then tucked her into bed.

"Thank you, honey," she said.

"For what?"

"For listening, for understanding . . . for getting me back out there
where I belong."

"You did it," I said. "I'm very, very proud of you, Gracie. Now
please . . . get some sleep."

"You'll wake me in a few hours?"

"Of course."

I shut her door softly and headed back to my own bedroom, where I
turned on the radio, then fell into a deep sleep of my own.

When I awoke I heard a strange but, by now, terrifyingly familiar
noise. It sounded like an animal crying.

Oh, God, I thought, she's not out there again.

I scrambled up, pulling the covers around my shoulders, and looked
out the window through the holly tree limbs to the old garage roof.

There on the roof was Grace, sitting on her prayer rug, dressed in her
bathrobe and slippers. It was a cold night, and I thought that my worst
fears had been realized. That taking part in the demonstration had un-
locked her subconscious and she was going to have a rash of spells. Maybe
worse then ever.

I started to throw on a sweater, then looked back down at the
rooftops again.

I blinked, rubbed my eyes.

What I saw couldn't be . . .

Grace was not alone.

G r a c e

There was a young black boy standing over her. The only problem was that his bare feet weren't exactly touching the garage rooftop. He hovered just above her in the air, his body encircled by the same bright light I'd seen in the hallway that night.

Even from my awkward vantage point I could see his large eyes. And the flaring, delicate nostrils Grace had described. And the head, slightly too large for the thin, sensuous body.

He hovered there above her, seeming to sway gently back and forth with the wind currents.

Then I saw her look up, and tears streamed down her face.

He showed no emotion at all but simply looked intently down at her for what must have been ten seconds.

Then he put out his two long, thin, elegant hands, and Grace slowly, fearfully reached up and took them in her own.

A warm, sweet smile broke across Wingate's face. Seemingly without effort he pulled my grandmother to her feet and gave her a ghostly embrace.

It seemed as though he was whispering something into her ear.

And suddenly, on the very edge of the roof, she collapsed, and he was gone.

I pulled myself up to the rooftop and ran breathlessly to Grace's side. I turned her over. She seemed not to be breathing.

Heart attack, I thought. Oh, God . . .

I began to beat on her chest. I hit her twice with my fist, hard, and I was crying out.

"Don't die. You can't . . . no!"

Grace's eyes popped open.

"What are you doing, dear?" she said.

"I'm saving your life," I said.

"Oh," she said. "That's good of you. But I think I'm okay."

I helped her up, and she looked at me. The moon shone down on us like a spotlight.

"He was here," she said.

"I know," I said. "I saw him."

She nodded.

"Well, thank God for that. I've been seeing him for thirty years. And believe me, most of the time he was not in a loving mood."

"No," I said. "It can't be."

"Yes, it is, honey. But tonight . . . tonight Wingate was different."

She was shivering, but she didn't want to leave yet, so I hugged her tightly.

"He held me, then he whispered something in my ear."

"What did he say?"

"He said, 'Grace, I forgive you.' Then he kissed me on the ear, and I guess I fainted."

I held her very close to me.

"I think we'd better go in," I said. "You're cold."

"Maybe," Grace said, "but I've never felt so warm in my life."

Together we made our way down the old rock to the back alley, and walked back by the holly tree to the house.

Grace went in first. I was about to join her when I felt something odd . . . as if someone's eyes were trained on my back.

I turned quickly and saw him there, standing just above the garage. He looked at me with a depth of sadness and understanding that tore at my heart. I stared back at him, and I felt his intensity, his passion filling my own heart. That, and sorrow. I felt that it was a sorrow for much more than his own shortened life. Indeed, he seemed to feel and embody the sorrow for all of us, for what we'd become, and how far we had to go.

I looked into those soulful eyes for some hint of the great mystery we all share, until I couldn't stand it any longer.

Then I looked down at the ground, just for a second . . . and when I gazed up at him again, he gave me a small, rueful smile and gallantly tipped his old straw hat. I waved shyly back to him.

Then he rose from the garage, straight up toward the moon, and in a flash of light he was gone.

G r a c e

I stayed out there in my grandmother's backyard, staring up at the sky, for quite a while. The stars seemed brighter that night, and the moon glowed pure, as if all of heaven's light was intensified by his presence.

Yes, I stood there in Grace's old backyard, watching and waiting, until I got so cold that it seemed to freeze my very bones. But he was gone . . . for now, though I felt that surely we would meet again sometime.

Then, as a cloud passed over the moon, I went inside to the kitchen to tend to Grace.

About the Author

Robert Ward grew up in Baltimore, Maryland. A novelist, scriptwriter, and television producer, he has written six acclaimed books, including *Cattle Annie and Little Britches,* which was made into a movie in 1981, and *Red Baker,* which won the PEN West Award for best novel of the year in 1985. He served first as a scriptwriter and later as story editor and producer for "Hill Street Blues," and then worked as executive producer for "Miami Vice." He has also written articles and stories for numerous newspapers and magazines. He lives with his wife and son in Los Angeles, California.